THE HUNGER ANGEL

ALSO BY HERTA MÜLLER

The Passport

Traveling on One Leg

Nadirs

The Land of Green Plums

The Appointment

THE
HUNGER ANGEL

a novel

HERTA MÜLLER

Translated by
PHILIP BOEHM

Portobello
BOOKS

Published by Portobello Books 2012

Portobello Books
12 Addison Avenue
London
W11 4QR
UK

First published in the United States in 2012 by Metropolitan Books, Henry Holt and
Company, New York

Originally published in Germany in 2009 under the title *Atemschaukel* by
Carl Hanser Verlag, Munich.

This is a work of fiction. All of the characters, organizations, and events portrayed in
this novel either are products of the author's imagination or are used fictitiously.

A CIP catalogue record is available from the British Library

9 8 7 6 5 4 3 2 1

ISBN 978 1 84627 332 2 (hardback)
ISBN 978 1 84627 298 1 (trade paperback)

www.portobellobooks.com

Designed by Kelly Too

Offset by Avon DataSet, Bidford on Avon, Warwickshire

Printed and bound by CPI Group (UK) Ltd, Croydon, CR0 4YY

CONTENTS

THE HUNGER ANGEL

On packing suitcases

All that I have I carry on me.

Or: All that is mine I carry with me.

I carried all I had, but it wasn't mine. Everything either came from someone else or wasn't what it was supposed to be. A gramophone box served as a pigskin suitcase. The light overcoat came from my father. The fancy coat with the velvet collar from my grandfather. The knickers from Uncle Edwin. The leather gaiters came from our neighbor Herr Carp, the green woolen gloves from Aunt Fini. Only the burgundy silk scarf and the toilet kit belonged to me, presents from the previous Christmas.

The war was still on in January 1945. In their dismay at my being shipped off in the dead of winter to who knows where in Russia, everyone wanted to give me something that might be of use, even if it couldn't help. Because nothing in the world could possibly help: I was on the Russians' list, and that was that. So everyone gave me something, and kept their thoughts to themselves. And I took what they gave. I was seventeen years old, and in my mind this going away couldn't have come at a better time. Not that I needed the Russians' list, but if things didn't turn out too badly, I thought, this leaving might even be a good thing. I wanted to get out of our thimble of a town, where every stone had eyes. Instead of fear I felt a secret impatience. And I had a bad conscience about it, because the same list that caused my relatives such despair was fine with me. They were afraid something might happen to me in a foreign country. I simply wanted to go to a place that didn't know who I was.

Something had just happened to me. Something forbidden. Something strange, filthy, shameless, and beautiful. It happened in the Alder Park, far in the back, on the other side of the short-grass mounds. Afterward, on my way home, I went to the pavilion in the middle of the park where the bands played on holidays. I sat there a while. Sunlight came stabbing through the finely carved wood. I stared at the empty circles, squares, and trapezoids, held together by white tendrils with claws, and I saw their fear. This was the pattern of my aberration, of the horror on my mother's face. In the pavilion I vowed: I'm never coming back to this park.

But the more I tried to stop myself, the faster I went back— after two days. For a rendezvous, as it was known in the park.

That next rendezvous was with the same first man. He was called THE SWALLOW. The second man was new, his name was THE FIR. The third was THE EAR. Then came THE THREAD. Then ORIOLE and CAP. Later HARE, CAT, GULL. Then THE PEARL. Only we knew which name belonged to whom. The park was a wild animal crossing, I let myself be passed from one man to the next. And it was summer with white skin on birch trees and shrubs of elderberry and mock orange leafing out to form an impenetrable wall of green.

Love has its seasons. Autumn brought an end to the park.

2

The trees grew naked, and we moved our rendezvous to the Neptune Baths. An oval sign with a swan hung next to the iron gate. Every week I met up with a married man twice my age. He was Romanian. I won't say what name he used or what name I used. We staggered our arrivals, so that no one and nothing could have any idea that we'd arranged to meet: not the cashier ensconced in the leaded-glass windows of her booth, nor the shiny stone floor, nor the rounded middle column, nor the water-lily tiles on the wall, nor the carved wooden stairs. We swam in the pool with all the others and didn't come together until we were both in the sauna.

Back then, before my time in the camp as well as after I returned, and all the way up to 1968 when I left the country, every rendezvous could have landed me in prison. Minimum five years, if I'd been caught. Some were. They went straight from the park or the baths to a brutal interrogation and then to jail. And from there to the penal colony on the canal. Today I know that almost nobody came back from there. The ones who did were walking corpses—old before their time and broken, of no use for any love in the world.

And in the camp—if I'd been caught in the camp I'd be dead.

After those five camp years I roamed the busy streets, day in and day out, silently rehearsing what to say in case I was arrested, preparing a thousand excuses and alibis to counter the verdict: CAUGHT IN THE ACT. I carry silent baggage. I have packed myself into silence so deeply and for so long that I can never unpack myself using words. When I speak, I only pack myself a little differently.

Once during the last rendezvous-summer I took a long way home from the park and found myself near the Holy Trinity

Church on the main square. This chance detour turned out to be significant: I saw the time that was coming. On a column next to the side-altar stood a saint in a gray cloak, with a sheep draped around his neck as a collar. This sheep draped around the neck is silence. There are things we do not speak of. But I know what I'm talking about when I say that silence around the neck is different from silence inside the mouth. Before, during, and after my time in the camp, for twenty-five years, I lived in fear—of my family and of the state. Fear of a double disgrace: that the state would lock me away as a criminal and that my family would disown me out of shame. On crowded streets I would stare at the glass panes of the shops, at the windows of streetcars, of houses, I would gaze into fountains and puddles—checking to make sure I wasn't transparent after all.

My father was an art teacher. With the Neptune Baths inside my head, whenever he used the word WATERCOLOR I'd flinch as though he'd kicked me. The words knew how far I'd already gone. At the dinner table my mother said: Don't stab the potato with your fork because it will fall apart, use your spoon, the fork is for meat. My temples were throbbing. Why is she saying meat when she's talking about forks and potatoes. What kind of meat does she mean. I was my own thief, the words came out of nowhere and caught me.

Like all the Germans in our little town, my mother, and especially my father, believed in the beauty of blond braids and white knee-stockings. They believed in the black square of Hitler's mustache and in the Aryan heritage of us Transylvanian Saxons. The physical part of my secret alone was a gross abomination. And with a Romanian there was the additional matter of *Rassenschande*.

I wanted to escape from my family, to a camp if need be.

4

But I felt sorry for my mother, who had no idea how little she knew me. And who would think of me more frequently when I was away than I of her.

Inside the church, next to the saint with the sheep of silence, I had seen the white alcove with the inscription: HEAVEN SETS TIME IN MOTION. Packing my suitcase, I thought: The white alcove has done its work. This is the time that's been set in motion. I was also happy I wasn't being sent off to war, into the snow at the front. Foolishly brave and obedient, I went on packing. And I took whatever was offered—leather gaiters with laces, knickers, the coat with the velvet collar—even though none of it was really right for me. Because this wasn't about clothes, but about the time that had been set in motion, about growing up, with one set of things or another. The world is not a costume ball, I thought, and no one who's forced to go to Russia in the dead of winter need worry about looking ridiculous.

A patrol consisting of two policemen—a Romanian and a Russian—went from house to house carrying a list. I no longer remember whether the word CAMP was uttered inside our home. Or what other word might have been spoken, except RUSSIA. If the word CAMP was mentioned, it didn't frighten me. Despite the war and the silence about my rendezvous draped around my neck, I was only seventeen years old and still living in my bright, silly childhood. The words WATER-COLOR and MEAT affected me. My brain didn't register the word CAMP.

Back then, at the table with the fork and potatoes, when my mother caught me with the word meat, I remembered how she used to shout down to the courtyard where I was playing: If you don't come to dinner right away, if I have to call you one more time, you can just stay where you are. But I didn't always come right away, and once, when I finally went upstairs, she said:

Why don't you just pack your satchel and go out into the world and do whatever you want. She pulled me into my room, grabbed my woolen cap and my jacket, and stuffed them inside my little backpack. I said, But I'm your child, where am I supposed to go.

A lot of people think packing a suitcase is something you learn through practice, like singing or praying. We had no practice and no suitcase. When my father was sent to join the Romanian soldiers on the front, there was nothing to pack. Soldiers are given everything they need, it's all part of the uniform. But we had no idea what we were packing for, except a long journey and a cold place. If you don't have the right things, you improvise. The wrong things become necessary. Then the necessary things turn out to be the only right things, simply because they're what you have.

My mother brought the gramophone from the living room and set it on the kitchen table. Using a screwdriver, I made it into a suitcase. First I took out the spindle and turntable. Then I corked up the hole for the crank. The fox-red velvet lining stayed. I also kept the triangular emblem with HIS MASTER'S VOICE and the dog facing the horn. I put four books on the bottom: a cloth-bound edition of *Faust*, the slim volume of Weinheber, *Zarathustra*, and my anthology of poems from eight centuries. No novels, since you just read them once and never again. After the books came my toilet kit, containing: 1 bottle eau de toilette, 1 bottle Tarr aftershave, 1 shaving soap, 1 razor, 1 shaving brush, 1 alum stone, 1 hand soap, 1 nail scissors. Next to the toilet kit I put: 1 pair wool socks (brown, darned), 1 pair knee-high socks, 1 red-and-white-checked flannel shirt, 2 short plain underpants. My new burgundy-colored silk scarf went on the very top so it wouldn't get crushed. It had a pattern of shiny checks alternating with matte. With that the case was full.

Then came my bundle: 1 day blanket off the sofa (wool, bright blue and beige plaid, a huge thing but not very warm). And rolled into that: 1 lightweight overcoat (salt-and-pepper, very worn) and 1 pair leather gaiters (ancient, from the First World War, melon-yellow, with laces).

Then came the haversack with: 1 tin of Scandia brand ham, 4 sandwiches, a few leftover Christmas cookies, 1 canteen of water with a cup.

Then my grandmother set the gramophone box, the bundle, and the haversack beside the door. The two policemen had said they'd come for me at midnight. My bags stood ready to go.

Then I got dressed: 1 pair long underwear, 1 flannel shirt (beige and green plaid), 1 pair knickers (gray, from Uncle Edwin, as I said), 1 cloth vest with knitted sleeves, 1 pair wool socks, and 1 pair lace-up boots. Aunt Fini's green gloves lay within easy reach on the table. As I laced up my boots I thought about a summer vacation years earlier in the Wench highlands. My mother was wearing a sailor suit that she had made. On one of our walks she let herself sink into the tall grass and pretended to be dead. I was eight years old. The horror: the sky fell into the grass. I closed my eyes so I wouldn't see it swallowing me. My mother jumped up, shook me, and said: So, do you love me. See, I'm still alive.

My boots were laced up. I sat at the table waiting for midnight. And midnight came, but the patrol was late. Three more

7

hours had to pass—that's almost too much for anyone. And then they were there. My mother held up the coat with the black velvet collar, and I slipped inside. She cried. I pulled on the green gloves. On the wooden walkway, just next to the gas meter, my grandmother said: I KNOW YOU'LL COME BACK.

I didn't set out to remember her sentence. I carried it to the camp without thinking. I had no idea it was going with me. But a sentence like that has a will of its own. It worked inside me, more than all the books I had packed. I KNOW YOU'LL COME BACK became the heart-shovel's accomplice and the hunger angel's adversary. And because I did come back, I can say: a sentence like that keeps you alive.

It was three in the morning, on the fifteenth of January, 1945, when the patrol came for me. The cold was getting worse: it was −15° C.

We rode in a canvas-topped truck through the empty town to the exhibition hall. The Transylvanian Saxons had used it as a banquet hall. Now it was an assembly camp. Some 300 people were crammed inside. Mattresses and straw sacks lay strewn on the floor. Vehicles arrived throughout the night, from the surrounding villages as well as from the town, and unloaded the people who'd been collected. It was impossible to count how many, there was no way to see everything, even though the light in the hall stayed on the whole night. Toward morning I counted nearly 500. People ran around looking for acquaintances. Word had it that carpenters were being requisitioned at the train station, that they were outfitting the cattle cars with plank beds made of fresh lumber. And that other craftsmen were equipping the trains with cylindrical stoves. And that others were sawing toilet holes into the floor. People talked a lot, quietly, with eyes wide open, and they cried a lot,

8

quietly, with eyes shut. The air smelled of old wool, sweaty fear and greasy meat, vanilla pastries, liquor. One woman took off her headscarf. She was obviously from the country, her braid had been doubled and pinned up to the top of her head with a semicircular horn comb. The teeth of the comb disappeared in her hair, but the two corners of its curved edge stuck out like little pointed ears. The ears and her thick braid made the back of her head look like a sitting cat. I sat like a spectator in the middle of all the legs and luggage. For a few minutes I fell asleep and dreamed:

My mother and I are in a cemetery, standing in front of a freshly dug grave. A plant half my height is growing in the middle of the grave. The leaves are furry, and its stem has a pod with a leather handle, a little suitcase. The pod is open the width of a finger and lined with fox-red velvet. We don't know who has died. My mother says: Take the chalk out of your coat pocket. But I don't have any, I say. I reach in my pocket and find a piece of tailor's chalk. My mother says: We have to write a short name on the suitcase. Let's write RUTH—we don't know anybody named that. I write RUHT—rests, as on a gravestone.

In my dream it was clear to me that I had died, but I didn't want to tell my mother just yet. I was startled out of my sleep by an older man with an umbrella who sat down on the straw sack next to me and spoke into my ear: My brother-in-law wants to come, but the place is guarded. They won't let him in. We're still in town, he can't come here, and I can't go home. A bird was flying on each silver button of the man's jacket—a wild duck, or rather an albatross, because the cross on his badge turned into an anchor when I leaned in closer. The umbrella stood between us like a walking stick. I asked: Are

9

you taking that along. Yes I am, he said, it snows even more there than it does here.

No one told us how or when we were supposed to leave the hall—or I should say, when we'd be allowed to leave, since I was anxious to get going, even if that meant traveling to Russia in a cattle car with a gramophone box and a velvet collar around my neck. I don't remember how we finally got to the station, just that the cattle cars were tall. I've also forgotten the boarding, we spent so many days and nights traveling in the cattle car, it seemed we'd been there forever. Nor can I remember how long we stayed on the train. I thought that traveling a long time meant we were traveling a great distance. As long as we keep moving, I thought, nothing can happen. As long as we keep moving, everything is fine.

Men and women, young and old, their bags stacked at the head of their plank beds, talking and keeping quiet, eating and sleeping. Bottles of liquor made the rounds. People grew accustomed to the journey, some even attempted to flirt. They made contact with one eye and looked away with the other.

I sat next to Trudi Pelikan and said: I feel like I'm on a ski trip in the Carpathians, in the cabin at Lake Bâlea, where half a high school class was swallowed up by an avalanche. She said: That can't happen to us, we didn't bring any skis. But with a gramophone box like that you can ride ride ride through the day through the night through the day, you know Rilke don't you, said Trudi Pelikan in her bell-shaped coat with the fur cuffs that reached to her elbows. Cuffs of brown hair like two half-dogs. Trudi Pelikan sometimes crossed her arms, hiding her hands in her sleeves, and then the two halves became a whole dog. That was before I'd seen the steppe, otherwise I would have thought of the little marmots we called steppe-dogs. Trudi Pelikan smelled like warm peaches, even her breath, and even after three or four days in the cattle car. She sat in her coat like a lady taking the streetcar to work and told me how she'd hidden for four days in a hole in the ground behind the shed in her next-door neighbor's garden. But then the snow came, and every step between house and shed and hole became visible. Her mother could no longer bring her food in secret. The footsteps were plain to see all over the garden. The snow denounced her, she had to leave her hiding place of her own accord, voluntarily forced by the snow. I'll never forgive that snow, she said. You can't rearrange freshly fallen snow, you can't fix snow so it looks untouched. You can rework earth, she said, and sand and even grass if you try hard enough. Water takes care of itself, because it swallows everything and flows back together once it's done swallowing. And air is always in place because you can't see it. Everything but snow would have kept quiet, said Trudi Pelikan. It's all the fault of the snow. The fact that it fell in town, as if it knew exactly where it was, as if it felt completely at home there. And the fact that it immediately sided with the Russians. The snow betrayed me, said Trudi Pelikan, that's why I'm here.

The train rolled on for 12 or 14 days, countless hours without stopping. Then it stopped for countless hours without moving. We didn't know where we were at any given moment. Except when someone on one of the top bunks could read a station sign through the narrow trap window: BUZĂU. The iron stove in the middle of the train car crackled. Bottles of liquor passed from hand to hand. Everyone was tipsy: some from drink, others from uncertainty. Or both.

The phrase HAULED OFF BY THE RUSSIANS came to mind, and all that might mean, but it didn't cause us despair. They couldn't line us up against the wall until we got there, and for the moment we were still moving. The fact that they hadn't lined us up against the wall and shot us long ago, as we had been led to expect from the Nazi propaganda at home, made us practically giddy. In the cattle car the men learned to drink just for the sake of drinking. The women learned to sing just for the sake of singing:

The daphne's blooming in the wood
The ditches still have snow
The letter that you sent to me
Has filled my heart with woe

Always the same solemn song, to the point where you no longer knew whether it was really being sung or not, because the air was singing. The song rocked back and forth inside your head, and fit the rhythm of the ride—a Cattle Car Blues, a Song of the Time Set in Motion. It became the longest song of my life, the women sang it for five whole years, until the song became as homesick as we were.

The sliding door, which had been sealed from the outside, was opened four times. Twice, when we were still on Romanian soil, they tossed half a goat inside the car. The animal had been skinned and sawed lengthwise in two. It was frozen stiff and crashed onto the floor. The first time we thought the goat was wood for burning. We broke the carcass into pieces and put it on the fire. It was so dry and scrawny it didn't stink at all, and it burned well. The second time we heard the word PASTRAMA: air-dried meat for eating. We burned our second goat, too, and laughed. It was every bit as stiff and blue as the first one, a ghastly bundle of bones. But we were too quick to laugh, it was arrogant of us to spurn those two kindly Romanian goats.

Familiarity increased as time passed. In the cramped space, people performed the little tasks: sitting down, getting up. Rummaging through suitcases, taking things out, fitting them back in. Going to the toilet hole behind two raised blankets. Every tiny detail brought another in its wake. Inside a cattle car, you lose the traits that make you distinct. You exist more among others than by yourself. There's no need for special consideration. People are simply there together, one for the other, like at home. Perhaps I'm only talking about myself when I say that today. Perhaps that wasn't even true for me. Perhaps the cramped quarters of the cattle car softened me, because I wanted to leave anyway, and I had enough to eat in my suitcase. We had no idea about the savage hunger that would soon attack us. During the next five years, when the hunger angel descended upon us, how often did we look like those stiff blue goats. And how mournfully did we long for them.

We were now in the Russian night, Romania lay behind us. We felt a strong jolt and waited for an hour while the train axles were switched to steppe-gauge, to accommodate the broader Russian track. There was so much snow outside it lit up the night. Our third stop was in an empty field. The Russian guards shouted UBORNAYA. All the doors of all the cars were opened. We tumbled out, one after the other, into the low-lying snowland, sinking in up to our knees. Without understanding the actual word, we sensed that ubornaya meant a communal toilet stop. High overhead, very high, the round moon. Our breath flew in front of our faces, glittering white like the snow under our feet. Machine pistols on all sides, leveled. And now: Pull down your pants.

The embarrassment, the shame of the world. How good that this snowland was so alone with us, that no one was watching it force us close together to do the same thing. I didn't need to, but I pulled down my pants and crouched. How mean and how still this nightland was, how it embarrassed us as we attended to our needs. How to my left Trudi Pelikan hoisted her bell-coat up under her arms and pulled her pants below her ankles, the hissing between her shoes. How the lawyer Paul Gast groaned as he tried to force a movement, how his wife Heidrun's bowels croaked from diarrhea. How all around the stinking warm steam immediately froze and glistened in the air. How the snowland meted out its drastic treatment, leaving each of us to our desolation, our bare bottoms, and the noise of our intestines. How pitiful our entrails became in their common condition.

Perhaps it was my terror, more than myself, that grew up so suddenly that night. Perhaps this was the only way for us to recognize our common condition. Because every one of us, without exception, automatically turned to face the track as we took care of our needs. All of us kept the moon to our backs, we refused to let the open door of the cattle car out of our sight, we needed it like the door to a room. We had the crazy fear that the doors might shut without us and the train drive away. One of us cried out into the vast night: So here we are, the Shitting Saxons. Wasting away in more ways than one. Well, you're all happy to be alive—I'm right, aren't I. He gave an empty laugh like tin. Everyone moved away from him. Then he had room around him and took a bow, like an actor, and repeated in a solemn, lofty tone: It's true, isn't it—you're all happy to be alive.

An echo rang in his voice. A few people started to cry, the air was like glass. His face was submerged in madness. The drool on his jacket had glazed over. Then I noticed his badge: it was the man with the albatross buttons. He stood all by himself, sobbing like a child. Now all that was next to him was the fouled snow. And behind him: the frozen world and the moon, as on an X-ray.

The locomotive let out a dull whistle. The deepest UUUUH I ever heard. Everyone pushed to get to the door. We climbed in and rode on.

I would have recognized the man even without his badge. But I never saw him in the camp.

Orach

None of the underclothes they issued us had buttons. The undershirts and the long underpants each had two small ties. The pillowcases had two sets of ties. By night the pillowcase was a pillowcase. By day it was a canvas sack you carried with you for whatever might come your way, also for stealing and begging.

We stole before, during, and after work, though never while begging—which we referred to as going door-to-door—and never from a neighbor in the barrack. Nor was it stealing when on the way home after work we combed the rubble heaps, picking weeds until our pillow was full. As early as March the women from the country spotted the edible orach with the serrated leaves they called MELDE. Here it was called LOBODA. We also picked wild dill, a kind of grass with feathery leaves. But none of it was any good unless you had salt. And you could only get salt by bartering at the market. The salt was gray and coarse like gravel, you had to break it up. Salt was worth a fortune. We had two recipes for orach:

Salt the leaves and tear the wild dill into tiny bits and sprinkle on top and eat raw, like field greens. Or else boil the stems whole, in salt water. Fished out of the pot with a spoon, orach stems make a delightful mock spinach. The broth can also be drunk, either as a clear soup or a green tea.

Spring orach is tender, the whole plant finger-high and silver-green. By early summer it's knee-high and the leaves are splayed. Each leaf can look like a different glove, always with the thumb pointing down. When silvery green like that, the orach is a cool plant, a food for spring. You have to watch out in summer, though, because it quickly grows tall and dense, with hard, woody stems. Then it tastes bitter, like loam. Eventually the plant forms a thick middle stalk that reaches up to your waist, and spreads out into a loose shrub. And by midsummer the leaves and stems start to take on color: first pink, then blood-red, later a reddish purple, and in the fall a deep indigo. Each stem develops clusters of flowers, just like stinging nettle. But the orach clusters don't hang, they stick out, angled upward. They, too, turn from pink to indigo.

It's strange: the orach isn't really beautiful until it begins to change color, long after it ceases to be edible. Then the plant lingers along the wayside, protected by its beauty. The time for eating orach is over. But not the hunger, which is always greater than we are.

What can be said about chronic hunger. Perhaps that there's a hunger that can make you sick with hunger. That it comes in addition to the hunger you already feel. That there is a hunger which is always new, which grows insatiably, which pounces on the never-ending old hunger that already took such effort to tame. How can you face the world if all you can say about yourself is that you're hungry. If you can't think of anything else. Your mouth begins to expand, its roof rises to the top of your skull, all senses alert for food. When you can no longer bear the hunger, your whole head is racked with pain, as though the pelt from a freshly skinned hare were being stretched out to dry inside. Your cheeks wither and get covered with pale fur.

I never knew whether the orach should be reproached for being inedible, for turning woody and refusing to cooperate. Did the plant know that it no longer served us and our hunger, but rather the hunger angel. The red flower clusters were jeweled ornaments around the neck of the hunger angel. From the first frost in early autumn, the orach put on more and more jewelry, until it froze to death. Poisonously beautiful colors that stabbed our eyes. The clusters, countless rows of red necklaces along every wayside, adorned the hunger angel. He had his jewels. And we had our mouths, which had grown so high and hollow that our steps echoed inside. A bright void in the skull, as if we'd swallowed too much glaring light. A light that sweetly creeps up your throat and swells and rises to your brain. Until you no longer have a brain inside your head, only the hunger echo. No words are adequate for the suffering caused by hunger. To this day I have to show hunger that I escaped his grasp. Ever since I stopped having to go hungry, I literally eat life itself. And when I eat, I am locked up inside the taste of eating. For sixty years, ever since I came back from the camp, I have been eating against starvation.

I looked at the orach that could no longer be eaten and tried to think about something else—about the last tired warmth of late summer, before the ice-winter came. But instead I thought about the potatoes we didn't have. And about the women who lived on the kolkhoz who probably did have potatoes in their daily cabbage soup. Though apart from that, no one envied them. They lived in holes in the earth and had to work much longer every day than we did: from dawn to dusk.

Springtime in the camp was the season for cooking orach picked off the rubble heap. The German name MELDE sounded as if it meant more than it did. In fact, MELDE was for us a word without any overtone, a word that left us in peace. It wasn't the MELDE DICH—present yourself—of roll call. This MELDE wasn't a roll-call weed, but a wayside word. If anything, it was a word for after evening roll call, an after-roll-call weed. Because we couldn't cook our orach until we had been counted, and that took forever because the numbers never came out right.

There were five work battalions, or ORBs—*Otdyel'niy Rabochiy Batal'on*—in our camp, each consisting of between five hundred and eight hundred internees. I was assigned to battalion number 1009, and my work number was 756.

For the *Appell*, or roll call, we stood in rank and file—what an expression for those five miserable regiments of swollen eyes, large noses, hollow cheeks. Our stomachs and legs were distended from the brown bog water. In freezing cold or searing heat, we spent entire evenings standing at attention. Only the lice were allowed to move. During the endless counting they could drink their fill, parade across our miserable flesh, crawl over us from head to pubic hair for hours on end. And after they were sated and resting in the seams of our quilted work clothes, we'd still be standing at attention. And Shishtvanyonov, our camp commandant, would still be screaming. We didn't know his first name. He was simply Tovarishch Shishtvanyonov. But that was long enough to make you stammer with fear whenever you said it. For me the sound always conjured the rumble of the deportation loco- motive. And the white alcove in the church at home, HEAVEN SETS TIME IN MOTION. Perhaps we had to stand so long to stop the time in motion. Our bones became heavy as iron. When the flesh on your body disappears, your bones become a burden, and the ground pulls you downward.

I practiced forgetting myself during roll call, to the point where I couldn't tell breathing out from breathing in. I prac- ticed rolling my eyes up without lifting my head, to look for a corner of cloud where I might hang my bones. If I was able to forget myself, and found the heavenly hook, it held on to me. But often there was no cloud, only blue sky, like open water.

Often there was nothing but an unbroken cover of clouds, a uniform gray.

Often the clouds were running, and no hook could hold fast.

Often the rain burned my eyes and glued my clothes to my skin.

Often the frost bit into my entrails.

On days like that the sky lifted my eyes up, and the roll call pulled them down—then my bones just hung inside me, with nothing to hold on to.

The kapo, Tur Prikulitsch, strutted back and forth between us and Commandant Shishtvanyonov, his lists slipping out of his hands, dog-eared from constant leafing. Every time he called out a number, his chest wobbled like a rooster's. His hands were still a child's. My hands grew in the camp: square, hard, and flat, like two boards.

If someone screwed up his courage after roll call and asked

one of the *nachal'niks*, or even Commandant Shishtvanyonov, when we would be going home, they would say curtly: SKORO— soon.

This Russian SOON robbed us of the longest time in the world.

Tur Prikulitsch had Oswald Enyeter, the barber, trim his nose hairs and fingernails. The two men came from the same region, near Rachiv in the Carpatho-Ukraine, where three lands meet. I asked if it was customary in that part of the world for barbers to trim the nails of their better clients. The barber said: No, it's not. That comes from Tur, not from home. What's from home is five coming after nine. What do you mean, I asked. That things are a little *balamuc*. What's that, I asked. All mixed up, like a madhouse.

Tur Prikulitsch spoke Russian as well as German. He wasn't Russian like Shishtvanyonov, nonetheless he belonged to the Russians, not to us. He was interned along with us, but he was the adjutant of the camp administration. He translated the Russian commands and added his own in German. He divided us into work battalions on a sheet of paper, assigning each name and work number to a specific battalion. That way he had an overview of everything. Each of us had to know his number day and night and never forget that we were not private individuals but numbered laborers.

In the columns next to our names Tur Prikulitsch wrote: kolkhoz, factory, rubble removal, sand transport, rail segment, construction, coal transport, garage, coke battery, slag cellar. Everything depended on what he wrote in that column. Whether we would end up tired, dog tired, or dead tired. Whether we would have time and energy to go door-to-door after work. Whether we'd be able to rummage around in the kitchen waste behind the mess hall unnoticed.

Tur Prikulitsch himself never went to work, never had to report to any battalion or brigade or shift. He ruled and was therefore alert and disparaging. When he smiled it was a trap. When you returned his smile—and everyone had to—you felt you were his fool. Tur Prikulitsch smiles because he's entered something in the column next to your name, some new and worse assignment. Between the barracks, along the main street of the camp, I avoid him, preferring to keep enough distance to make speaking impossible. He lifts his legs high when he walks and carefully places his shiny shoes on the ground like two patent-leather purses, as if the empty time were dropping out of him, right through his soles. He notices everything. People say that even what he forgets becomes an order.

At the barber's I'm no match for Tur Prikulitsch. He says whatever he wants, there's no risk. It's in his interest to insult us. He knows he has to keep us in our place, so things stay the way they are. He stretches out his neck and always talks down to us. He has the whole day to admire himself. I admire him as well: he's athletically built, with brass-colored eyes and an oily gaze, small ears that lie flat like two brooches, a porcelain chin, nostrils pink like tobacco flowers, a neck like candle wax. He's fortunate that he never has to get dirty. And this good fortune makes him more attractive than he deserves to be. He doesn't know the hunger angel, so he can give commands at roll call, strut around the camp, smile cunningly in the barber room. But he can't take part in our conversation. I know more about Tur Prikulitsch than he would like, because I know Bea Zakel well. She is his mistress.

The Russian commands sound like the name of the camp commandant, Shishtvanyonov: a gnashing and sputtering collection of ch, sh, tch, shch. We can't understand the actual words, but we sense the contempt. You get used to contempt. After a while the commands just sound like a constant clearing of the throat—coughing, sneezing, nose blowing, hacking up mucus. Trudi Pelikan said: Russian is a language that's caught a cold.

While everyone else was suffering at attention during the evening roll call, the shift workers who didn't have to be counted tended their orach or other delicacies over little fires—built with coal between two bricks—in the corner of the camp behind the well. Beets, potatoes, even millet, if a clever barter had paid off—ten beets for a jacket, three measures of millet for a sweater, half a measure of sugar or salt for a pair of woolen socks.

For a special meal the pot needed to be covered, but there weren't any lids. At best a piece of tin, and even that might exist more in the mind than anywhere else. But however they did it, people always managed to create a lid out of something. And even though it was never really a lid except in words, they kept repeating: That pot needs a lid. Perhaps memory has put a lid on itself when you can no longer say what the lid was made of, and when there was never but always a lid, no matter where it came from.

In any case, as evening fell, some fifteen to twenty little fires flickered in the corner of the camp behind the well. The rest of us had no food except what was served in the mess hall, nothing to cook on our own. The coal smoked, and the cooks watched their pots, spoon in hand. The pots came from the mess hall, pitiful mess kits of local manufacture. Gray-brown-enameled tin dishes full of pockmarks and dents. On the fire in the yard they were pots, and on the tables in the mess hall they were bowls. As soon as one person finished cooking his meal, other people with pots were waiting to take over the fire.

When I had nothing to cook, the smoke snaked through my mouth. I drew in my tongue and chewed on nothing. I swallowed my spit with the evening smoke and thought about bratwurst. When I had nothing to cook, I walked close to the pots and pretended I was on my way to brush my teeth at the well before going to bed. But by the time I put the toothbrush in my mouth I'd already eaten twice. First I ate the yellow fire with the hunger of my eyes and then the smoke with the hunger of my mouth. As I ate, everything around me went still, all I could hear was the rumble of the coke ovens from the factory yard. The faster I tried to leave the well, the slower I went. I had to tear myself away from the little fires. In the rumble of the coke ovens I heard my stomach growling, the whole scene was filled with hunger. The sky sank black onto the earth, and I staggered back to the yellow light of the barrack.

You didn't need toothpaste to brush your teeth. The toothpaste from home was quickly gone. And salt was far too valuable, no one would have spit that out, it was worth a fortune. I can remember the salt, and how much it was worth. But I can't remember my toothbrush at all. I had one in my toilet kit. But that couldn't have lasted four years. And I wouldn't have been able to buy a new one until the fifth and last year, when we were given some money, cash for our work. In any case, I can't remember a new toothbrush, if there was one. Perhaps I preferred to spend my money on new clothes instead of a new toothbrush. I'm sure that the first toothpaste, the one I took from home, was called CHLORODONT. The name wants to be remembered. But I've forgotten the brushes—the one I must have taken from home and the one that probably replaced that one. The same with my comb. I'm sure I had one. I can remember the word BAKELITE. At the end of the war, all the combs we had at home were made of Bakelite.

Can it be that I forgot the things I brought from home sooner than I forgot the things I acquired in the camp. And if so, is that because they traveled with me. Is it because they were my own and therefore I didn't give them any more thought, just went on using them until they were used up, and even longer. As though with them I was at home and not somewhere else. Can it be that I remember the objects that belonged to others better because I had to borrow them.

I definitely remember the aluminum combs. They came during the time of lice. The lathe operators and metalworkers made them in the factory and gave them to the women. They had jagged teeth and felt moist in your hand and on your scalp, because they were cold to the touch. When you worked with them they quickly took on your body warmth, and they smelled bitter, like radish. Their smell clung to your hand long after you'd put down the comb. The aluminum combs made nests in your hair, you had to tug and pull. They caught more hair in their teeth than lice.

But for lice there were also square horn combs with teeth on both sides. The village girls had brought them from home. On one side thick teeth for parting the hair, on the other fine teeth for nits. The horn combs were solid and heavy in the hand. Your hair didn't catch in the teeth, it came out sleek and smooth. You could borrow the horn combs from the village girls.

For sixty years now, at night I try to recall the objects from the camp: the things I carry in my night-suitcase. Ever since I came back, the sleepless night is a suitcase made of black leather. And the suitcase is lodged in my forehead. For sixty years now I don't know if I can't sleep because I'm trying to recall the objects, or whether I struggle to recall them because I can't sleep. One way or the other, the night always packs its black suitcase against my will. And it's against my will that I have to remember. And even if I didn't have to, but wanted to, I'd rather not have to want to.

Occasionally the objects from the camp attack me, not one at a time, but in a pack. Then I know they're not—or not only—after my memory, but that they want to torment me. Scarcely do I remember that I had brought along some sewing things in my toilet kit than a towel barges in, a towel whose appearance I no longer remember. And then comes a nail brush I'm not sure I had. A pocket mirror that was either there or not. And a watch I may have taken with me, but I can't remember what became of it. I'm pursued by objects that may have had nothing to do with me. They want to deport me during the night, fetch me home to the camp. Because they come in a pack, there isn't room enough in my head. I feel pressure in my stomach rising to the roof of my mouth. My breath teeters over, I have to pant. A toothcombneedlescissormirrorbrush is a monster, just as hunger is a monster. And these objects would not gang up on me if hunger were not one of them.

When the objects gang up on me at night, choking me, I fling open the window and hold my head out in the fresh air. A moon is in the sky like a glass of cold milk, it rinses my eyes.

My breath again finds its rhythm. I swallow the cold air until I'm no longer in the camp. Then I close the window and lie back down. The bedding knows nothing and warms me. The air in the room looks at me and smells of warm flour.

Cement

There was never enough cement. But always more than enough coal. Also enough cinder blocks, gravel, and sand. But the cement always ran out. It dwindled all by itself. You had to beware of the cement—it could become a nightmare. Not only did it disappear all by itself but also into itself. Then everything was full of cement and there was no cement left.

The brigade leader shouted: Take care with the cement.

The foreman shouted: Be sparing with the cement.

And when the wind was blowing: Don't let the cement fly away.

And when it rained or snowed: Don't let the cement get wet.

Cement sacks are made of paper. But the paper is too thin to hold a full sack. Whether carried by one person or two, by its belly or its four corners—it tears. If the sack tears, you can't be sparing with the cement. If the torn sack is dry, half the cement winds up on the ground. If the torn sack is wet, half the cement sticks to the paper. There's nothing to be done: the more you try to be sparing with the cement, the more it wastes itself. The cement is treacherous, just like dust on the road, and fog, and smoke—it flies into the air, crawls on the ground, sticks to the skin. It can be seen everywhere and grasped nowhere.

You have to be sparing with the cement, but what you really have to watch out for when it comes to cement is yourself. You carry the sack with care, but even so, the cement inside grows less and less. You get accused of destroying the economy, of being a Fascist, a saboteur, a cement thief. You stumble ahead, deaf to all the yelling. You shove the wheelbarrows full of mortar up a slanted board onto the scaffold. The board sways, you grip the wheelbarrow tightly. The swaying might send you flying into the sky, because your empty stomach is climbing into your head.

What are the cement guards worried about. A forced laborer has nothing but his quilted work clothes—his *fufaika*—on his body, and a suitcase and a bunk inside his barrack. Why would anyone steal cement. It's not something we take because we're stealing, it's dirt that forces itself onto our bodies. Every day we feel this blind hunger, but cement cannot be eaten. We freeze and we sweat, but cement doesn't warm and doesn't cool. It stirs suspicion because it flies and crawls and sticks, because it loses all form, vanishes soft and gray for no reason, like a wild hare.

The construction site was behind the camp, next to a stable that hadn't housed a horse in years, only empty troughs. Six houses were being built for Russians—six two-family dwellings, each with three rooms. So we were told, but we imagined there'd be at least five families in each house, because from going door-to-door we had seen how poor the people were, and the many emaciated schoolchildren. Both girls and boys had shaved heads and light-blue smocks. Always lined up in pairs, holding hands, singing patriotic songs as they marched

29

through the mud beside the construction site. A silent, rotund schoolmistress traipsed back and forth, looking morose and swinging her buttocks like a ship.

Eight brigades were assigned to the site. They dug foundations, hauled cinder blocks and sacks of cement, stirred the lime slurry and the concrete, poured the foundations, mixed the mortar, carried it in hods, carted it to the scaffold in the wheelbarrow, made the plaster for the walls. All six houses were going up at the same time, people were constantly running here and there, it was utter mayhem and nothing got done. You could see the workers, and you could see the mortar and the bricks, but you couldn't see the walls going up. That's the funny thing about construction: you never actually notice the walls growing, even if you watch the whole day. And then three weeks later, all of a sudden, they're up, so they must have been growing—perhaps during the night, all on their own, just like the moon. They grow every bit as inexplicably as the cement disappears.

The cement guards order you around, but no sooner do you start one thing than they chase you off to do another. You get slapped and kicked. You become dour and melancholy on the inside and slavish and cowardly on the outside. The cement eats away at your gums. When you open your mouth your lips tear like the cement-sack paper. So you keep your mouth shut and obey.

Mistrust grows higher than any wall. In our construction-site misery everyone suspects everyone else of taking advantage, of protecting himself, of carrying the lighter end of the cement sack. Everyone is humiliated by the shouting, deceived by the cement, betrayed by the construction site. If someone dies, the most the foreman says is: *Zhalko, ochyen' zhalko*—

What a pity. Right after that he changes his tone and barks: *Vnimanye*—Attention.

We slog away and hear our own heartbeats and: Take care with the cement. Be sparing with the cement. Don't let the cement fly away. Don't let the cement get wet. But the cement scatters on its own, it squanders itself, it could not be more miserly toward us. We live the way the cement wants us to. Cement is the thief, he has robbed us, not the other way around. Not only that: the cement makes you spiteful. It sows mistrust when it scatters itself, cement is a schemer.

Every evening on the way home, as soon as the work site was far enough behind me and I had enough distance from the cement, I realized that we weren't betraying one another. We were all being betrayed by the Russians and their cement. But even though I knew this, the very next day I suspected everybody all over again. And they felt it. They suspected me, too. And I felt it. The cement and the hunger angel are accomplices. Hunger pulls open your pores and crawls in. Once it's inside, the cement seals them back shut and there you are, cemented in.

In the cement tower the cement can turn deadly. The structure is 40 meters high, with no windows. Considering the height, there isn't much inside, but there is enough to drown in. The cement is loose, not in sacks. We use our bare hands to scoop it into buckets. This cement is old but spry, nasty, and alert. It lies in wait for us, slides onto us, gray and silent, faster than we can jerk back and run away. Cement can flow, and when it does it runs faster and smoother than water. It can carry you off and drown you.

I became cement-sick. For weeks I saw cement everywhere: the clear sky was cement that had been smoothed out, the

31

cloudy sky was rough cement. Rain tied threads of cement to the earth. My metal bowl flecked with gray was made of cement. The watchdogs had cement fur, as did the rats in the kitchen waste behind the mess hall. The lizards crawling between the shacks were clad in cement. The mulberry trees were covered with tentworm nests, funnels of silk and cement. I tried wiping them out of my eyes when the sun was glaring but that's not where they were. And in the evenings a cement bird perched on the edge of the well at the roll-call grounds. His song was scratchy, a cement song. Paul Gast the lawyer recognized the bird from back home—a calandra lark. I asked: Is it made of cement there, too. He hesitated before saying: Back home it comes from the south.

I didn't ask him the other question, because you could see it in the pictures in the barracks and hear it from the loudspeakers: Stalin's cheekbones and voice may have been made of steel, but his mustache was pure cement.

In the camp every type of work made you dirty. But nothing was as relentless as the cement. Cement is as impossible to escape as the dust of the earth, you can't tell where it comes from because it's already there. And apart from hunger, the only thing in our minds that's as quick as cement is homesickness. It steals from you the same way cement does, and you can drown in it as well. It seems to me there's only one thing in our minds quicker than cement, and that's fear. And that's the only explanation I can give for why, as early as the beginning of the first summer, I had to jot this down in secret on a piece of thin brown cement-sack paper:

SUN HIGH IN THE HAZE
YELLOW CORN, NO TIME

I didn't write more because cement has to be spared. Actually I wanted to write something completely different:

Deep and crooked and lurking reddish
the half-moon stands in the sky
already setting

But I didn't write that, just said it quietly under my breath, where it shattered, the cement grinding in my teeth. Then I was silent.

You have to be sparing with paper, too. And keep it well hidden. Anyone caught writing on paper was sent to detention—a concrete box, eleven steps belowground, so narrow all you can do is stand. Stinking of excrement and full of vermin. Iron bars at the top.

In the evening, in the shuffle of footsteps on the way home, I often thought: There's less and less cement, it can disappear all by itself. I'm made of cement, too, and there's less and less of me. So why can't I disappear.

The lime women

The lime women are one of eight brigades at the site. First they haul the wagon with the lumps of lime up the steep hill next to the stable, then down to the edge of the construction site, where the slaking pit is located. The wagon consists of a large trapezoidal wooden box on wheels. On each side of the shaft, five women are harnessed with leather straps around their shoulders and hips. A guard walks alongside. The women's eyes are thick and wet from the strain of pulling, and their mouths are half open.

Trudi Pelikan is one of the lime women.

When rain spills over the steppe for weeks and the mud around the slaking pit dries into furry flowers, the alderflies become unbearable. Trudi Pelikan says they smell the salt in your eyes and the sweetness in your mouth. And the weaker you are, the more your eyes tear up and the more sugar is in your spit. Trudi Pelikan was harnessed in the rearmost position, because she was too weak for the front. The alderflies didn't alight on the corners of her eyes but right on her pupils, and not on her lips but right inside her mouth. Trudi Pelikan stumbled. When she fell, the wagon rolled over her toes.

A motley crew

Trudi Pelikan and I, Leopold Auberg, came from Hermannstadt. We didn't know each other before we had to climb inside the cattle car. Artur Prikulitsch and Beatrice Zakel—Tur and Bea—had known each other since they were children. They came from the village of Lugi in the mountains, in the Carpatho-Ukraine, where three lands meet. Oswald Enyeter came from the same region, from Rachiv. And so did the accordion player Konrad Fonn, from the little town of Sucholol. My truck companion Karli Halmen came from Kleinbetschkerek, and Albert Gion, with whom I was later in the slag cellar, came from Arad. Sarah Kaunz with the silky hairs on her hands came from Wurmloch, and Sarah Wandschneider with the wart on her ring finger came from Kastenholz. They didn't know each other before the camp, yet they looked as if they could be sisters. In the camp they were nicknamed the two Zirris. Irma Pfeifer came from the small town of Deta, and deaf Mitzi—Annamarie Berg—from Mediasch. Paul Gast the lawyer and his wife Heidrun Gast were from Oberwischau. Anton Kowatsch the drummer came from the

Banat mountain region, from Karansebesch. Katharina Seidel, whom we called Kati Sentry, came from Bakowa. She was feebleminded and for all five years didn't realize where she was. The mechanic Peter Schiel, who died from drinking coal alcohol, came from Bogarosch. Ilona Mich—Singing Loni— came from Lugosch. Herr Reusch, the tailor, from Guttenbrunn. And so on.

We were all Germans and had been rounded up at home. All except Corina Marcu, who arrived at the camp with bottle curls, a fur coat, patent-leather shoes, and a cat brooch on her velvet dress. She was Romanian; the transport guards had picked her up the night we stopped in Buzău and stuck her in the cattle car. Presumably they had to fill a gap in the list, replace a woman who had died during the trip. Corina Marcu froze to death in the third year while shoveling snow on a railroad embankment. And David Lommer, known as Zither Lommer because he played the zither, was Jewish. Because his tailor shop had been expropriated, he traveled around the country, plying his trade, stopping at the better homes. He had no idea how he wound up as a German on the Russians' list. His home was in Dorohoi, in Moldavia. His parents and his wife and four children had fled the Fascists. He didn't know where they were, and they didn't know where he was, even before he was deported. He was sewing a woolen suit for an officer's wife in Grosspold when he was picked up.

None of us were part of any war, but because we were Germans, the Russians considered us guilty of Hitler's crimes. Even Zither Lommer. He had to spend three and a half years in the camp. One morning a black car pulled up in front of the construction site. Two strangers wearing fine karakul caps climbed out and spoke with the foreman. Then they took

Zither Lommer away. From that day on, his bed in the barrack was empty. Bea Zakel and Tur Prikulitsch probably sold his trunk and his zither at the market.

Bea Zakel said the men in the karakul hats were high-ranking party officials from Kiev. They supposedly took Zither Lommer to Odessa, and from there shipped him back to Romania.

Because he came from the same region as Tur Prikulitsch, Oswald Enyeter could get away with asking why Odessa. Tur said: Lommer had no business being here, and from Odessa he can go wherever he wants. Addressing the barber, and not Tur, I said: But where is he supposed to go. There's no one left for him at home. At that point Tur Prikulitsch was holding his breath, to keep still while Oswald Enyeter pruned his nose hairs with a rusty pair of scissors. The barber finished the second nostril and brushed the snippets of hair off Tur's chin like so many ants, then turned away from the mirror so Prikulitsch couldn't see that he was winking. Are you satisfied, he asked. Tur said: With my nose, yes.

Outside in the yard the rain had stopped. The bread cart came clattering up the drive, through the puddles. Every day the same man pulled the cart with the large loaves through the camp gate to the yard behind the mess hall. The loaves were always covered with a white linen cloth, like a pile of corpses. I asked what rank the bread man had. The barber said none at all, that he had either inherited or stolen the uniform. With so much bread and so much hunger he needed the uniform to gain some authority.

The cart had two high wooden wheels and two long wooden arms. It resembled the big cart the scissor-grinders rolled through the streets from town to town, all summer long. As soon as the bread man stepped away from the cart, he limped.

According to the barber, he had a wooden leg made of shovel handles that had been nailed together. I envied the bread man; it's true he had one leg too few, but he had more than enough bread. Like me, Oswald Enyeter the barber also watched the bread cart pass by. But he only knew half-hunger; he probably made deals with the bread man every now and then. Even Tur Prikulitsch, whose stomach was full, watched the bread man, either to monitor his movements or simply out of absentmindedness. I didn't know why, but I had the impression that the barber wanted to call Tur Prikulitsch's attention away from the bread cart. Otherwise why would he have said, just as I sat on the stool: What a motley crew we are here in the camp. Everybody coming from someplace else, just like a hotel you live in for a while.

That was in the time of the construction site. But what did words like MOTLEY CREW, HOTEL, and A WHILE have to do with us. The barber was not an accomplice of the camp administration, but he was privileged. He was allowed to live and sleep in his barber room, while we were stuck in our barracks, our brains clogged with cement. Of course, during the day, Oswald Enyeter didn't have the place to himself, since we were always coming and going. He had to cut and shave every wretch who stepped inside, and some men cried when they saw themselves in the mirror. Month after month he had to watch us coming through his door looking seedier and seedier. Throughout the five years he knew exactly who was still coming but whose body was already half wax. And who was no longer coming because he was too exhausted, or homesick, or dead. I don't think I could have put up with that. On the other hand, Oswald Enyeter didn't have to put up with work brigades or days cursed with cement, or night shifts in the cellar. He was besieged by our misery, but not betrayed by the cement. He had to console us, and we took advantage of him, because we couldn't help it. Because we were blinded by hunger and sick for home, withdrawn from time and outside ourselves and done with the world. Just as the world was done with us.

That day I jumped up from the chair and shouted that unlike him I didn't have a hotel room, just cement sacks. Then I kicked the stool so hard it nearly fell over, and said: And believe me, Herr Enyeter, I'm not one of the owners of this hotel, like you are.

Leo, sit down, he said, I thought we were on a first-name basis. You're wrong, the owner is Tur Prikulitsch. And Tur stuck the pinkish-red tip of his tongue out of the corner of his mouth and nodded. He was so stupid he felt flattered. Then he checked himself in the mirror, combed through his hair, and blew through the comb. After that, he placed the comb on the table and the scissors on the comb, then the scissors next to the comb and the comb on top of the scissors. Then he left. Once Tur Prikulitsch was outside, Oswald Enyeter said: Did you see that, he's the owner, he's the one who keeps us in check, not me. Sit back down. You know, you don't have to say anything to the cement sacks, but I have to say something to everybody. Be happy you still know what a hotel is. By now everything people think they remember has long since changed into something else. Everything except the camp, I said.

That day I didn't sit back down on the stool. I held firm and walked away. Back then I wouldn't have admitted it, but I was just as vain as Tur Prikulitsch. I felt flattered that Enyeter had become conciliatory, though he didn't need to be. The more he pleaded with me to stay, the more determined I was to leave unshaven. With stubble on my face, the cement was even more unrelenting. It wasn't until four days later that I went back and sat down on the stool, as if nothing had happened. I was so tired from the construction work, I couldn't care less about his hotel. He didn't mention it either.

Weeks later, when the bread man pulled the empty cart up to the gate, I remembered about the HOTEL. By then I liked the idea. I used it against the dreariness. Coming back from unloading cement on the night shift, I trotted like a calf through the morning air. In our barrack, three people were still asleep. As dirty as I was, I lay down on my bed and said to myself: At least nobody needs a key in this hotel. There's no key check, either, no locks, it's all open living, just like in Sweden. My barrack and my trunk are always open. My valuables are sugar and salt. Under my pillow is the dried bread I've rescued from my mouth. It's a treasure and guards itself. I am a calf in Sweden and a calf always does the same thing upon entering its hotel room— before anything else, it looks under the pillow to make sure the bread is still there.

For half a summer I was assigned to the cement, and trotted around like a calf in Sweden. I came off the day or night shift and played hotel in my head. Some days I had to laugh to myself. And some days the HOTEL just caved in completely, in me, that is, and tears came to my eyes. I wanted to right myself, but I no longer knew who I was. HOTEL was a cursed word we couldn't inhabit because we were living inside another word, one that sounded close but was very far away: APPELL.

Wood and cotton wool

There were two types of shoes. The rubber galoshes were a luxury, the wooden shoes a catastrophe. Only the sole was made of wood, a piece of board two fingers thick. The upper part consisted of gray sackcloth nailed to the sole along a narrow strip of leather. Because the cloth was too weak for the nails, it always tore, first at the heels. The wooden shoes were high, with eyelets for lacing, but there were no laces. We used thin wire instead, which we threaded through the eyelets and tightened by twisting the ends. Within a few days the sackcloth around the eyelets was also in tatters.

You can't flex your toes in wooden shoes. You can't lift your feet, either, you have to slide them. Your knees get stiff from the shuffling. It was a relief when the cloth tore at the heels, because then your toes had a little more room, and you could bend your knees more easily.

The wooden shoes had no right or left, and only three sizes: tiny, gigantic, and, very rarely, medium. To find two shoes of the same size you sifted through the pile of wood and sackcloth in the clothes room. Not only was Bea Zakel Tur Prikulitsch's mistress—she was mistress of our clothes. Some people she helped rummage for two well-nailed shoes. With others she merely slid her chair closer to the pile of shoes, without so much as bending over, and lurked there to make sure nothing was stolen. She herself had a good pair of low shoes made of leather, and felt boots for when it was icy cold. If she had to run through the mud she'd pull on her rubber galoshes.

The camp administration expected the wooden shoes to last half a year. But the cloth tore at the heels after three or four days. So, in addition, everyone tried to barter his way into a pair of galoshes. These were flexible and light, several sizes larger than your foot. There was ample room for several layers of rags—footwraps—which we used instead of socks. To keep your feet from slipping out of the galoshes, you ran wire under the sole and tied it off on top, at the instep. The wire knot chafed, so the top of your foot was always raw. And that sensitive spot always got the first chilblains. Throughout the winter, both the wooden shoes and the galoshes froze to the footwraps. And the footwraps froze to the skin. The rubber galoshes were even colder than the wooden shoes, but they lasted for months.

Our work clothes—we had nothing else—in other words, the camp uniforms, were distributed every six months. They were the same for men and women. Apart from the wooden shoes and rubber galoshes, we were given underwear, padded suits, work gloves, footwraps, bedding, towels, and one piece of soap that had been chopped off a bar and smelled strongly of lye. The soap burned the skin and had to be kept away from any open sores.

The underclothes were made of unbleached linen: 1 pair long underwear, with ties at the ankles and in front at the stomach, 1 pair short underwear with ties, 1 undershirt with ties, which was really an all-purpose, underoverdaynightsummerandwintershirt. The fufaikas had rolls of padding that ran the length of the garment. The pants had a wedge cut for fat stomachs and tight cuffs that laced at the ankles. There was a single button in front, at the waist, and pockets on either side. The jacket was shaped like a sack with a standing collar known as a *rubashka*-collar, and had cuffs with one button on each sleeve, a row of buttons in front, and two square pockets sewn onto the sides. For a head covering, both men and women were issued quilted caps with earflaps and laces.

The fufaikas were blue-gray or green-gray, depending on how the dye had taken. But after a week's work, they all turned brown and stiff from the dirt. The fufaikas were a good thing, the warmest clothing for the dry winter, when the frost sparkled and your breath froze on your face. And in the scorching summer they were roomy enough to let the air circulate and the sweat dry. But in wet weather they were miserable. The padding soaked up the rain and snow and stayed wet for weeks. Our teeth chattered and we suffered from extreme cold until evening, when we could finally return to the barrack. And in the barrack, given the 68 bunks and 68 internees with their 68 fufaikas, 68 caps, 68 pairs of footwraps, and 68 pairs of shoes, the air was stuffy and oppressive. We lay awake and stared at the lightbulb. The yellow gleam seemed to contain melting snow. And in the melting snow was the stench of the night, covering us with forest earth and moldy leaves.

Exciting times

After work, instead of going back to the camp, I went begging in the Russian village. At the UNIVERMAG the door was open but the store was empty. The saleswoman was bending over a shaving mirror on the counter, checking her head for lice. A gramophone was playing next to the shaving mirror, taa-tatata-taa. I recognized the melody from the radio back home: Liszt, announcing special bulletins from the war. My father had bought the Blaupunkt with the green cat eyes in 1936 for the Berlin Olympics. In these exciting times, he had said. The Blaupunkt paid off, because the times got even more exciting.

Three years later, at the beginning of September, it was once again time for cold cucumber salad in the shade on the veranda. The Blaupunkt sat on the little corner table, hanging on the wall next to it was the large map of Europe. Taa-tatata-taa: Special News Bulletin. Father tipped his chair to reach the knob on the radio and turned up the volume. We all went silent and stopped clattering with our silverware. Even the wind listened through the windows on the veranda. What had started on September 1, my father called Blitzkrieg. My mother called it the Polish Campaign. My grandfather, who had sailed around the world as a cabin boy on a big frigate out of Pola, was a skeptic. He was always interested in what the English had to say. When it came to Poland, he preferred to keep quiet and take another spoonful of cucumber salad. My grandmother said that dinner was a family affair and not the place for politics on the radio.

My father had cut out several little red triangular flags—victory banners—and affixed them to pins with colorful heads. He kept them in the ashtray next to the Blaupunkt. For 18 days Father moved his little flags eastward on the map. That was it for Poland, said Grandfather. And for the little flags. And for the summer. My grandmother plucked the little flags off the map of Europe and returned the pins to her sewing box. The Blaupunkt migrated to my parents' bedroom, three walls away. At the crack of dawn I heard the wake-up broadcast from Radio Munich. The program was called Morning Gymnastics, and the floor began to vibrate rhythmically. Led by the gymnastics instructor in the Blaupunkt, my parents performed their exercises. And since I was too chubby and they wanted me to be more soldierly, my parents sent me once a week to a private exercise class that most people called Gymnastics for Cripples.

Yesterday an officer wearing a green cap the size of a cake platter gave a speech at the roll-call grounds, the Appellplatz. He spoke about peace and FUSSKULTUR, which sounded to us like the culture of feet. Tur Prikulitsch couldn't interrupt, he stood next to the man like a devout acolyte, then summarized the contents of the speech: Fusskultur strengthens our hearts. And in our hearts beats the heart of the Soviet Socialist Republics. Fusskultur steels the strength of the working class.

45

Through Fusskultur the Soviet Union will blossom in the strength of the Communist Party and in the peace and happiness of the people. Konrad Fonn, the accordion player, who came from the same region as Tur Prikulitsch, told me that Y in the Cyrillic alphabet was like our U, and that the speech was all about the power of physical training, which the Russians call FISKULTURA. The officer had evidently tried to re-create the word in German and come up with PHYS-KULTUR, but had read the German Y like a Cyrillic U, and Tur didn't dare correct him.

I knew all about FUSSKULTUR from the cripple gymnastics and from our *Volk* course in high school, which we had to attend every Thursday. We drilled in the schoolyard: lie down, stand up, climb the fence, squat, lie down, push up, stand up. Left, right, march, sing songs. Wotan, Vikings, Germanic ballads. On Saturdays or Sundays we would go on marches out of town. We trained in the brush on the hills, we used branches for camouflage, we practiced finding our way with owl calls and dog barks, and played war games wearing red and blue woolen threads. If you tore the thread off an enemy you had killed him. The person with the most threads was decorated as a hero, a blood-red rose hip serving as a medal.

Once I simply decided not to go. It wasn't easy. There had been a big earthquake the night before. An apartment house had collapsed in Bucharest and buried a number of people. In our town all that collapsed were a few chimneys, and at home two pipes fell off the stove, but I used the earthquake as an excuse. The gym instructor didn't inquire further, but I was already feeling the effects of my special training: my act of disobedience only reinforced my sense of being crippled.

In these exciting times my father photographed girl gymnasts and Transylvanian Saxon girls in folk costume. He had even purchased a Leica to do so. And he became a Sunday hunter. On Mondays I'd watch him skin the hares he had shot. Stretched out without their fur, stiff and tinged with blue, the hares looked like the Saxon gymnast girls at the barre. The hares were eaten. The pelts were nailed to the wall of the shed and after drying got stored in a tin chest in the attic. Every six months Herr Fränkel came to pick them up. Then he stopped coming. No one wanted to know anything more. He was Jewish, reddish-blond, tall, and nearly as slender as a hare. Little Ferdi Reich and his mother, who lived in the rear of the building, were no longer there either. No one wanted to know anything more.

It was easy not to know anything. Refugees arrived from Bessarabia and Transnistria, they were given lodging, stayed a while, and went on. Then German soldiers came from the Reich, were given lodging, stayed a while, and went on. Neighbors and relatives and teachers went off to fight for the Romanian Fascists or for Hitler. Some came home on leave from the front and others didn't. There were also rabble-rousers who avoided the front but stirred things up at home and wore their uniforms to the ballrooms and cafés.

Our science teacher, too, wore a uniform when he taught us about the yellow lady's slipper growing in the moss. And the edelweiss. The edelweiss was more than a plant, it was a fashion. Everyone wore some kind of talisman: badges and pins with edelweiss and gentian, or airplanes and tanks, or various types of weapons. I collected and traded different types of insignia, learning the order of ranks by heart. My favorite was private first class. I thought it meant someone who was very good in private, because we had Dietrich from the Reich billeted in our house. My mother sunbathed on the roof of the shed, and Dietrich watched her through the skylight with a pair of binoculars. And my father watched him from the veranda, dragged him to the courtyard, took a hammer, and smashed his binoculars on the pavement next to the shed. My mother moved to my Aunt Fini's for two days with a small bag of clothes under her arm. A week earlier, Dietrich had given my mother two coffee demitasses for her birthday. It was all my fault, I had told him she collected demitasses, and had gone with him to the porcelain store, where I pointed out two little cups my mother was bound to like. They were pale pink, like the most delicate cartilage, with a silver rim and a drop of silver on the top of the handle. My second favorite insignia was made of Bakelite and had an edelweiss coated with phosphorus that glowed in the dark like the alarm clock.

Our science teacher went off to fight and didn't come back. Our Latin teacher came home on leave from the front and dropped by our school. He sat at the teacher's desk and taught a Latin class. It was soon over, and things didn't go as he had expected. One student who had often been decorated with rose hips said right at the beginning of class: Sir, tell us what it's like at the front. The teacher bit his lips and said: It's not what you think. Then his face went rigid and his hands started to shake. We'd never seen him like that before. It's not what you think, he repeated. And then he laid his head on the table, let his arms droop next to his chair like a rag doll, and cried.

The Russian village is small. When you go begging you hope not to run into another beggar from the camp. Everyone begs with coal. If you're a practiced beggar, you carry your chunk of coal wrapped in a rag, cradled in your arm like a sleeping child. You knock on a door, and if it opens, you lift the rag and show your wares. From May through September the prospects for the coal trade aren't very good. But coal is all we have.

Going door-to-door, I saw petunias in someone's garden: an entire bed full of pale-pink little cups with silver rims. As I walked on I closed my eyes and said, DEMITASSES, then counted the letters in my head: ten. Next I counted ten steps, then twenty, for both cups. But where I stopped there was no house. So I counted to one hundred for all ten demitasses my mother had in her china cabinet, and found myself three houses farther along. There were no petunias. I knocked on the door.

On the road

Riding somewhere was always a happy thing.

First of all: as long as you're moving, you haven't arrived. As long as you haven't arrived, you don't have to work. Riding in a truck gives you time to recover.

Second: when you ride, you come to some place that couldn't care less about you. You can't be yelled at or beaten by a tree. Under a tree, yes, but the tree can't help that.

When we arrived at the camp, our only point of reference was NOVO-GORLOVKA, which could be the name of the camp or a town or the entire region. It couldn't be the name of the factory, though, since we knew that was KOKSOKHIM-ZAVOD. I did find a cast-iron manhole cover beside the well in the camp yard, and used my school Greek to decipher the Cyrillic letters as DNEPROPETROVSK, but that could be a nearby city, or some foundry at the other end of Russia. Whenever you were able to leave the camp, you got to see more than letters—the wide steppe and the villages on the steppe. For that reason, too, riding somewhere was a happy thing.

Every morning, a transport crew was assigned to the vehicles in the garage behind the camp, mostly two men at a time. Karli Halmen and I wound up on a four-ton LANCIA from the 1930s. There were five trucks in the garage, and we knew the pros and cons of each. The Lancia was a good truck, not too tall and fully metal, no wood. The five-ton MAN, whose wheels came up to your chest, wasn't as good. And with the Lancia came the driver Kobelian, who had a crooked mouth. He was a good-natured man.

When Kobelian said KIRPICH we understood he meant bricks, and that we would be driving through the boundless steppe to pick up a load. If it had rained the night before, the burned-out wreckage of automobiles and tanks would flash in the hollows. The steppe-dogs darted away from the wheels. Karli Halmen sat with Kobelian inside the cab. I preferred to stand in the truck bed and hold on to the top. In the distance I saw a seven-story redbrick tenement with empty windows and no roof. Half in ruins and all by itself, but very modern. Maybe it was the first building of a new settlement that had been scrapped overnight. Maybe the war had arrived before the roof.

The road was bumpy, the Lancia rattled past the scattered farms. Waist-high stinging nettle grew in some of the yards, and white chickens, thin as cloud wisps, roosted on iron bedsteads. Nettles only grow where there are people, my grandmother had told me, and burdocks only grow where there are sheep.

I never saw anyone in the farmyards. I wanted to see people who didn't live in the camp, who had a home, a fence, a yard, a room with a carpet, maybe even a carpet beater. Where carpets are beaten, I thought, you can trust the peace. There, life is civilized. There, people are left alone.

On our very first drive with Kobelian I'd seen a frame for beating carpets in one of the farmyards. It had a roller so the carpet could be moved up and down. And next to that I saw a large white enameled watering can that looked like a swan, with its beak and slender neck and heavy belly. That was so beautiful that I kept a lookout for carpet-beating frames on every ride, even far out on the steppe, in the empty wind. But I never saw another carpet frame, or a swan.

Beyond the farmyards on the outskirts we came to a small town of yellow-ochre houses with crumbling stucco walls and rusty tin roofs. Streetcar rails could be seen in the remnants of asphalt, and now and then two-wheeled carts from the bread factory moved along the rails, pulled by horses. The carts were covered with white linen, like the bread cart in the camp. But the half-starved horses made me wonder whether it was bread the cloth was covering and not fully starved bodies.

Kobelian said: The town is called Novo-Gorlovka. So the town has the same name as the camp, I asked. He said: No, the camp has the same name as the town. There were no signs. Anyone who drove here knew the name of the place, just as Kobelian and the Lancia did. Strangers like Karli Halmen and myself had to ask. And whoever didn't have anyone to ask didn't wind up here and had no business being here in the first place.

We had to pass through the town to pick up the bricks. They take a while to load: one and a half hours, if you have two people and can park the Lancia close by. You carry four at a time, pressing them together like an accordion. Three are too few and five are too many. You could carry five, but the middle one would slip out. You'd need a third hand to hold it. You fill the entire truck bed, making sure there are no gaps, stacking

the bricks in three or four layers. Bricks have a bright reso-
nance, each one sounds a little different, but the red dust is
always the same and settles on your clothes. Brick dust is dry,
it doesn't envelop you like cement dust, and it isn't as oily as
coal dust. The brick dust made me think of sweet red paprika,
though it has no smell.

On the way back, the Lancia never rattled: it was too heavily weighed down. We again drove through Novo-Gorlovka,
over the streetcar rails, past the farmyards in the outskirts, and
down the road under the wisps of clouds drifting over the
steppe. All the way to the camp. And then past the camp to the
construction site.

Unloading went faster than loading. The bricks did have to
be stacked, but not so carefully, because they'd be hauled off
the next day to the masons on the scaffold.

With the travel time there and back, and the loading and
unloading, we managed two trips a day. Then it was evening.
Occasionally Kobelian would take us out one more time,
without saying anything. Then Karli and I knew it was a private delivery. We only filled half the truck bed with a single
layer of bricks, and drove back to the seven-story ruin. There
we turned off into a low-lying area where the houses were bordered by rows of poplars. At that time of day the clouds were
as red as the bricks. We drove between a fence and a wood-
shed into Kobelian's yard. The truck jerked to a stop, and I
found myself standing up to my waist in the middle of a withered fruit tree, its branches full of shrunken balls from the
previous summer, or the one before. Karli climbed up to me.
The last bit of daylight dangled fruit in front of our faces, and
Kobelian let us pick some before we unloaded.

The balls were dry as wood, you had to lick and suck at

them before they tasted like sour cherries. If you chewed them well, the pit felt very smooth and hot on the tongue. Those night cherries were a happy thing, but they only sharpened our hunger.

On the way home the night was made of ink. It was good to arrive late at the camp. Roll call was over, and supper had long since started. The thin soup from the top of the kettle had been served to others. There was a better chance of getting something more substantial.

But arriving too late was bad. Then the soup was all gone. Then you had nothing except this big empty night, and the lice.

On strict people

I'm sitting on the bench with the backrest. Bea Zakel has washed her hands at the well and is walking down the path. She sits down next to me. Her eyes slowly drift off to the side, almost as if she were cross-eyed. But she isn't, she lets them slide like that because she knows it makes her look more striking. So striking that I feel self-conscious. Then she starts talking, just like that. She speaks as fast as Tur Prikulitsch, but not as capriciously. She turns her drifting eyes toward the factory, follows the cloud from the cooling tower, and tells me about the mountains where the three lands meet: Galicia, Slovakia, and Romania.

When she lists the mountains from home she talks more slowly: the Lower Tatra, the Beskids, which flow into the Eastern Carpathians, by the headwaters of the river Tisza. My village is called Lugi, she says, a poor village stashed away near Kaschau. There the mountains stare down through our heads until we die. The people who stay are given to brooding. Many move away. That's why I left, to attend the conservatory in Prague.

The cooling tower is a tall matron, wearing her dark wooden

casing like a corset. The white clouds pass through her narrow waist and rise out of her mouth day and night. And they move away, like the people leaving Bea Zakel's mountains.

I tell Bea about the mountains around Transylvania, which are also part of the Carpathians, I say. Except our mountains have deep, round lakes. People call them sea-eyes, and they're so deep that their bottoms connect to the Black Sea far underground. When you stare into a mountain lake you have your feet on the mountain and your eyes in the sea. My grandfather says that far below the earth the Carpathians are carrying the Black Sea on their arm.

Then Bea talks about Artur Prikulitsch, how he's part of her childhood. That he comes from the same village and lived on the same street and even sat at the same desk with her in school. When they played together she had to be the horse and Tur was the coachman. The street was steep, and one day she fell and though she didn't realize it until later, she had broken her foot. Tur goaded her on with his whip and claimed that she was just pretending to be in pain because she didn't want to be his horse anymore. Whenever she played with Tur he was always a sadist, she says, and I tell her about the Millipede Game. The children were divided into two millipedes. One was supposed to pull the other across a chalked line in order to eat it. In each of the millipedes the children were told to put their arms around each other's waists and pull with all their strength. We were practically torn apart, I got bruises on my hips and a dislocated shoulder.

I'm not a horse, and you're not a millipede, says Bea. If you are what you play, you're bound to get punished for it, that might as well be a law. And you can never escape the law, even if you move to Prague. Or to a camp, I say. Yes, because Tur moves with you, says Bea. He also left our village and went off to Prague to study. At first he wanted to become a missionary but ended up switching to business instead. You know, the laws of the small village, and even the laws of Prague, are strict, says Bea. That's why you can't escape them, because they were made by strict people.

Once again Bea lets her eyes slide into a sidelong glance and she says:

I love people who are strict.

At least one of them, I think, but I have to hold my tongue, because she lives off this strictness, and her strict person has given her this job in the clothes room, which is a lot nicer than what he's assigned to me. She complains about Tur Prikulitsch, she wants to live like him but still be one of us. When she talks fast she sometimes comes close to denying the difference between us and her. But at the last moment she slips back into her safe place. Maybe it's her sense of safety that causes her eyes to drift. It's possible that she's always thinking about her privileged position when she talks with me. And that she talks so much because in addition to her strict person, she wants to have a little freedom—freedom he doesn't know about. Or maybe she's coaxing me out of my reserve, maybe she confides everything we talk about to him.

Bea, I say, the song of my childhood goes like this:

Sun high in the haze,
yellow corn,
no time

Because the strongest scent from my childhood is the rotten stench of germinating corn. In summer we'd go to the Wench highlands for eight weeks of vacation. By the time we came back, the corn we'd left on the sand pile in the courtyard had sprouted. I pulled it out of the sand, the cobs were falling apart, with smelly yellow kernels dangling off to the side from white, threadlike roots.

Bea repeats: Yellow corn, no time. Then she sucks on her finger and says: Growing up is a good thing.

Bea Zakel is taller than me by half a head. Her braids are rolled around her head, a silk cord thick as an arm. Perhaps her proud look doesn't only come from sitting in the clothes room, but because she has to carry this heavy hair. She probably had this heavy hair as a child, so that in her poor, stashed-away village, the mountains wouldn't stare down through her head until she died.

But she won't die here in the camp. Tur Prikulitsch will see to that.

Onedroptoomuchhappiness
for Irma Pfeifer

By the end of October it was sleeting icy nails and snow. Our guard and the site inspector gave us our quotas and went straight back to the camp, to their warm rooms. At the construction site a quiet day began, without the dread of shouted orders.

But this quiet day was interrupted when Irma Pfeifer screamed. Perhaps HELPHELP or ICAN'TTAKEANYMORE—we couldn't make out the exact words. We grabbed shovels and wooden boards and ran to the mortar pit, but not fast enough, the supervisor was already there. Raising his shovel, he ordered us to drop everything: *Ruki nazad*—Hands behind your backs. He forced us to stand there and look into the mortar pit. There was nothing we could do.

Irma Pfeifer was lying facedown in the bubbling mortar. First it swallowed her arms, then the gray mass came oozing over the backs of her knees. For an eternity, a few seconds, the mortar rippled and waited. Then the mixture suddenly sloshed up to her hips, and then wobbled between her head and her cap. Her head began to sink and her cap floated away, with outspread earflaps, drifting slowly to the edge of the pit like a fluffed-up pigeon. Shaved bare and scabbed with lice bites, the back of her head hovered a moment like half a melon. When that, too, went under, all we could see was her back, and the supervisor said: Zhalko, ochyen' zhalko.

Then he brandished his shovel, drove the whole group to the edge of the construction site, where the lime women worked, and shouted: Vnimanye, lyudi. Attention, people—if a saboteur is looking for death that's fine with us. She jumped in, he said, the bricklayers saw it all from up on the scaffold. Konrad Fonn the accordion player had to translate for the supervisor.

After that we had to line up, march into the camp, and stand in formation to be counted. It was still early morning, still raining ice-nails, and we stood there, aghast, silent outside and in. Shishtvanyonov ran yelling out of his office, foaming at the mouth like an overheated horse. He hurled his leather gloves at us. Wherever one landed, someone had to bend down and take it back to him. Again and again. Then Shishtvanyonov turned us over to Tur Prikulitsch. He was wearing an oilcloth coat and rubber boots. He had us count off, step forward, step back, count off, step forward, step back, into the evening.

No one knows when Irma Pfeifer was fished out of the mortar pit or where they scraped a little dirt away to bury her. The next morning the sun was cold and bare. There was fresh mortar in the pit, everything was as usual. No one mentioned the previous day. I'm sure more than one person thought about Irma Pfeifer and her fine cap and her good quilted work jacket, since she was probably laid to rest in her clothes, and the dead have no need of clothes when the living are freezing.

Irma Pfeifer wanted to take a shortcut. She was carrying a sack of cement in front of her and couldn't see where she was going. The sack had soaked up the icy rain and went down before she did, which is why we didn't see any sack when we came to the mortar pit. At least that's what Konrad Fonn the accordion player thought. You can think all kinds of things. But you can't know for sure.

Black poplars

It was the night of December 31, New Year's Eve, in our second year. Halfway through the night the loudspeakers summoned us to the Appellplatz. We were chased down the main street of the camp, flanked by eight guards with rifles and dogs, and followed by a truck hauling a trailer. In the tall snow behind the factory, where the empty fields began, we were told to line up in rows along the brick wall and wait. We thought: This is the night we will be shot.

I pushed into the front row so I could be one of the first. That way I wouldn't have to load corpses onto the truck, which was already waiting off the road. Shishtvanyonov and Tur Priku-litsch had crawled into the cab, the motor was running to keep them warm. The guards paced up and down. The dogs huddled together, their eyes squeezed shut by the cold. Now and then they lifted a paw so it wouldn't get frostbitten.

We stood there, our faces aged, our eyebrows covered with frost, our lips shivering. Some of the women mumbled prayers. This is the end, I told myself. My grandmother's farewell was: I know you'll come back. That, too, was in the middle of the night, but also in the middle of the world. At home they've already welcomed the New Year, maybe raised a glass to me, a midnight toast to my being alive. I hope they thought about me in the first hours of the New Year and then climbed into their warm beds. By now my grandmother's wedding ring should be lying on the nightstand, she takes it off every evening because it's too tight. And I am standing here, waiting to be shot.

I saw all of us standing in a giant box. Its top was made of sky, lacquered black by the night and decorated with sharply whetted stars. The bottom was lined knee-deep with cotton wool, so that we would fall into softness. And the sides of the giant box were draped with stiff, icy brocade, silken tangles of fringe, endless lace. Toward the back of the box, between the watchtowers, a catafalque of snow was lying on the wall of the camp. And on top of that, as tall as the towers, a stack of bunk beds reached to the sky, a tiered coffin with room for all of us to be laid out, just like in the barracks. And over the topmost tier was the black-lacquered cover of the night. From the towers at the head and foot of the catafalque, two honor guards dressed in black kept watch over the dead. At the head, nearest the camp gate, the guard lights shined like a candelabra. At the darker foot end, the snow-draped crown of the mulberry tree made a magnificent bouquet, with all our names on countless paper bows. Snow muffles sound, I thought, almost no one will hear the shooting. Our families are slumbering away, tipsy, unsuspecting, worn out from celebrating New Year's Eve in the middle of the world. Maybe they're dreaming about our enchanted burial in the New Year.

I had no desire to leave the box with the tiered coffins. Fear of death can become a kind of trance if you try to master it but don't quite succeed. Even the icy cold that keeps you from moving softens the horror. Death by freezing lulled me into a state where I could surrender to death by shooting.

But then two of the heavily wrapped Russians from the trailer tossed shovels at our feet. Tur Prikulitsch and one of the Russians laid out four knotted ropes parallel to the factory wall, forming two corridors between the looming darkness and the snowy brightness. Shishtvanyonov had fallen asleep in the cab. Perhaps he was drunk. He slept with his chin on his chest, like a forgotten passenger left in the train at the last station. He slept the whole time we shoveled. No, we shoveled the whole time he slept, because Tur Prikulitsch had to wait for his instructions. The whole time he slept, we went on digging two ditches between the ropes, for our execution. I don't know how long we dug, until the sky turned gray. And that's how long I heard my shovel repeating: I know you'll come back, I know you'll come back. The shoveling had shaken me awake, I now preferred to go on starving and freezing and slaving away for the Russians rather than get shot. My grandmother was right: I will come back. Although I qualified that with: But do you know how hard this is.

Then Shishtvanyonov climbed out of the cab, rubbed his chin, and shook his legs, perhaps because they were still asleep. He waved the heavily wrapped guards over. They opened the tailgate and threw down pickaxes and crowbars. Shishtvanyonov spoke unusually briefly and quietly, gesticulating with his index finger. He climbed back inside and the empty truck drove away with him.

Tur had to give Shishtvanyonov's mumbling the tone of a command and shouted: Dig holes for trees.

We searched for the tools in the snow as if they were presents. The earth was frozen hard as bone. The pickaxes bounced off the ground, the crowbars clanged like iron against iron. Nut-sized clods sprayed into our faces. I sweated in the cold, and froze as I sweated. I split into two halves, one ember, one ice. My upper body was scorched with fire, it bent and blazed away automatically for fear of the quota. My lower body was numb with frost, my legs pressed cold and dead into my gut.

By afternoon our hands were bloody, but the holes were only knuckle-deep. And that's how we left them.

The holes didn't get finished until late spring, when two long rows of trees were planted. They grew quickly. These trees didn't grow anywhere else, not on the steppe, not in the Russian village, nowhere nearby. Throughout our time in the camp no one knew what they were called. The taller they grew, the whiter their branches and trunks became. Not delicate and wax-white translucent like birches, but robust, with dull skin like plaster paste.

During my first summer home, I saw these plaster-white camp trees in the Alder Park, old and huge. Uncle Edwin looked in his tree atlas and found: Stout and sturdy, this rapid-growing tree can shoot up to a height of 35 meters, with a trunk reaching two meters in diameter. Specimens can attain an age of 200 years.

Uncle Edwin had no idea how correct, or rather, how fitting the description was, when he read out the word SHOOT. He said: This tree doesn't seem to need a lot of care and it's quite beautiful. But its name is a royal lie. Why is it called BLACK POPLAR when its trunk is so white.

I didn't contradict him. I only thought to myself: If you've spent half the night under a black-lacquered sky, waiting to be shot, the name isn't a lie at all.

Handkerchief and mice

In the camp there were many kinds of cloth. Life moved from one cloth to the next. From the footwrap to the hand towel, to the bread cloth, the orach pillowcase, the door-to-door begging cloth, and even to a handkerchief, if you happened to have one.

The Russians in the camp had no need of handkerchiefs. They pressed one nostril shut with their index finger and blew the snot out through the second like dough, right onto the ground. Then they shut the cleaned nostril and the snot sprayed out the other. I practiced this but without success. No one in the camp used a handkerchief to wipe his nose. Whoever had one used it for sugar and salt, and when it was all in tatters, as toilet paper.

One time a Russian woman gave me a handkerchief as a present. It was after work, very cold. Hunger had driven me back to the Russian village. I went door-to-door with a piece of anthracite coal, which people used for heating. I knocked at one dwelling. An old Russian woman answered, took my coal, and let me in. The room was low, the window set in the wall at

66

the level of my knee. Two scrawny, gray-white spotted chickens were perched on a stool. One of them had a comb hanging over its eyes. It flipped its head like a person without hands whose hair has fallen into his face.

The old woman spoke for some time. I only understood a word here and there but could sense what it was about. She was afraid of her neighbors, she'd been living all alone for a long time with just her two chickens, yet she'd rather talk to them than to her neighbors. She had a son my age named Boris who was as far from home as I was, but in the opposite direction, in a camp in Siberia, a penal battalion, because a neighbor had denounced him. Perhaps you and my son Boris will be lucky, she said, and you'll be able to go home soon. She pointed to the chair, and I sat down at the end of the table. She took the cap off my head and laid it on the table. She set a wooden spoon next to the cap. Then she went to the stove and ladled potato soup out of a pot into a tin bowl. She must have given me a whole liter. I spooned away; she stood over my shoulder and watched.

The soup was hot, I slurped it down, watching her out of the corner of my eye. And she nodded. I wanted to eat slowly, because I wanted the soup to last. But my hunger crouched in front of the bowl like a ravenous dog. The two chickens had fluffed out their feathers, pulled in their feet, and were asleep. The soup heated me down to my toes. My nose was dripping. *Podozhdi*, wait, said the Russian woman, then went into the next room and came back with a snow-white handkerchief. She placed it in my hand and closed my fingers around it as a sign I should keep it. It was a gift. But I didn't dare blow my nose. What happened in that moment went beyond going door-to-door, beyond me and her and a handkerchief. It was about her son. And it made me feel good and it didn't, because she or I or both of us had gone slightly too far. She had to do something for her son because I was there, and because he was as far away from home as I was. I felt bad that I was there, that I wasn't him. And I was embarrassed that she felt the same way but couldn't show it because she could no longer bear worrying about him. And I could no longer bear being two people at once, two people who had been deported—that was too much for me. That wasn't as simple as two chickens roosting next to each other on a stool. I was already one burden too many for myself.

Afterward, back on the street, I used my coarse, dirty coal cloth as a handkerchief. After blowing my nose I wrapped it around my neck, it became my scarf. As I went on, I used the two ends of the scarf to wipe my eyes, several times and very quickly, so no one would notice. Of course no one was watching me, but I didn't want to notice it either. I was all too aware that there's an unspoken law that you should never start to cry if you have too many reasons to do so. I told myself that my tears were due to the cold, and I believed myself.

The snow-white handkerchief was made of the most delicate batiste. It was old, a nice piece from the time of the tsars, with a hand-embroidered silk *ajour* border. The openwork between the stitches was very precise, and there were little rosettes in the corners. I hadn't seen anything that beautiful in a long time. At home, the beauty of normal everyday objects wasn't worth mentioning. And in the camp it was better to forget such beauty. But the beauty of this handkerchief got to me. It made my heart ache. Would he ever come home, this old Russian woman's son, this man who was himself but also me. To keep these thoughts at bay I started singing. For the sake of both of us, I sang the Cattle Car Blues:

> The daphne's blooming in the wood
> The ditches still have snow
> The letter that you sent to me
> Has filled my heart with woe

The sky was running by—plump, cushiony clouds. Then the early moon looked at me with the face of my mother. The clouds moved one cushion underneath her chin and another one just behind her right cheek. Then they pulled that cushion back out through her left cheek. And I asked the moon: Is my mother now so frail. Is she sick. Is our house still there. Is she still at home, or is she in a camp as well. Is she even still alive. Does she know that I'm alive, or is she already weeping for her dead son whenever she thinks of me.

That was my second winter in the camp, we weren't allowed to write letters home, or send any sign of life. The birch trees in the Russian village were bare, under their branches the snowy rooftops looked like crooked beds in an open-air barrack. And in the early twilight, the birch skin showed a different paleness than during the day, and a different whiteness from the snow. I saw the wind swimming gracefully through the branches. A small, wood-brown dog came trotting toward me down the path along the woven willow fence. He had a triangular head and long legs, straight and thin as sticks. White breath came flying out of his mouth as though he were eating my handkerchief while drumming with his legs. The little dog ran past me as if I were nothing more than the shadow of the fence. And he was right: on my way home to the camp I was just another ordinary Russian object in the twilight.

No one had ever used the white batiste handkerchief, and I didn't either. I kept it in my suitcase to the last day, as a kind of relic from a mother and a son. And eventually took it home.

A handkerchief like that has no business in the camp. Each year I could have traded it at the market for something to eat, for sugar or salt, or even millet. The temptation was there, and the hunger was blind enough. What kept me from doing so was the belief that the handkerchief was my fate. And once you let your fate pass out of your hands, you're lost. I was convinced that my grandmother's parting sentence I KNOW YOU'LL COME BACK had turned into a handkerchief. I'm not ashamed to say that the handkerchief was the only person who looked after me in the camp. I'm certain of that even today.

Sometimes things acquire a tenderness, a monstrous tenderness we don't expect from them.

At the head of my bed, behind my pillow, is my trunk, and underneath my pillow, wrapped in the bread cloth, is the bread I've saved from my mouth, precious beyond belief. One morning I heard a squeal inside the pillow, right under my ear. I lifted my head and looked in wonder: between the bread cloth and the pillow was a bright pink tangle the size of my ear. Six blind mice, each smaller than a child's finger. With skin like silk stockings that twitch because they're living flesh. Mice born out of nothingness, a gift for no reason. All of a sudden I felt proud of them, as if they, too, might feel proud of me. Proud because my ear had had children, because out of all the 68 beds in the barrack these mice were born in mine, and out of all people they wanted me as their father. They lay there by themselves, I never saw a mother. They made me ashamed, because they trusted me so fully. I immediately felt that I loved them and I knew that I had to get rid of them right away, before they ate up the bread and before anyone else woke up and noticed.

I lifted the tangle of mice onto the bread cloth, cupping my fingers like a nest in order not to hurt them. I crept out of the barrack and carried the nest across the yard. My legs shook as I hurried to keep from being spotted by a guard or smelled by a dog. But my eyes never left the cloth, so that I wouldn't drop a single mouse. Then I stood in the latrine and shook the cloth out over the hole. The mice splashed into the pit. Not a peep. I took a deep breath. Done.

When I was nine I found a newborn gray-green kitten on an old carpet in the farthest corner of our washroom. Its eyes were stuck together. I picked it up and stroked its belly. It hissed and bit my little finger and wouldn't let go. I saw blood. I squeezed back with my thumb and index finger—I think I squeezed as hard as I could, around its neck. My heart was pounding, like after a fight. Because it died, the kitten caught me in the act of killing. The fact that it wasn't intentional only made it worse. Monstrous tenderness gets tangled in guilt differently from intentional cruelty. More deeply. And for longer.

What that kitten has in common with the mice: not a peep.

And what sets the kitten apart from the mice: with the mice it was all about intent and compassion. With the kitten it was resentment: wanting to pet and winding up bitten. That's one thing. The other is compulsion. Once you start to squeeze, there's no going back.

On the heart-shovel

There are many shovels, but the heart-shovel is my favorite. It's the only one I named. The heart-shovel can't do anything except load or unload coal, and only loose coal at that.

The heart-shovel has a blade as big as two heads side by side. It's shaped like a heart, with a large scoop deep enough for five kilos of coal or the hunger angel's entire backside. The blade has a long, welded neck where it joins the handle. For such a big blade, the heart-shovel's handle is short. It has a wooden crossbar at the top.

With one hand you hold the neck and with the other you clasp the crossbar at the top. Actually I should say at the bottom, because I think of the blade as being the top, the handle isn't so important, it can be held closer to the ground or off to the side. So, I grip the heart-blade high on its neck, and the crossbar low on the handle. I keep the two ends in balance, the heart-shovel teeters in my hand like a seesaw, the way my breath teeters inside my chest.

The heart-shovel has to be broken in, until the blade is

completely shiny, until the weld on its neck feels like a scar on your hand and the shovel becomes an extension of your arm, its weight in balance with your body.

Unloading coal with the heart-shovel is completely different from loading bricks. With the bricks all you have are your hands, it's a matter of logistics. But when it comes to coal, the tool you use—the heart-shovel—turns logistics into artistry. Unloading coal is an elegant sport, more so than riding, high diving, or even the noble game of tennis. It's like figure skating. Or perhaps pair skating, with the shovel as your partner. A single encounter with a heart-shovel is enough for anyone to get swept away.

Unloading coal begins like this: when the dump gate comes crashing open, you stand off to the left and jab your shovel in at a slant, with one foot on the heart-blade as though it were a spade. You clear a good two feet of room and then climb onto the wooden bed. Now you can start shoveling. All your muscles work together to create a swaying, swinging motion. You hold the crossbar with your left hand and the neck of the blade with your right, so that your fingers rest on the seam of the weld. Then you jab underneath the coal and swing your shovel in an arc, toward the back of the truck. As you turn, your weight shifts, and you let the length of the handle slide through your right hand, out over the edge of the gate, so you can dump the coal into the deep. Then you bring the empty shovel back up. Then you plunge the shovel back inside for another load, another swing, another dump.

Once most of the coal has been unloaded and what's left is too far from the gate, this rotating swing is no longer effective. Now you need to take up a fencing position, with your right

foot set gracefully forward, while your left serves as a support-
ing axis in back, toes gently turned out. You hold the crossbar
with your left hand, but this time you don't hold on to the
metal seam with your right hand, you just let the handle slide
up and down as you balance the load. You plunge the shovel
in, shifting your weight onto your left leg as you add a little
push from your right knee. Then you pull the shovel back out,
carefully, so that not one piece of coal falls off the heart-blade.
You step back onto your right foot, continuing to turn with
your whole body. This brings you to a new, third, position,
with your left foot gracefully poised, its heel lifted as though
dancing, so nothing but the tip of your big toe has any
purchase—ready to lunge forward as you fling the coal off the
heart-blade into the clouds. For a second the shovel hangs
horizontally in the air, only the crossbar is still attached to
your left hand. The movements are as beautiful as a tango, a
series of ever-changing acute angles against a constant rhythm.
And if the coal has to fly even farther, the fencing gives way to
waltzing: you move in a triangle, your weight shifting from
one leg to the other, and you bend as low as 45 degrees. You
fling your coal and it scatters in flight like a flock of birds.
And the hunger angel flies as well. He is in the coal, in the
heart-shovel, in your joints. He knows that nothing warms the
whole body more than the very shoveling that wears it down.
But he also knows that hunger devours nearly all the artistry.

Unloading was always a job for two or three people. Not
counting the hunger angel, because we weren't sure whether
there was one hunger angel for all of us or if each of us had his
own. The hunger angel approached everyone, without restraint.
He knew that where things can be unloaded, other things can
be loaded. In terms of mathematics, the results could be horri-

fying: if each person has his own hunger angel, then every time someone dies, a hunger angel is released. Eventually there would be nothing but abandoned hunger angels, abandoned heart-shovels, abandoned coal.

On the hunger angel

Hunger is always there.

Because it's there, it comes whenever and however it wants to. The causal principle is the work of the hunger angel.

When he comes, he comes with force.

It's utterly clear:

1 shovel load = 1 gram bread.

I myself could do without the heart-shovel. But my hunger depends on it. I wish the heart-shovel were my tool. But the shovel is the master, and I am the tool. I submit to its rule. Nevertheless it's my favorite shovel. I've forced myself to like it. I submit because it is a better master when I'm compliant, when I don't hate it. I ought to thank it, because when I shovel for my bread I am distracted from my hunger. Since hunger never goes away, the heart-shovel makes sure that shoveling gets put ahead of hunger. Shoveling takes priority when you are shoveling, otherwise your body can't manage the work.

The coal gets shoveled away, but fortunately there's never any less of it. New shipments arrive every day from Yasinovataya, so it says on the coal cars. Every day the head becomes possessed by shoveling. The body, steered by the head, becomes the tool of the shovel. And nothing more.

Shoveling is hard. Having to shovel and not being able to is one thing. Wanting to shovel and not being able to brings a double despair—first bowing to the coal and then buckling under. I'm not afraid of the shoveling, but of myself. Afraid my mind might wander while I'm shoveling. That sometimes happened to me early on, sapping the strength I needed for shoveling. The heart-shovel notices right away if I'm not there exclusively for it. Then a thin cord of panic begins to choke me. The double stroke beats away in my temples, stark and severe, it picks up my pulse and becomes a jangle of horns. I'm on the verge of breaking down, my throat swells. The hunger angel climbs to the roof of my mouth and hangs his scales. He puts on my eyes and the heart-shovel goes dizzy, the coal starts to blur. He wears my cheeks over his chin. He sets my breath to swinging, back and forth. The breath swing is a delirium—and what a delirium. I look up, the sky is filled with summer cotton wool, embroidered clouds, very still. My brain twitches, pinned to the sky with a needle, at the only fixed point it has left, where it fantasizes about food. I can see the tables in the air, decked in white, and the gravel crunches beneath my feet. And the sunlight comes stabbing through the middle of my brain. The hunger angel looks at his scales and says:

You're still not light enough for me. Why don't you just let go.

I say: You're deceiving me with my own flesh. It has become your slave. But I am not my flesh. I am something else and I won't let go. Who I am is no longer the question, but I won't tell you what I am. What I am is what's deceiving your scales.

The second winter in the camp was often like that. Early in

the morning I come back from the night shift, dead tired, thinking: It's my time off, I ought to sleep. And I lie down, but I can't sleep. All 68 beds in the barrack are empty, everyone else is at work. I'm drawn outside into the empty yard of the afternoon. The wind tosses thin snow that crackles against my neck. With open hunger the angel leads me to the garbage pile behind the mess hall. I stumble after him, trailing a little way behind, dangling from the roof of my mouth. Step after step, I follow my feet, assuming they aren't his. Hunger is my direction, assuming it isn't his. The angel lets me pass. He isn't turning shy, he just doesn't want to be seen with me. Then I bend my back, assuming it isn't his. My craving is raw, my hands are wild. They are definitely my hands: the angel does not touch garbage. I shove the potato peelings into my mouth and close both eyes, that way I can taste them better, the frozen peels are sweet and glassy.

The hunger angel looks for traces that can't be erased, and erases traces that can't be saved. Fields of potatoes pass through my brain, the farm plots angled between the grassy meadows in the Wench, mountain potatoes from back home. The first pale, round, new potatoes, the gnarled glass-blue late potatoes, the fist-sized, leather-shelled, yellow-sweet flour potatoes, the slender, smooth-skinned oval rose-potatoes that stay firm when boiled. Their flowers in the summer: yellow-white, pinkish-gray, or waxy purplish clusters on bitter-green plants with angular stalks.

How quickly I devour the frozen potato peels, spread my lips and shove them into my mouth, one after the other, without stopping, just like the hunger. All of them, so that they form a single long ribbon of potato peel.

All of them, all of them.

Evening comes. And everyone comes home from work. And they all climb into their hunger. Hunger is a bunk, a bed frame, when one hungry person is watching the others. But that is deceptive, I can sense in myself that hunger is climbing into us. We are the frame for the hunger. All of us eat with closed eyes. We feed the hunger all night long. We fatten him up, for the shovel.

I eat a short sleep, then wake up and eat the next short sleep. One dream is like the next, each involves eating. Our compulsion to eat finds a merciful outlet in our dreams, though that, too, is a torment. I eat wedding soup and bread, stuffed peppers and bread, baumtorte. Then I wake up in the barrack, peer at the shortsighted lightbulb. I fall back asleep and eat kohlrabi soup and bread, hasenpfeffer and bread, strawberry ice cream in a silver bowl. Then hazelnut noodles and fancy kipfel pastries. And then sauerkraut stew and bread, rum cake. Then boiled pig's head with horseradish and bread. And just when I'm about to start in on a haunch of venison with bread and apricot compote, the loudspeaker begins to blare away, and it's already morning. I eat and eat, but my sleep stays thin, and my hunger shows no sign of tiring.

When the first three of us died of hunger, I knew exactly who they were and the order of their deaths. I thought about each of them for several long days. But three never stays three. One number leads to another. And the higher the number gets, the more hardened it becomes. When you're nothing but skin and bones and in bad shape yourself, you do what you can to keep the dead at a distance. The mathematical traces show that by March of the fourth year 330 people had died. With numbers like that you can no longer afford separate feelings. We thought of the dead only briefly.

Before it even had a chance to settle, we cast off the dreary mood, chased away the weary sadness. Death always looms large and longs for all. You can't give him any of your time. He has to be driven away like a bothersome dog.

Never was I so resolutely opposed to death as in the five years in the camp. To combat death you don't need much of a life, just one that isn't yet finished.

The first three deaths in the camp were:

Deaf Mitzi crushed by two coal cars.

Kati Meyer buried alive in the cement tower.

Irma Pfeifer drowned in the mortar.

And in my barrack, the first to die was the machinist Peter Schiel, from coal alcohol poisoning.

In every case the cause of death was different, but hunger was always part of it.

In pursuit of the mathematical traces, I once looked at Oswald Enyeter, the barber, in the mirror and said: Everything simple is pure result, and every one of us has a mouth with a roof. The hunger angel places everyone on his scales, and when someone lets go, he jumps off the heart-shovel. Those are his two laws: causality and the lever principle.

Of course you can't ignore them, the barber said, but you can't eat them either. That's also a law.

I looked in the mirror and said nothing.

Your scalp is covered with little flowers, the barber said. We'll have to use the clippers, that's the only thing that can help.

What kind of flowers, I asked.

Little pus flowers, he said.

It was a blessing when he started to clip my hair close to the scalp.

One thing is certain, I thought: the hunger angel knows

who his accomplices are. He pampers them and then drops them. Then they shatter. And he with them. He's made of the same flesh that he's deceiving. This is consistent with his lever principle.

And what am I to say to that now. Everything that happens is always simple. And there's a principle to how things proceed, assuming that they last. And if things last for five years you can no longer discern or even notice any principle. And it seems to me that if someone is inclined to talk about it later, there's nothing that can't be included: the hunger angel thinks straight, he's never absent, he doesn't go away but comes back, he knows his direction and he knows my boundaries, he knows where I come from and what he does to me, he walks to one side with open eyes, he never denies his own existence, he's disgustingly personal, his sleep is transparent, he's an expert in orach, sugar, and salt, lice and homesickness, he has water in his belly and in his legs.

All you can do is list.

If you don't let go, things will be only half as bad, you think. To this day, the hunger angel speaks out of your mouth. But no matter what he says, this remains utterly clear:

1 shovel load = 1 gram bread.

Except you're not allowed to talk about hunger when you're hungry. Hunger is not a bunk or a bed frame, otherwise it could be measured. Hunger is not an object.

Coal alcohol

During a ransacked night, when there was no thought of sleep, no merciful outlet for our hunger, because the lice would not stop their torture, during such a night Peter Schiel noticed that I wasn't sleeping either. I sat up in my bed and he sat up in his bed diagonally opposite and asked:

What does give-and-take mean.

I said: Sleep.

Then I lay back down. He stayed sitting up, and I heard a gurgling sound. Bea Zakel had traded Peter Schiel's wool sweater at the market for some alcohol made from anthracite. He drank it. And didn't ask me any more questions.

The next morning Karli Halmen said: He asked a few more times what give-and-take meant. You were sound asleep.

The zeppelin

Behind the factory is a place with no coke ovens, no extractor fans, no steaming pipes, where the tracks come to an end, where all we can see from the mouth of the coal silo is a heap of rubble overgrown with flowering weeds, a pitiful bare patch of earth at the edge of the wilderness, crisscrossed by well-trodden paths. There, out of sight to all but the white cloud drifting from the cooling tower far across the steppe, is a gigantic rusted pipe, a discarded seamless steel tube from before the war. The pipe is seven or eight meters long and two meters high and has been welded together at the end closest to the silo. The end that faces the empty fields is open. A mighty pipe, no one knows how it wound up here. But everyone knows what purpose it has served since we arrived in the camp. It's called THE ZEPPELIN.

This zeppelin may not float high and silver in the sky, but it does set your mind adrift. It's a by-the-hour hotel tolerated by the camp administration and the nachal'niks—a trysting place where the women from our camp meet with German POWs who are clearing the rubble in the wasteland or in the bombed-out factories. Wildcat weddings was how Anton

Kowatsch put it: Open your eyes sometime when you're shoveling coal, he told me.

As late as the summer of Stalingrad, that last summer on the veranda at home, a lovethirsty female voice had spoken from the radio, her accent straight from the Reich: Every German woman should give the Führer a child. My Aunt Fini asked my mother: How are we to do that, is the Führer planning to come here to Transylvania every night, or are we supposed to line up one by one and visit him in the Reich.

We were eating jugged hare, my mother licked the sauce off a bay leaf, pulling the leaf slowly out of her mouth. And when she had licked it clean, she stuck it in her buttonhole. I had a feeling they were only pretending to make fun of him. The twinkle in their eyes suggested they'd be more than a little happy to oblige. My father noticed as well: he wrinkled his forehead and forgot to chew for a while. And my grandmother said: I thought you didn't like men with mustaches. Send the Führer a telegram that he better shave first.

Since the silo yard was vacant after work, and the sun still glaring high above the grass, I went down the path to the zeppelin and looked inside. The front of the pipe was shadowy, the middle was very dim, and the back was pitch-dark. The next day I opened my eyes while I was shoveling coal. Late in the afternoon I saw three or four men coming through the weeds. They wore quilted work jackets like ours, except theirs had stripes. Just outside the zeppelin they sat down in the grass up to their necks. Soon a torn pillowcase appeared on a stick outside the pipe—a sign for occupied. A while later the little flag was gone. Then it quickly reappeared and disappeared once more. As soon as the first men had gone, the next three or four came and sat down in the grass.

I also saw how the women in the work brigades covered for each other. While three or four wandered off into the weeds, the others engaged the nachal'nik in conversation. When he asked about the ones who had left they explained it was because of stomach cramps and diarrhea. That was true, too, at least for some—but of course he couldn't tell for how many. The nachal'nik chewed on his lip and listened for a while, but then kept turning his head more and more frequently in the direction of the zeppelin. At that point I saw the women resort to a new tactic, they whispered to our singer, Loni Mich, who began singing loud enough to shatter glass, drowning out all the noise made by our shoveling—

Evening spreads across the vale
Softly sings the nightingale

—and suddenly all the women who had disappeared were back. They crowded in among us and shoveled away as if nothing had happened.

I liked the name zeppelin: it resonated with the silvery forgetting of our misery, and with the quick, catlike coupling. I realized that these unknown German men had everything our men were lacking. They had been sent by the Führer into the world as warriors, and they also were the right age, neither childishly young nor overripe like our men. Of course they, too, were miserable and degraded, but they had seen battle, had fought in the war. For our women they were heroes, a notch above the forced laborers, offering more than evening love in a barrack bed behind a blanket. Evening love in the barrack remained indispensable. But for our women it smelled of their own hardship, the same coal and the same longing for home.

And it led to the same worn-out give-and-take, with the man providing the food, while the woman cleaned and consoled. *Love in the zeppelin was free of all concerns except for the hoisting and lowering of the little white flag.*

Anton Kowatsch was convinced I would disapprove of the women going to the zeppelin. No one could have guessed that I understood them all too well, that I knew all about arousal in disheveled clothes, about roving desire and gasping delight in the Alder Park and the Neptune baths. No one could imagine that I was reliving my own rendezvous, more and more often: SWALLOW, FIR, EAR, THREAD, ORIOLE, CAP, HARE, CAT, SEAGULL. Then PEARL. No one had any idea I was carrying so many cover names in my head, and so much silence around my neck.

Even inside the zeppelin, love had its seasons. The wildcat weddings came to an end in our second year, first because of the winter, and later because of the hunger. When the hunger angel was running rampant during the skinandbones time, when male and female could not be distinguished from each other, coal was still unloaded at the silo. But the paths in the weeds were overgrown. Purple tufted vetch clambered among the white yarrow and the red orach, the blue burdocks bloomed, and the thistles as well. The zeppelin slept and belonged to the rust, just as the coal belonged to the camp, the grass belonged to the steppe, and we belonged to hunger.

On the phantom pain
of the cuckoo clock

One evening in the summer of the second year, a cuckoo clock appeared on the wall above the tin bucket that contained our drinking water, right next to the door. No one could figure out how it got there. It belonged to the barrack and to the nail it hung from, and to no one else. But it bothered all of us together and each of us individually. In the empty afternoons, the ticking listened and listened, whether we were coming or going or sleeping. Or simply lying in bed, lost in our thoughts, or waiting because we were too hungry to fall asleep and too drained to get up. But after the waiting nothing came, except the ticking in the back of our throat, doubled by the ticking from the clock.

Why did we need a cuckoo clock here. Not to measure the time. We had nothing to measure, the anthem from the loud-speaker woke us every morning, and in the evening it sent us off to bed. Whenever we were needed, they came to get us, from the yard, the mess hall, from our sleep. The factory sirens were a clock for us, as were the white cooling tower cloud and the little bells from the coke oven batteries.

Presumably it was Anton Kowatsch, the drummer, who had dragged in the cuckoo clock. Although he swore he had nothing to do with it, he wound it every day. As long as it's hanging there it might as well run, he said.

It was a perfectly normal cuckoo clock, but the cuckoo wasn't normal. At three-quarters past the hour it called the half hour, and at a quarter past it called the hour. When it reached the hour, it either forgot everything or sounded the wrong time, calling twice as much or only half of what it should. Anton Kowatsch claimed that the cuckoo was calling the right time, but in different parts of the world. He was infatuated with the clock and its cuckoo, the two fir-cone weights made of heavy iron, and the speedy pendulum. He would have happily let the cuckoo call out the other parts of the world all through the night. But no one else in the barrack wanted to lie awake or sleep in the lands called by the cuckoo.

Anton Kowatsch was a lathe operator in the factory, and in the camp orchestra he was a percussionist and played the drum for our pleated version of La Paloma. It pained him that no one in the camp orchestra could play big-band swing the way his partners had back in Karansebesch. He was also a tinkerer, and had fashioned his instruments at the lathe in the metal shop. He wanted the worldly cuckoo clock to conform to the Russian day-and-night discipline. By narrowing the voice aperture in the cuckoo mechanism he tried to give the cuckoo a short, hollow night sound that was one octave lower than its bright day sound, which he hoped to lengthen. But before he could get a handle on the habits of the cuckoo, someone tore it out of the clock. The little door was wrenched partly off its hinge. When the clockwork wanted to animate the bird to sing, the little door opened up halfway, but instead of the cuckoo all that came out of the housing was a small piece of rubber, like an earthworm. The rubber vibrated, and you could hear a pitiful rattling noise that sounded just like the coughing, throat-clearing, snoring, farting, and sighing we did in our sleep. In that way the rubber worm protected our nighttime rest.

Anton Kowatsch became as excited about the worm as he was about the cuckoo, and especially about the sound it made. Each evening, when the loudspeaker anthem chased us into the barrack, Anton Kowatsch used a bent wire to switch the little piece of rubber to its nighttime rattle. He'd linger next to the clock, look at his reflection in the water bucket, and wait for the first rattle, as if hypnotized. When the little door opened, he'd hunch over a bit, and his left eye, which was slightly smaller than his right, would sparkle right on time. One evening, after the worm had rattled, he said to himself more than to me: Well well, it looks like our worm has picked up a little phantom pain from the cuckoo.

I liked the clock.

I didn't like the crazy cuckoo, or the worm, or the speedy pendulum. But I did like the two fir-cone weights. They were nothing more than heavy, inert iron, but I saw the fir forests in our mountains at home. The dense black-green mantle of needles high overhead. And below, strictly aligned, as far as the eye can see, the trunks—wooden legs that stand when you stand and walk when you walk and run when you run. But not the way you do, more like an army. You feel afraid, your heart starts pounding beneath your tongue, and then you notice the shiny needle-fall underfoot, this bright calm scattered with fir cones. You bend over and pick up two and stick one in your pocket. The other you hold in your hand, and suddenly you're no longer alone. The fir cones help you remember that the army is nothing but a forest, and that being lost in the forest is nothing more than going for a walk.

My father took great pains to teach me how to whistle, and how to tell where a whistle was coming from, so you could find a person who was lost in the woods by whistling back. I understood the usefulness of whistling, but I didn't understand the right way to blow the air through my lips. I did it backward, filling my chest with air instead of sending sound to my lips. I never learned to whistle. Every time he tried to show me, all I could think about was what I saw, how men's lips glisten on the inside, like rose quartz. He said that sooner or later I'd realize how useful it was. He meant the whistling. But I was thinking about the glassy skin inside the lips.

Actually the cuckoo clock belonged to the hunger angel. What was important in the camp was not our time, but rather the question: Cuckoo, how much longer will I live.

Kati Sentry

Katharina Seidel came from Bakowa in the Banat. Either someone from her village paid to be taken off the list and some scoundrel grabbed her instead, or the scoundrel was a sadist and she was on the list from the beginning. Kati was born feebleminded and all five years in the camp she had no idea where she was. A small version of a large woman, she had stopped growing while still a child, except in girth. She had a long brown braid, and her head was circled with a wreath of tightly curled hair. At first the women combed her hair every day, and later, after the lice plague began, every few days.

Kati Sentry wasn't suited for any type of work. She didn't understand what a quota was, or a command, or a punishment. She disrupted the course of the shift. During the second winter, to keep her busy, they came up with a sentry job. She was to go from one barrack to the next, keeping watch.

For a while she'd come to our barrack, sit at the small table, cross her arms, screw up her eyes, and peer into the prickly light from the bulb. The chair was too high for her, her feet didn't reach the floor. When she got bored she held on to the edge of the table and rocked back and forth. She could hardly stand that for more than an hour, then she'd be off to another barrack.

By summer she had stopped going to any barrack but ours, because she liked the cuckoo clock, although she didn't know how to tell time. She'd spend the night sitting under the light, arms crossed, waiting for the rubber worm to come out of his little door. When the worm started to rattle, she would open her mouth as if to join in, but wouldn't make any sound. By the time the worm came out again she'd be asleep with her face on the table. Before falling asleep she always laid her braid on the table and held on to it all night long. Maybe that way she wasn't so alone. Maybe she was afraid in this forest of beds for sixty-eight men. Maybe the braid helped her the way the fir cones helped me in the forest. Or perhaps she held her braid simply to make sure no one stole it.

The braid did get stolen, but not by us. As punishment for falling asleep, Tur Prikulitsch had her taken to the sick barrack, where the female medic was told to shave Kati Sentry's head. That evening Kati came to the mess hall with her cut-off braid and laid it on the table like a snake. She dunked the upper end in her soup and held it to her bare head so it would take root. Then she tried to feed the bottom end, and cried. Heidrun Gast took the braid away and told her it would be better to forget it. After dinner Heidrun Gast tossed the braid into one of the little fires in the yard and Kati Sentry looked on in silence as it burned.

Even with a shaved head Kati Sentry liked the cuckoo clock, and even with a shaved head she fell asleep after the rubber worm's first rattle, her hand clasping the missing braid. And she continued holding her hand that way even after her hair started growing back. But she also continued to fall asleep on duty, and several months later her head was shaved once again. After that her hair grew back so sparse that you saw more lice bites than hair. But that still didn't stop her from falling asleep on duty, until Tur Prikulitsch finally understood that you can put any human being to the drill, no matter how wretched, but you can't bend a feeble mind to your will. The sentry post was abolished.

Once during roll call, before her head was first shaved, Kati Sentry was standing in the middle of a row. She took off her cap, placed it on the snow, and sat down. Shishtvanyonov shouted: Get up, Fascist! Tur Prikulitsch jerked her up by her braid, but when he let go she sat down again. He kicked her in the small of her back until she lay doubled up on the ground, holding her braid in her fist and her fist in her mouth. The end of her braid stuck out as though she'd bitten off half a little brown bird. She lay there until after the Appell, when one of us helped her up and took her to the mess hall.

Tur Prikulitsch could order us around as he wished, but he disgraced himself with his coarse treatment of Kati Sentry. And when that backfired, he disgraced himself with his show of sympathy. Because she was beyond correction and beyond help, Kati Sentry showed how hollow his authority really was. In order to save face, Tur Prikulitsch softened. He had Kati Sentry sit next to him on the ground during roll call. For hours she would sit on her quilted cap and watch him in amazement as though he were a marionette. After roll call, her cap would be frozen to the snow and had to be pried off the ground.

For three summer evenings in a row Kati Sentry disrupted the roll call. For a while she sat quietly next to Prikulitsch, then scooted close to his feet and started polishing his shoe with her cap. He stepped on her hand. She pulled it away and polished the other shoe. Then he stepped on her hand with his other foot. When he lifted his foot she jumped up and ran through the assembled ranks, fluttering her arms and cooing like a dove. We all held our breath, and Tur let out a hollow laugh like a big turkey-cock. Three times Kati Sentry managed to polish his shoes and become a dove. After that she was no longer allowed at roll call. Instead she had to mop the floors in the barracks. She took a bucket of water from the well, wrung out the rag, wrapped it around the broom, and changed the dirty water after every barrack. She worked without hesitation, her mind unclouded by any distraction. The floor was cleaner than ever before. She mopped thoroughly, without haste, perhaps out of habit from home.

Nor was she all that crazy. For roll call, instead of Appell she said APFEL—apple. When the little bell rang at the coke batteries she thought it was time for mass. She didn't have to invent illusions, because her mind wasn't in the camp to begin with. The way she behaved didn't conform to camp regulations, but it did fit the circumstances. There was something elemental about her that we envied. Even the hunger angel was baffled when faced with her instincts. He visited her as he did all of us, but he did not climb into her brain. Kati performed the most basic tasks without thinking, abandoning herself to whatever came her way. She survived the camp without going door-to-door. She was never seen rummaging through the kitchen waste behind the mess hall. She ate what could be found in the yard and on the factory grounds. Seeds, leaves, and flowers in the weeds. And all kinds of insects—worms and caterpillars, maggots and beetles, spiders and snails. And in the snowy yard inside the camp the frozen excrement of the watchdogs. We were amazed at how the dogs trusted her, as if this human were one of them as she tottered about, her cap flapping over her ears.

Kati Sentry's madness never went beyond what we could put up with. She was neither clinging nor aloof. Through all the years in the camp she seemed as much at home as a house pet. There was nothing alien about her. We liked her.

One September afternoon after my shift, the sun was still blazing hot in the sky. I drifted along the overgrown paths behind the mouth of the coal silo. Singed by the summer, the skeletons of wild oats shimmered like fish bones as they swayed among the fiery orach, which had long since turned inedible. Inside the hard husks, the kernels were still milky. I ate. On my way back I didn't want to swim through the weeds again and so I decided to go a different way. Kati Sentry was sitting by the zeppelin. Her hands were on an anthill swarming with black ants. She was licking them off and eating them. I asked: Kati, what are you doing.

She said: I'm making gloves for myself, they tickle.

Are you cold, I asked.

She said: Not today, tomorrow. My mother baked poppy-seed rolls, they're still warm. Don't step on them with your feet, you can wait, you're not a hunter. When the rolls are all gone the soldiers will be counted at the apple. Then they'll go home.

By then her hands were swarming black again. Before she licked off the ants, she asked: When is the war over.

I said: The war's been over for two years. Come, let's go back to the camp.

She said: Can't you see I don't have any time now.

The case of the stolen bread

Fenya never wore a fufaika, she wore a white work apron, and a crocheted wool sweater over that—a different sweater every day. One was nut brown, another a dirty purple, like unpeeled beets, one was muddy yellow and another speckled with whitish gray. Each was too loose in the sleeve and too tight at the stomach. We never knew which sweater was meant for which day, or why Fenya wore them at all, or why she wore them over the apron. They couldn't have kept her warm, they had more holes than wool. The wool was from before the war, repeatedly knitted and unraveled, but still good for crocheting. The yarn may have been salvaged from all the worn-out sweaters of a single large family, or else inherited from everyone in it who had died. We knew nothing about Fenya's family, or whether she even had one, before or after the war. None of us was interested in Fenya personally. But we were all devoted to her, because she doled out the bread. She was the bread, the mistress from whose hands we ate, like dogs, day after day.

Our eyes clung to her, as though she might create the bread for us. Our hunger examined everything about her very closely.

Her eyebrows like two toothbrushes, her face with its powerful chin, her too-short horse lips that didn't quite cover her gums, her gray fingernails gripping the large knife she used to fine-tune the rations, her kitchen scale with its two beaks.

Most of all, her heavy eyes, as lifeless as the wooden beads on the abacus she rarely touched. The fact that she was repulsively ugly was something we couldn't admit even to ourselves. We were afraid she might see what we were thinking.

As soon as the beaks of her scale started moving up and down, I followed them with my eyes. My tongue twitched along with the beaks. I closed my mouth, but parted my lips so Fenya could see my toothy smile. We smiled out of necessity and out of principle, our smiles were genuine and false, helpless and underhanded at the same time, so as not to lose Fenya's favor. So as not to challenge her sense of justice but encourage it, and if possible even increase it by a few grams.

But nothing helped, she was always in a foul mood. Her right leg was so much shorter than her left that we said she was lame, and this limp seemed to cause the right corner of her mouth to twitch up and down, while twisting the left into a permanent grimace. When she hobbled up to the bread counter, her bad mood appeared to come from the dark bread, and not from her short leg. Her mouth gave her face an agonized appearance—especially the right half.

And because she was the one who gave us our bread, her limping and her tormented face struck us as something fateful, like the staggering gait of history. Fenya seemed to exude a Communist saintliness. She was undoubtedly a loyal member of the camp's administrative cadre, otherwise she would never have become mistress of the bread and accomplice of the hunger angel.

All alone she stood behind the counter in her whitewashed chamber, between abacus and scales, wielding the large knife. She must have carried lists in her head. She knew exactly who should get six hundred grams, who eight hundred grams, and who was to receive the thousand-gram ration.

I was overcome by Fenya's ugliness. But in time I came to see that it was beauty turned inside out, and that made her the object of my veneration. Disgust would have made me bitter and would have been risky in view of her scales. I scraped and bowed, and often hated myself for doing so, but only after I'd savored her bread and felt halfway sated for a few minutes.

Today I imagine Fenya having administered all the bread I ever ate. First was the daily bread from Transylvania, the in-the-sweat-of-thy-face sour bread of the Lutheran God. Second was the wholesome brown bread from Hitler's golden ears of grain in the German Reich. Third was the ration of *khlyeb* on the Russian scales. I believe the hunger angel knew of this trinity of the bread, and that he exploited it.

The bread factory made the first deliveries at dawn. By the time we arrived at the mess hall, between six and seven, Fenya had already measured out the portions. She placed each person's ration back on the scales and balanced it against the weight, adding a bit more or cutting off a corner. Then she pointed her knife at the beaks, cocked her heavy chin, and looked at you as if she were seeing you for the first time in four hundred days.

Early on—around the time of the stolen bread—it dawned on me that Fenya's saintliness, cold and cruel, had crept inside the bread, which is why we were capable of killing in the name of hunger.

By reweighing the bread like that, Fenya showed us that she

was just. The ready portions lay on the shelves, covered with linen sheets. Before doling out a ration she would lift the cloth a little bit and then put it back, exactly as the practiced beggars did with their coal when going door-to-door. In her white-washed chamber, with her white apron and white sheets, Fenya was like a priestess celebrating bread hygiene as a pillar of camp civilization. Of world civilization. The flies had no choice but to land on the fabric instead of the bread. They couldn't get to the bread until we were holding it. And if they didn't fly away quickly enough we ate their hunger along with our bread. At the time, I never thought about the flies' hunger, or even about the hygienic rites with the white bread linens.

Fenya's sense of justice, this combination of bitter resent-ment and accurate weighing, made me utterly submissive. There was perfection in her very repulsiveness. Fenya was neither good nor bad, she was not a person but the law in a crocheted sweater. It never would have occurred to me to compare her to other women, because no other woman was so agonizingly disciplined and so immaculately ugly. She was like the rationed loaves we coveted—appallingly wet, sticky, and disgracefully nourishing.

Each morning we received our ration for the whole day. Like most people, I belonged to the eight-hundred-gram group—that was the normal ration. Six hundred was for light work inside the camp: moving waste from the latrines into cisterns, sweeping snow, spring and fall cleaning, whitewash-ing the rocks along the main street. Only a few people were given a thousand grams, that was the exceptional ration for the heaviest labor. Even six hundred grams sounds like a lot, but the bread was so heavy that a single slice as thick as the length of your thumb weighed eight hundred grams, if cut from the center of the loaf. If you were lucky enough to get the heel, with the dry crusty corners, the slice was two thumbs thick.

The first decision of the day was: Am I steadfast enough to not eat my entire portion at breakfast with my cabbage soup. Can I, in all my hunger, save a little piece for the evening. At midday there was nothing to decide, since we were at work and there was no meal. In the evening after work, assuming I'd been steadfast in the morning, came the second decision: Am I steadfast enough just to check that my saved bread is still under my pillow, only look and nothing more. Can I hold off eating it until I'm in the mess hall, after evening roll call, which could take another two hours, or even longer.

If I hadn't been steadfast in the morning, I had no leftover bread in the evening and no decision to make. Then I would fill my spoon just halfway and slurp deeply. I had learned to eat slowly, to swallow a little spit after every spoonful of soup. The hunger angel said: Spit makes the soup longer, and going to bed early makes the hunger shorter.

I went to bed early but woke up constantly, because my throat was swollen and pulsing. Whether I kept my eyes open or closed, whether I tossed around or stared at the lightbulb, whether someone was snoring as if he were drowning, whether the rubber worm from the cuckoo clock was rattling or not— the night was boundlessly vast, and in the night Fenya's bread cloths were endlessly large, and beneath them lay the abundant, unreachable bread.

In the morning, after the anthem, hunger hurried off with me to breakfast, to Fenya. To the heroic first decision: Am I steadfast today, can I save a piece of bread for the evening, and on and on.

But how far on.

Each day the hunger angel gnawed at my brain. And one day he raised my hand. And with my hand I nearly struck Karli Halmen dead—because of the bread he had stolen.

Karli Halmen had the day off. He had the barrack all to himself, since everyone was at work. He'd eaten his entire ration of bread at breakfast. And that evening, when Albert Gion came off his shift, he found his saved bread had disappeared. Albert Gion had been steadfast for five days in a row, he'd saved five little pieces of bread, a whole day's ration. He had been on our shift the entire day and, like everyone else who'd saved his bread, he had spent the entire day thinking about eating it with his evening soup. Like everyone else, the first thing he did when he came off the shift was to look under his pillow. His bread was no longer there.

Albert Gion's bread wasn't there, and Karli Halmen was sitting on his bed in his underwear. Albert Gion positioned himself in front of Karli Halmen and without saying a word punched him in the mouth three times. Without saying a word, Karli Halmen spat two teeth onto his bed. The accordion player dragged Karli by the neck to the water bucket and held his head under water. Bubbles came out of his mouth and nose, then gasping sounds, and after that it was quiet. The drummer then pulled Karli's head out of the water and choked him until his mouth started twitching as hideously as Fenya's. I pushed the drummer away, but then I pulled off my wooden shoe. And I raised my hand, so high I would have killed the bread thief. Up to that moment Paul Gast the lawyer had been watching from his upper bunk. He jumped on my back, tore the shoe out of my hand, and threw it against the wall. Karli Halmen had wet himself and was lying next to the bucket, spitting up bready slime.

My bloodlust had swallowed my reason. And I wasn't the only one, we were a mob. We dragged Karli in his bloody, piss-soaked underwear out into the night, next to the barrack. It was February. We stood him against the barrack wall, he staggered and fell over. Without any discussion, the drummer and I undid our pants, then Albert Gion and all the others. And because we were all getting ready for bed anyway, one after the other we pissed on Karli Halmen's face. Paul Gast the lawyer joined in as well. Two watchdogs barked, and a guard came running after them. The dogs smelled the blood and growled, the guard cursed. The lawyer and the guard carried Karli to the sick barrack. We watched them leave and used the snow to wipe the blood off our hands. Everyone went back to the barrack in silence and crawled into bed. I had a spot of blood on my wrist, I turned it toward the light and thought, How bright red Karli's blood is, like sealing wax, as if it came from the artery and not the vein. In the barrack it was dead silent, and I heard the rubber worm rattling in the cuckoo clock, sounding so close it could be inside my head. I no longer thought about Karli Halmen, or about Fenya's endlessly white linen, or even about the unreachable bread. I fell into a deep, calm sleep.

The next morning Karli Halmen's bed was empty. We went to the mess hall as always. The snow was empty as well, no longer red, fresh snow had fallen. Karli Halmen spent two days in the sick barrack. After that he was back with us in the mess hall just as before, except with pus-filled wounds, swollen eyes, and blue lips. The business with the bread was over, everyone acted the same as always. We didn't hold the theft against Karli Halmen. And he never held his punishment against us. He knew he had earned it. The bread court does not deliberate, it punishes. It knows no mitigation, it needs no legal code. It is a law unto itself, because the hunger angel is also a thief who steals the brain. Bread justice has no prologue or epilogue, it is only here and now. Totally transparent, or totally mysterious. In any case, the violence meted out by bread justice is different from hungerless violence. You cannot approach the bread court with conventional morality.

The bread court took place in February. By April, Karli Halmen was sitting on a chair in Oswald Enyeter's barber room, his wounds had healed, his beard had grown like trampled grass. My turn was next, and I waited behind him in the mirror, the way Tur Prikulitsch usually waited behind me. The barber placed his furry hands on Karli's shoulders and asked: Since when are we missing two front teeth. Karli Halmen answered, speaking not to me, nor to the barber, but to the barber's furry hands: Since the case of the stolen bread.

After his beard had been shaved off, I sat down on the chair. It was the only time that Oswald Enyeter ever whistled a kind of serenade as he shaved, and a spot of blood came spilling out of the lather. Not bright red like sealing wax, but dark red, like a raspberry in the snow.

Crescent Moon Madonna

When our hunger is at its peak, we talk about childhood and food. The women at greater length than the men. And no one talks at greater length than the women from the countryside. Each of their recipes takes three acts, like a play. The dramatic tension builds as opinions differ over ingredients. And it really heats up over a bread-bacon-and-egg stuffing, when a whole onion is called for, and a half just won't do, when you need six and not just four cloves of garlic, and when the onions and garlic better be grated and not just minced. And when old rolls make better crumbs than bread, and caraway is better than pepper, and marjoram is better than anything including tarragon, which of course goes with fish but not duck. The play reaches its climax when the mixture clearly has to be inserted just under the skin to absorb the fat during roasting, or absolutely has to be spooned into the stomach cavity so it won't soak up all the fat. Sometimes the Lutheran stuffed duck wins out, and sometimes the Catholic one.

And when the women from the country make soup noodles out of words, they spend at least half an hour thrashing out how many eggs are needed and whether the dough should be stirred with a spoon or kneaded by hand before it gets rolled out glassy thin but doesn't tear and is left to dry on the noodle board. And then it's another quarter hour before the dough gets rolled and cut, before the noodles move off the board and into the soup, before the soup is slowly stirred or quickly brought to a rolling boil and is finally served with either a good handful or just a pinch of freshly chopped parsley sprinkled on top.

The women from the city don't argue about how many eggs to put in the dough but how few. Because they're always scrimping on everything, their recipes aren't even enough for a curtain-raiser.

Telling a recipe takes greater art than telling a joke. The punch line has to hit home even though it's not funny. Here in the camp it's already a joke as soon as you say: FIRST TAKE. The punch line is that there's nothing to take. But no one bothers to say that. Recipes are the jokes of the hunger angel.

To get inside the women's barracks you have to run a gauntlet. As soon as you step inside you have to say who you're looking for, without waiting to be asked. Your best bet is to ask a question yourself: Is Trudi here. And while you're asking you head for Trudi Pelikan's bed, in the third row on the left. The beds are two-story iron bunks, just like in the men's barracks. Some have blankets draped as a screen, for evening love. I'm never interested in going behind the blanket, though, all I'm after are recipes. The women think I'm too shy, because I once had books. They believe that reading makes you delicate and sensitive.

I never read the books I brought to the camp. Since paper is strictly forbidden, I kept my books hidden under some bricks behind the barracks until the middle of the first summer.

Then I auctioned them off. For 50 pages of *Zarathustra* cigarette paper I received 1 measure of salt, and 70 pages fetched 1 measure of sugar. For the clothbound *Faust* in its entirety Peter Schiel made me my own lice comb out of tin. I consumed the lyrical anthology from eight centuries in the form of corn flour and lard and converted the slim volume of Weinheber into millet. That doesn't make you delicate, just discreet.

Discreetly, after work, I look at the young Russians on duty taking a shower. I'm so discreet that I forget why I'm looking. They would kill me if I remembered.

Once again I was not steadfast. I ate all my bread in the morning. Once again I'm sitting next to Trudi Pelikan on the edge of her bed. The two Zirris sit opposite us, on Corina Marcu's bed. She's been at the kolkhoz for weeks. I look at the little golden hairs and the black wart on the emaciated fingers of the Zirris and, so as not to start right in on food, I talk about my childhood.

Every summer we used to take a long vacation in the country—we, meaning my mother, myself, and the servant girl Lodo. We had a summerhouse in the Wench highlands, across from Schnürleibl Mountain. We stayed for eight weeks. During these eight weeks we always took one day-trip to Schässburg, the nearest town. We had to go down into the valley to catch the train. Our station was called Hétur in Hungarian, and Siebenmänner in German. When the bell rang on the roof of the station attendant's hut, we knew that the train had left Danesch and would be arriving in five minutes. We had to board right from track level, because there was no platform, so when the train pulled up, the door was as high as my chest. Before we climbed on I inspected the car from underneath, the black wheels with the shiny rims, the chains, hooks, and buffers.

Then we rode past our swimming place, past Toma's house and past the field that belonged to old Zacharias—to whom we gave two packs of tobacco each month for letting us walk through his barley to get to the river. Next came the iron bridge, with the yellow water rolling below. Then the eroded sand cliffs, topped by Villa Franca. And then we were in Schässburg, where we always went straight to the elegant Café Martini on the market square. We stood out a little among the guests because we were dressed a bit too casually—my mother in culottes and I in my shorts with knee-high socks, gray so they wouldn't show dirt so quickly. Only Lodo wore the Sunday clothes she'd brought from her village, a white peasant blouse and a black headscarf with a border of roses and a green silk fringe. Red-shaded roses, as big as apples, bigger than real roses. On that day we could eat whatever we wanted, and as much as we could. We could choose among marzipan truffles, chocolate cake, savarins, cream cake, nut cake roll, Ischler tartlet, cream puffs, hazelnut crisps, rum cake, napoleons, nougat, and doboschtorte. And ice cream—strawberry ice cream in a silver dish or vanilla ice cream in a glass dish or chocolate ice cream in a porcelain bowl, always with whipped cream. And, finally, if we were still able, sour-cherry cake with jelly. My arms felt the cool touch of the marble tabletop and the backs of my knees felt the soft plush of the chair. And up on the black buffet, teetering in the wind of the fan, wearing a long red dress, standing on her tiptoes atop a very thin moon, was the Crescent Moon Madonna.

After I'd finished telling that, all our stomachs started to teeter. Trudi Pelikan reached behind me and took her saved bread from under her pillow. The women picked up their metal bowls and stuck their spoons inside their jackets. I had mine on me, together we went to supper. We took our place in the line in front of the soup kettle. No one said a thing. From the end of the table Trudi Pelikan asked over the clatter of tin: Leo, what was that café called.

Café Martini, I shouted.

Two or three spoonfuls later she asked: And what was that woman on her tiptoes called.

I shouted: Crescent Moon Madonna.

On the bread trap

Everyone gets caught in the bread trap.

In the trap of being steadfast at breakfast, the trap of swapping bread at supper, the trap of saved bread under your pillow at night. The hunger angel's worst trap is the trap of being steadfast: to be hungry and have bread but decline to eat it. To be hard against yourself, harder than the deep-frozen ground. Every morning the hunger angel says: Think about the evening.

In the evening, over cabbage soup, bread gets swapped, because your own bread always appears smaller than the other person's. And this holds true for everyone.

Before the swap you feel light-headed, right after the swap you feel doubt. After swapping, the bread I traded seems bigger in the other person's hand than it did in mine. And the bread I got in return has shrunk. Look how quickly he's turning away, he has a better eye, he's come out on top, I better swap again. But the other person feels the same way, he thinks that I've come out on top, and now he's on his second trade as well. Once more the bread shrinks in my hand. I look for a third person and swap with him. Some people are already eating. If my hunger can just hold out a little longer, there'll be a fourth swap, and a fifth. And if nothing works, I'll make one more swap and wind up back with my own bread.

Trading bread is something we need to do. The exchange happens fast and never hits the mark. Bread deceives you like the cement. And just as you can become cement-sick, bread can make you swap-sick. The evening hubbub is all about swapping bread, a business of glinting eyes and jittery fingers. In the mornings it's the beaks on the scales that weigh the bread, in the evening it's your eyes. To make your trade you not only have to find the right piece of bread, you have to find the right face. You size up the mouth of the other person. The best mouths are long and thin like a scythe. You size up the hollows of the cheeks, to see if the hunger-fur is growing, if the fine white hairs are long and thick enough. Before someone dies of hunger, a hare appears in his face. You think: Bread is wasted on that one, it doesn't pay to nourish him anymore since the white hare is already on its way. That's why we call the bread from someone with the white hare cheek-bread.

In the morning there's no time, but there's also nothing to trade. The freshly cut slices look alike. By evening, though, each slice has dried differently, either straight and angular or crooked and bulging. The shifting appearance of your bread as it dries gives rise to the feeling that your bread is deceiving you. Everyone has this feeling, even if they don't swap. And swapping only heightens the feeling. You move from one optical illusion to another. Afterward you still feel cheated, but tired. The swapping that takes you from your own bread to cheek-bread stops the way it began, suddenly. The commotion is over, your eyes move on to the soup. You hold your bread in one hand and your spoon in the other.

Utterly alone inside the pack, each person tries to make his soup go further. The spoons, too, are a pack, as are the tin plates and the slurping and the shoving of feet under the table. The soup warms, it comes alive in your throat. I slurp out loud, I have to hear the soup. I force myself not to count the spoonfuls. Uncounted, there'll be more than sixteen or nineteen—numbers I have to forget.

One evening the accordion player Konrad Fonn swapped bread with Kati Sentry. She gave him her bread, but he handed her a rectangular piece of wood. She bit into it, was stunned, and swallowed air. No one but the accordion player laughed. And Karli Halmen took the little piece of wood away from Kati Sentry and dropped it in the accordion player's cabbage soup. Then he returned Kati's bread to her.

Everyone gets caught in the bread trap. But no one is allowed to take Kati Sentry's cheek-bread. This, too, is part of the bread law. In the camp we've learned to clear away the dead without shuddering. We undress them before they turn stiff, we need their clothes so we won't freeze to death. And we eat their saved bread. Their death is our gain. But Kati Sentry is alive, even if she doesn't know where she is. We realize this, so we treat her as something that belongs to all of us. We make up for what we do to one another by standing up for her. We're capable of many things, but as long as she is living among us, there's a limit to how far we actually go. And this probably counts for more than Kati Sentry herself.

On coal

There's as much coal as there is earth, more than enough.

FAT COAL comes from Petrovka. It's full of gray rock, heavy, wet, and sticky. It has a sour, burnt smell and flaky lumps like graphite. Large amounts of waste rock remain after it is ground in the *molina* and washed in the *moika*.

SULFUR COAL comes from Kramatorsk, and generally arrives around noon. The *yama* is a kind of pit that serves as a giant underground coal silo, covered with a screening grate and protected by an open-air roof. The coal cars are driven onto the grate one by one. Each coal car is a sixty-ton Pullman freight wagon with five bottom chutes. The chutes are opened with hammers, and when each strike hits its mark it sounds like the gong at the cinema. If all goes well, you don't have to go inside the car at all, the coal comes rattling out in one swoop. The dust makes everything go dark, the sun turns gray in the sky like a tin dish. You breathe in and swallow more dust than air, it grinds in your teeth. Unloading sixty tons of coal takes only fifteen minutes. All that's left on the grate are a few oversized chunks. Sulfur coal is light, brittle, and dry. It has a crystalline sheen like mica, and consists of lumps and dust, nothing that classifies as nut- or grain-sized. Its name comes from its sulfur content but it has no odor. The sulfur doesn't show until much later, and then as yellow deposits in the sludge puddles in the factory yard. Or at night, as yellow eyes on the slag heap, glowing like carved-up bits of moon.

MARKA-K-COAL, used for coking, comes from the nearby Rudniy mine. It is neither fat nor dry, not stony, not sandy, not granular. It is everything at once and nothing special and utterly despicable. True, it has a lot of anthracite, but no character. Supposedly it's the most valuable grade of coal. Anthracite was never a friend to me, not even an annoying one. It was sneaky and difficult to unload, as if you were jabbing your shovel into a knot of rags or a tangle of roots.

The yama is like a train station, only half-covered and just as drafty. Biting wind, piercing cold, short days, electric light even at midday. Coal dust and snow dust mixed together. Or wind and rain slanting into your face, with thicker drops coming through the roof. Or singeing heat and long days with sun and coal until you drop. Marka-k-coal is as difficult to pronounce as it is to unload. The name can only be stuttered, not whispered like the name for gas coal: *gazoviy.*

GAS COAL is agile. It comes from Yasinovataya. The Ukrainian nachal'nik softens it into HAZOVIY. But to us it sounds like: hase-vey. And that sounds like a hare in pain. Which is why I like it. Every car contains walnuts, hazelnuts, corn kernels, and peas. The five chutes open easily, with the mere swipe of a glove, so to speak. The hazoviy rustles five times, very easy, slate-gray, clean, no waste rock. You watch and think: this hazoviy has a soft heart. Once it's unloaded, the grate is as clean as if nothing had passed through. We stand overhead on the grate. Below, in the belly of the yama, must be whole mountain ranges and chasms of coal. The hazoviy gets deposited there as well.

My head has deposits of its own. The summer air trembles over the yama just like at home, and the sky is silky just like at home. But no one at home knows I'm still alive. At home Grandfather is eating cold cucumber salad and thinks that I am dead. Grandmother is clucking to the chickens, scattering their feed in the room-sized shade beside the shed, and thinks that I am dead. Mother and Father may be at the summer-house in the Wench. Mother is wearing her homemade sailor suit. She's lying in the tall grass of a mountain meadow and thinks that I'm already in heaven. And I can't shake her and say: So, do you love me. See, I'm still alive. And Father is sitting in the kitchen, slowly filling his shells with shot, tiny balls of tempered lead for hunting hares in the waning summer. Hase-vey.

How the seconds drag

I went hunting.

Kobelian had left me alone out on the steppe, in the second waning summer, and I killed a steppe-dog with my shovel. It let out a short whistle, like a train. How the seconds drag, when a forehead has been split in two, right over the snout. Hase-vey.

I wanted to eat it.

There's nothing here but grass. But you can't stake things with grass, and you can't skin things with a shovel. I didn't have the tools, and I didn't have the heart.

Or the time. Kobelian was back, he'd seen what I had done. I left the animal just the way it was, how the seconds drag, when a forehead has been split in two, right over the snout. Hase-vey.

Father, once you wanted to teach me how to whistle back to find someone who is lost.

On yellow sand

Sand can be any shade of yellow, from peroxide blond to canary, or even with a tinge of pink. Yellow sand is tender, it makes you sad to see it get mixed in the gray cement.

It was late in the evening, once again Kobelian was taking Karli Halmen and me out for a private delivery, this time of yellow sand. He said: We're going to my house. I'm not building anything, but the holiday's coming up and, after all, people aren't animals, you have to have a little beauty, a little culture.

Karli Halmen and I understood that yellow sand meant culture. Even in the camp yard and at the factory they strewed it along the pathways after spring and fall cleaning. The ornamental spring sand was for the end of the war and the ornamental fall sand was for the October Revolution. May 9 was the first anniversary of the peace. But neither the peace nor the anniversary was of any use to us, here in our second year in camp. Then came October. The ornamental spring sand was long gone, carried off by the wind on dry days, and washed away by the torrents of rain. Now the yard was strewn with fresh yellow fall sand, like sugar crystals. Sand to beautify the great October, but by no means a sign that we'd be allowed to go home.

Not all our deliveries were made for beautification. We hauled yellow sand by the ton, the construction sites devoured it. The sand quarry was called the *kar'yer*. It was inexhaustible, at least three hundred meters long and twenty to thirty meters deep, nothing but sand everywhere. An arena of sand inside an open quarry of sand. Enough to serve the entire district. And the more sand that was hauled, the higher the arena grew, as the quarry ate deeper and deeper into the earth.

If you were *khitriy*, or clever, you steered the truck so it backed right into the slope, then you didn't have to shovel the sand upward, but could casually load it on the same level, or even comfortably scoop it down into the bed.

The kar'yer was fascinating, like the imprint of some giant toe. Pure sand, not a crumb of earth. Layers of sand, straight and level, one on top of the other: wax-white, skin-pale, pallid-yellow, bright-yellow, ochre, and pink. Cool and moist. As you shoveled, the sand fluffed up, drying as it flew through the air. It practically shoveled itself. The truck was quickly filled. And because it was a dump truck, it unloaded itself as well. So Karli Halmen and I stayed behind in the quarry until Kobelian came back for the next load.

When he did return, he lay down in the sand and stayed that way while we loaded up. He even closed his eyes, perhaps he fell asleep. Once the truck was full, we gently nudged his shoe with the tip of a shovel. He jumped up and stomped over to the cab. The imprint of his body stayed in the sand, as if there were two Kobelians, a hollow one lying down and another standing by the cab, with damp trousers. Before he climbed inside he spat twice into the sand, grabbed the steering wheel with one hand, and rubbed his eyes with the other. Then he got in and drove off.

Now Karli and I let ourselves drop into the sand and listened to it trickling around us, felt it clinging to our bodies. The sky curved overhead, a grassy scar marked where it met the sand. Time was still and smooth, a microscopic twinkling all around. Faraway places came to mind, as if we'd escaped and belonged to any sand anywhere in the world but not here in this place of forced labor. We fled by lying still. I looked all around: I had managed to slip below the horizon without danger and without consequences. The sand cradled my back from below, and the sky drew my face upward. Soon the sky became blind, and my eyes pulled it back down and my head was filled with its motionless blue through and through. I was blanketed by the sky and no one had any idea where I was. Not even homesickness could find me. In the sand, heaven did not set the time in motion, but neither could heaven turn back the time, just as the yellow sand couldn't make the peace mean more than it did, not after three years, and not after four. We were in the camp after the fourth peace anniversary as well.

Karli Halmen lay facedown in his own hollow. The scars left from the bread theft shimmered like wax through his short hair. The sunlight lit up his ear, revealing the red silk of tiny veins. I thought about my last rendezvous in the Alder Park and the Neptune Baths with the twice-my-age married Romanian. How long had he waited for me that first time I didn't appear. And how often did he wait before he realized that I wasn't coming back the next time, or the time after that, or ever again. It would be at least half an hour before Kobelian came back.

And once again something raised my hand, I wanted to

caress Karli Halmen. Luckily he helped me out of my temptation. He raised his face—he had bitten into the sand. He chewed the sand, it grated in his mouth, and he swallowed. I froze, and he filled his mouth a second time. The grains spilled from his cheeks as he ate. And the sand left the imprint of a sieve on his cheeks and nose and on his forehead. And the tears on both cheeks left a pale brown string.

As a child I'd take a peach and bite into it, he said, then I'd drop it on the ground so it would land where I'd bitten. Then I'd pick it up and eat the sandy spot and drop it again. Until all that was left was the pit. My father took me to the doctor because I wasn't normal, because I liked the taste of sand. Now I have more than enough sand and can't remember what a peach looks like at all.

I said: Yellow, with delicate fuzz and a little red silk around the pit.

We heard the truck coming and got up.

Karli Halmen began shoveling. Tears were running down his face as he filled his shovel. When he sent the sand flying, the tears ran left, into his mouth, and right, into his ear.

The Russians have
their ways, too

Karli Halmen and I were once again riding across the steppe in the Lancia. Steppe-dogs darting off in all directions. Tire tracks everywhere, flattened bundles of grass, lacquered reddish-brown with dried blood. Everywhere swarms of flies, parading over squashed fur and spilled entrails, some with a fresh blue-white sheen like coiled strings of pearls, others bluish red and half gone to rot, and others withered, like dried flowers. Some dogs had been hurled to the side of the tire tracks, seemingly untouched by the wheels, as though asleep. Karli Halmen said: When they're dead they look like flatirons. In no way did they look like flatirons. How did that ever occur to him, I'd already forgotten the word flatiron.

There were days when the steppe-dogs didn't fear the wheels as much as they should. Perhaps on those days the wind whooshed like the truck, and the similarity confused their instincts. As the wheels approached they'd start to run, but in a daze, not at all as if their life depended on it. I was certain that Kobelian never took the trouble to avoid hitting a steppe-dog. And equally certain that he had never hit one, never caused one to whistle underneath his wheels. Not that you would have heard its high-pitched squeal—the Lancia was too loud.

Even so, I know how a steppe-dog whistles when it gets hit by a truck, because I hear it in my mind on every trip. A short, heartbreaking sound, three syllables in a row: ha-se-vey. Exactly like when you kill one with the shovel, because it happens just as quickly. And I also know how at that spot the earth trembles in fright and sends out ripples, like a fat stone falling into water. And I know how your lip burns right afterward, because you bite into it when you strike with all your strength and kill with one blow.

Ever since I left that one dog lying there, I've been telling myself that you can't eat steppe-dogs, even if you don't feel a trace of compassion for the living ones or the slightest disgust for the dead. If I felt either, it wouldn't be about the steppe-dogs but about me. The disgust would be with myself, for hesitating out of compassion.

But if we have time on our next trip, if Kobelian lets Karli and me out of the truck even for a little while, just for as long as it takes him to stuff three or four sacks full of young grass for his goats. Only I don't think Karli Halmen would do it, not with me there. I'd end up wasting several minutes trying to talk him into it, and then it would be too late, even if we did have enough time. I'd have to tell him: There's no reason to be ashamed in front of a steppe-dog, or in front of the steppe. I think he'd be embarrassed in front of himself, at least more than I would be in front of myself. And more than I would be in front of Kobelian. I'd probably have to ask him why he was making Kobelian out to be some kind of standard, and tell him that if Kobelian were as far from home as we are, he'd undoubtedly eat steppe-dogs too.

Some days the steppe was covered with brown-lacquered crushed bundles of grass that looked as though they had appeared overnight. And overnight all the clouds had melted away. The only things left were the skinny cranes in the sky and the wild, fat blowflies on the ground. But not a single dead steppe-dog lying in the grass.

What do you think happened to them, I'd ask Karli. What are all those Russians doing, walking through the steppe and bending over and sitting down like that. Do you think they're just resting, that they're all tired. They have a tangled nest inside their skulls just like we do, and the same empty stomach. The Russians have their ways, too, I'd say to him. And they have all the time they need, they live here on the steppe. Believe me, I'd say to Karli, Kobelian doesn't have anything against eating steppe-dogs. Why else would he keep a short-handled shovel in the cab next to the brake—after all, he picks his grass by hand. When we're not with him, he doesn't just stop to pick goat grass. I'd say all that to Karli, and I wouldn't be lying, because I'd have no idea what the truth was. Even if I did know, it would only be one truth, and the opposite would be another. Besides, I'd say, you and I are different when we're with Kobelian than we are without him. And I'm different without you. You're the only one who thinks you're never different. But when you stole bread you were different, and I was different, and all the others, too—but that I'd never say to him, because it would sound like a reproach.

Fur stinks when it burns. Hurry up and build the fire, I'd say, if Karli Halmen did decide to join in, I'll skin the animal.

Another week had passed. Karli Halmen and I were once again riding across the steppe in the Lancia. The air was pale, the grass orange, the sun was turning the steppe into late fall.

Night frost had sugared the steppe-dogs that had been run over. We drove past an old man. He was standing in a whirl of dust, waving to us with a shovel. It had a short handle. A sack was slung over his shoulder, it was only a quarter full and looked heavy. Karli said: That's not grass he's getting. If we have time on our next trip, if Kobelian lets us out of the truck even for a little while. I know Kobelian wouldn't mind, but you, you'd rather be tenderhearted, you'd never join in.

They don't call it blind hunger for no reason. Karli Halmen and I didn't know much about each other. We were together too much. And Kobelian didn't know anything about us and we didn't know anything about him. We were all different than we are.

Fir trees

Shortly before Christmas I was sitting next to Kobelian in the Lancia. It was getting dark, and we were making another illegal trip, this time to his brother's. We were hauling a load of coal.

Cobblestones and the ruins of a train station marked the beginning of a small town. We turned onto a rough, crooked street at the edge of the settlement. Behind a cast-iron fence a cluster of fir trees stood out against the last band of light in the sky, black as night, slender and pointed, rising high above everything else and very distinct. Kobelian drove past two houses and pulled up in front of the third.

When I started to unload the coal he gave a relaxed wave as if to say: Not so fast, we have time. He went into a house that was probably white but which the headlights had turned yellow.

I put my coat on the roof of the cab and shoveled as slowly as I could. But the shovel was my master, it set the time, and I had to follow. And it was proud of me. For years now, shoveling was the only thing left to be proud of. Soon the truck was empty and Kobelian was still inside the house with his brother.

Sometimes plans hatch slowly, but sometimes you make a decision so fast you start acting before you even know you can do it, and that can be electrifying. My coat was already back on. I told myself that stealing could land me in the concrete box, but my feet carried me even faster toward the fir trees. The gate—it must have been an overgrown park or a cemetery—wasn't locked. I broke off the lower branches, then removed my coat and wrapped them inside. Leaving the gate open, I hurried back to Kobelian. His brother's house now loomed white in the darkness, the truck's headlights were no longer on, the tailgate was already closed. My bundle smelled strongly of sap and sharply of fear when I tossed it over my head into the back of the truck. Kobelian was sitting in the cab, stinking of vodka. At least that's what I'd say today, but at the time I thought to myself: He smells of vodka, but he's not a real drunk, he only drinks with heavy meals. Still, he could have shared some with me.

When it's that late you never know what's going to happen at the entrance to the camp. Three guard dogs barked. The guard knocked the bundle out of my arms with the barrel of his rifle. The branches fell to the ground, on top of my fancy coat with the velvet collar. The dogs sniffed first at the branches and then just at the coat. The strongest one, he may have been the leader, bit into the coat and dragged it like a corpse halfway across the camp to the roll-call grounds. I ran after the dog and was able to save the coat, but only because he let go.

Two days later the bread man passed me, pulling his cart. And lying on the white linen was a brand-new broom, made from a shovel handle and my fir branches. In three days it would be Christmas—a word that puts green fir trees in every room. All I had were Aunt Fini's torn green woolen gloves stashed away in my trunk. Because Paul Gast the lawyer had been working as a machine operator for the past two weeks, I asked him for some wire. He brought me a bundle of wire snippets, all cut to the width of a hand and tied at one end like a tassel. I used his wire to make a tree, then unraveled my gloves and tied bits of green yarn onto the branches, very close together, like fir needles.

Our Christmas tree stood on the little table below the cuckoo clock. Paul Gast the lawyer hung two brown bread-balls as ornaments. At the time I didn't ask myself how he had enough bread for ornaments, first because I was sure he'd eat them the next day, and also because as he was kneading the little balls, he told us a story from home:

Our high school in Oberwischau used to have an Advent wreath that hung right over the teacher's desk. The candles were lit every morning, before our first-period class, which was Geography. Our teacher, Herr Leonida, was completely bald. One morning the candles were burning and we started singing: *O Tannenbaum, O Tannenbaum, wie grün sind deine Blä*— And all of a sudden Herr Leonida let out a shriek: the pink wax had dripped onto his bald head. Blow out those candles, he screamed. Then he jumped over to his chair, grabbed his coat, and pulled out a small knife—a little silver fish. He looked right at me and yelled: Come here. He opened the little knife and lowered his head for me to scrape off the wax. I managed to do it without nicking him, but as soon as I was sitting at my desk, he came up and slapped me. When I tried to wipe the tears from my eyes, he screamed: Hands behind your back.

10 rubles

Bea Zakel had persuaded Tur Prikulitsch to give me a *propusk*—a pass—so I could go to the market. The chance of getting a pass is something you don't mention to a hungry person. I didn't mention it to anybody. I took my pillowcase and Herr Carp's leather gaiters. As always, it was a matter of finagling the best deal for the most calories. At eleven o'clock I set off, that is to say we set off, my hunger and I.

The day was still hazy from the rain. Peddlers stood in the mud, showing their wares: men with rusty screws and gear wheels, and wrinkled old women with tin dishes and little piles of blue pigment for house paint. The puddles around the paint were blue. Right nearby were other piles, of sugar and salt, dried prunes, corn flour, millet, barley, and peas. Even corn-flour cakes with sugar-beet paste, set on green horseradish leaves. Women without teeth were selling thick sour milk in metal containers, and a one-legged boy with a crutch was standing by a bucket full of red raspberry water. A few young drifters ran around hustling bent knives, forks, and fishing rods. Little silver fish flitted like living safety pins inside empty tin cans from America.

I pushed through the crowd with my leather gaiters on my arm, pausing in front of an old man in uniform with bald patches on his head and a dozen war medals on his chest. He had two books displayed at his feet: one was about Popocatépetl, and the other had a cover showing two fat fleas. I skimmed through the flea book because it had lots of pictures. Two fleas on a seesaw, next to them the trainer's hand wielding a tiny whip, a flea on the back of a rocking chair, a flea harnessed to a wedding coach fashioned from a nutshell, the chest of a boy with two fleas between his nipples and two parallel chains of fleabites of even lengths running from the fleas down to his navel.

The man in uniform reached out and grabbed my leather gaiters and held them up first to his chest, then to his shoulders. I showed him they were meant for the legs. He let out a hollow laugh, from his belly, the way Tur Prikulitsch sometimes did during roll call, like big turkeys do. His upper lip kept catching on the stump of a tooth. The peddler selling next to him came over and rubbed the leather laces of the gaiters between his fingers. Then a man appeared carrying a handful of knives, which he stuck in his coat pocket. He took the gaiters and held them up to his left hip and his right, then placed them on his bottom and hopped around like a fool, while the man in uniform made farting noises. And then another man came whose neck was all bundled up. He walked on a crutch with an armrest made from a broken scythe wrapped in rags. He slipped his crutch into one of the gaiters and hurled it into the air. I ran after it and picked it up. A little farther down the other gaiter came flying. I bent over to pick that one up and there, lying in the mud next to my gaiter, was a crumpled banknote.

Somebody's lost that, I thought. With luck he hasn't noticed it's missing. Or maybe he's already looking for it, maybe while that mob was teasing me one of them saw it or saw me bend over and is waiting to see what I'll do next. They were still laughing at me and my gaiters, but the money was already in my fist.

I had to quickly make myself scarce and so I pressed into the crowd. I clutched the gaiters tightly under my arm and smoothed out the bill, it was 10 rubles.

10 rubles was a fortune. Don't waste time calculating, just eat, I thought, what doesn't get eaten can go in the pillowcase. I'd had enough of the gaiters—those embarrassing leftovers from another universe, they only made me stick out. So I just dropped them on the ground and flitted off with my 10 rubles like a little silver fish. .

My throat was throbbing, I was sweating with fright and paid two rubles for two cups of red raspberry water, which I drank down in one gulp. Then I bought two corn-flour cakes with sugar-beet paste. I even ate the horseradish leaves, thinking that because they were bitter, they must be good for the stomach, like medicine. Then I bought four Russian pancakes with cheese filling. Two for me and two for the pillowcase. After that I drank one small canful of thick sour milk and bought two pieces of sunflower-seed cake, both of which I ate. Then I saw the one-legged boy again and drank another cup of red raspberry water. After that I counted how much money I had left: 1 ruble and 6 kopeks, not enough for sugar, or even salt. While I was counting, I could feel the woman with the dried prunes watching me. She had one brown eye and one eye that was completely white and without a pupil, like a bean. I showed her my money. She pushed my hand away, saying no and waving her arms as if she were shooing flies. I stayed rooted where I was and kept holding up my money. I started to shiver, then crossed myself and mumbled as if praying: Our Father, save me from this goddamned hideous hag. Lead her into temptation and deliver me from evil. As I mumbled, I thought about Fenya's cold saintliness, and when I was done I said a hard, clear AMEN, to give some form to my prayer. The woman was moved and fixed me with her bean eye. Then she took my money and filled an old green Cossack cap with prunes. I dumped half of them in my pillowcase and the rest in my quilted cap, to eat right away. And after I finished the prunes in the cap, I ate the two pancakes I had left. And then there was nothing in the pillowcase except a handful of prunes.

The wind flew warmly through the acacias, the mud in the puddles curled up into gray cups. On the path that ran beside the road to the camp a goat was tethered to a stake. Its neck was rubbed raw from constantly chafing against the rope, which had circled the stake so many times the goat could no longer reach the grass. The goat had a sidelong gaze like Bea Zakel and a tormented quality like Fenya. It tried to follow me. I thought about the blue, dry-frozen goats that had been split in two and tossed into the cattle car and which we had used for heating. I was only halfway to the camp, I was going to be late, and on top of that I'd be showing up with prunes in my pillowcase. To keep them away from the guards I ate the rest. Through the poplars behind the Russian village I could already see the cooling tower. Above its white cloud the sun grew square and slipped into my mouth. My throat was walled shut, I gasped for air. My stomach ached, my intestines rumbled and twisted in my belly like scimitars. My eyes teared up, and the cooling tower began to spin. I leaned against a mulberry tree, and the earth beneath it began to spin. A truck began to flutter on the road, and on the path three stray dogs began to blur together. I threw up all over the tree, and I felt so bad about wasting all the expensive food that I cried even as I threw up.

Then it all lay glistening beside the mulberry tree.

All of it, all of it.

I leaned my head against the trunk and stared at the glistening chewed-up food, as if I could eat it all over again with my eyes. Then I passed under the first watchtower in the empty wind, with an empty pillowcase and an empty stomach. The same as before, except without my leather gaiters. My lucky gaiters. The guard was spitting sunflower-seed husks from the tower, they sailed through the air like flies. The emptiness inside me was bitter as gall, I felt sick. But the minute I was in the yard I was already wondering if there was any cabbage soup left in the mess hall. The mess hall was closed. And I chanted to the drumming clatter of my wooden shoes:

The Matron with her white cloud is real. My shovel is real. My bunk in the barrack is real. And I'm sure there's a gap between being hungry and dropping dead. I just have to find it, since the urge to eat is stronger than I am. Fenya limps but thinks straight. Her chilly saintliness is just. She gives me my share of food. Why go to the market, the camp keeps me locked up for my own good. I can only be made a laughing-stock where I don't belong. I'm at home in the camp. The guard from this morning recognized me, he waved me through the gate. And his dog knows me too, he didn't budge from the warm pavement. And the roll-call grounds know me, and I can find my way to my barrack even with my eyes closed. I don't need a day pass, I have the camp, and the camp has me. All I need is a bunk and Fenya's bread and my tin bowl.

I don't even need Leo Auberg.

On the hunger angel

Hunger is an object.

The angel has climbed into my brain.

The angel doesn't think. He thinks straight.

He's never absent.

He knows my boundaries and he knows his direction.

He knows where I come from and he knows what he does to me.

He knew all of this before he met me, and he knows my future.

He lingers in every capillary like quicksilver. First a sweetness in my throat. Then pressure on my stomach and chest. The fear is too much.

Everything has become lighter.

The hunger angel leans to one side as he walks with open eyes. He staggers around in small circles and balances on my breath-swing. He knows the homesickness in the brain and the blind alleys in the air.

The air angel leans to the other side as he walks with open hunger.

He whispers to himself and to me: where there is loading there can also be unloading. He is of the same flesh that he is deceiving. Will have deceived.

He knows about saved bread and cheek-bread and he sends out the white hare.

He says he's coming back but stays where he is.

When he comes, he comes with force.

It's utterly clear:

1 shovel load = 1 gram bread.

Hunger is an object.

Latin secrets

After wolfing down our food in the mess hall, we shove the long wooden tables and the benches against the wall. Now and then on Saturday nights we're allowed to dance until a quarter before midnight, then we have to put everything back. At twelve on the dot, when the loudspeaker plays the Russian anthem, everyone has to be in his barrack. On Saturdays the guards are feeling happy from drinking sugar-beet liquor and their fingers can be light on the trigger. If someone's found dead in the yard on Sunday morning the word is: attempted escape. The fact that he had to run to the latrine in his underwear because his guts were worn out and could no longer digest the cabbage soup is no excuse. Even so, we shuffle out a tango now and then on our mess-hall Saturdays. When you dance you're like the Crescent Moon Madonna at Café Martini, living on your tiptoes in the world you come from—the world of ballrooms and garlands and Chinese lanterns, of evening dresses, brooches, ties, pocket squares, and cuff links. My mother is dancing. She has her hair in a bun braided like a little basket, with two curls spiraling down her cheeks. She's wearing light-brown sandals with high heels and straps as thin as pear peels, a green satin dress, and a brooch right over her heart—four emeralds in the shape of a lucky clover. And my father is wearing his sand-gray suit with a white square in his pocket and a white carnation in his buttonhole.

But I'm wearing lice in my fufaika and footwraps that stink inside my rubber galoshes, I'm a forced laborer getting dizzy from the ballroom back home and the emptiness in my stomach. I dance with Zirri Kaunz, the one with the silky hair on her hands. The other Zirri, with the olive-sized wart under her ring finger, is Zirri Wandschneider. While we're dancing, Zirri Kaunz assures me that she comes from the village of Kastenholz—or Boxwood—and not from Wurmloch— Wormhole—like the other Zirri. And that her father came from Wolkendorf—or Cloudville. That before she was born her parents moved to Kastenholz because her father bought a large vineyard there. I tell her there's also a village called Liebling—Darling—and a town called Gross-Scham or Big-Shame, but they're in the Banat, not Transylvania. I don't understand the first thing about the Banat, says Zirri. I don't either, I say, spinning around her in my sweaty fufaika, while her sweaty fufaika spins around me. The whole mess hall is spinning. There's nothing to understand when everything is spinning. And then I mention the wooden cabins behind the camp, which for some reason are called Finnish cabins though the people who live there are Russian Ukrainians. There's nothing to understand about that either, I say.

After the break comes La Paloma. I dance with the other Zirri. Loni Mich, our singer, stands half a step in front of the musicians. For La Paloma she takes another half step forward, because she wants to have the song all to herself. She keeps her arms and legs completely still, but her eyes roll and her head sways. Her small goiter trembles, her voice turns raw like the undertow of deep water:

A ship can go down very fast
And all of us sooner or later
Will breathe our last
So it's anchors aweigh
We all reach the day
When we're claimed by the sea
And what the waves take away
Never comes back

Everyone has to keep silent while dancing our pleated Paloma. You go mute and think what you have to think, even if you don't want to. We shove our homesickness across the floor like a heavy crate. Zirri lets her feet drag, I press my hand against the small of her back until she regains the rhythm. She's had her head turned away from me for some time, so I can't see her face. But her back is quivering, and I can tell that she's crying. The shuffling is loud enough so that I don't have to say anything. What could I say other than she shouldn't cry.

It's impossible to dance without toes, so Trudi Pelikan sits on a bench off to the side, and I sit down next to her. In the first winter her toes froze. The following summer they were squashed by the lime wagon. That fall they were amputated because worms got under the bandage. Since then Trudi Pelikan has walked on her heels, so she compensates by tilting her shoulders forward. That makes her back a little hunched, and her arms as stiff as shovel handles. She couldn't work at the construction site or in a factory or in the garage, and during the second winter she was assigned to the sick barrack.

We talk about the sick barrack, that it's nothing more than a place to die. Trudi Pelikan says: Ichthyol salve is the only thing we have that's of any use. Even the Russian medic has remarked that the Germans die in waves. The winter wave is the biggest. The second biggest comes in summer, when the diseases spread. The autumn wave comes when the tobacco ripens. People poison themselves with tobacco broth, it costs less than coal alcohol. And it doesn't cost a thing to open your vein with a shard of glass, or to slice off your hand or foot. It doesn't cost anything to run headfirst into a brick wall until you collapse, either, although that's a little harder to do, says Trudi Pelikan.

Most people only knew each other by sight, from the mess hall or the Appell. I realized many were missing. But unless they'd collapsed right in front of me I didn't consider them dead. And I took care not to ask where they might be. Still, when the evidence is staring you in the face, when you know so many have died, fear becomes a powerful thing, even overpowering after a while—and therefore remarkably similar to indifference. This is what allows you to act so fast when you're the first to discover a dead person. You have to undress him quickly, before the body gets too stiff to bend, and before someone else makes off with his clothes. You have to take his saved bread out of his pillowcase before someone else beats you to it. Clearing away the dead person's things is our way of mourning. When the stretcher arrives in the barrack, there should be nothing to haul away but a body.

If you don't know the dead person, then you only stand to gain. There's nothing wrong with clearing things away: if the situation were reversed, the corpse would do the same to you, and you wouldn't begrudge him that, either. The camp is a practical place. You can't afford to feel shame or horror. You proceed with steady indifference, or perhaps dejected contentment. And this has nothing to do with schadenfreude. I believe that the less skittish we are around the dead, the more we cling to life. And the more we fall prey to illusions. You convince yourself that the missing people have simply been moved to another camp. It doesn't matter what you know, you believe the opposite. Just like the bread court, the act of clearing away happens only in the present moment. But there is no violence, everything proceeds matter-of-factly and peacefully.

> Outside my father's house there stands a linden
> Outside my father's house there is a chair
> And if I find my way back home again
> Then I will spend my whole life there

So sings our singer Loni Mich, the sweat beading up on her forehead. David Lommer has his zither on his knees, the metal ring on his thumb. After each line he plucks a quiet echo and sings along. And Anton Kowatsch inches his drum forward until he can squint at Loni's face through his drumsticks. The couples stumble awkwardly through the song, hopping like birds trying to land in a heavy wind. Trudi Pelikan says we're no longer capable of walking anyway, all we can do is dance, we're nothing but quilted jackets filled with sloshing water and clattering bones, weaker than the drumbeats.

To prove her point she offers me a list of Latin secrets from the sick barrack.

Polyarthritis. Myocarditis. Dermatitis. Hepatitis. Encephalitis. Pellagra. Slit-mouth dystrophy, called monkey-skull face. Dystrophy with stiff cold hands, called rooster claw. Dementia. Tetanus. Typhus. Eczema. Sciatica. Tuberculosis. Then dysentery with bright bloody stools, boils, ulcers, muscular atrophy, dry skin with scabies, shriveled gums with decayed and missing teeth. Trudi Pelikan doesn't mention frostbite, doesn't talk about the brick-red skin and angular white patches that turn dark brown at the first spring warmth and are already showing on the faces of the people dancing. And because I don't say anything or ask anything, nothing at all, Trudi Pelikan pinches my arm hard and says:

Leo, I mean it, don't die in the winter.

And the drummer sings in harmony with Loni:

Sailor, leave your dreaming
Don't think about your home

All winter long—Trudi is speaking through the singing—the dead are stacked up in the back courtyard and shoveled over with snow, and left there for a few days until they're frozen hard enough. And then the gravediggers, who she says are lazy louts, chop the corpses into pieces so they don't have to dig a grave, just a hole.

I listen carefully to Trudi Pelikan and start to feel that I've caught a little bit of each of her Latin secrets. The music makes death come alive, he locks arms with you and sways to the rhythm.

I flee from the music to my barrack. I glance at the two watchtowers where the camp faces the road, the guards are standing thin and rigid. They look as though they just stepped off the moon. Milk flows from the guard lights, laughter flies from the guardhouse, they're drinking sugar-beet liquor again. A guard dog is sitting on the main street of the camp. He has a green glow in his eyes, and a bone between his paws. I think it's a chicken bone, I'm envious. He senses what I'm after and growls. I have to do something so he doesn't pounce on me, so I say: Vanya.

I'm sure that's not his name, but he looks at me as though he could say my name, too, if he only wanted to. I have to get away, before he actually says it. I take several large steps and turn around a few times to make sure he isn't following me. At the door to my barrack I see he still hasn't returned to his bone. His eyes are following me, or my voice, and the name Vanya. Guard dogs, too, have a memory that goes away and comes back. And hunger doesn't go away but comes back. And loneliness is like hunger. Maybe Russian loneliness is named Vanya.

Still wearing my clothes, I crawl into my bunk. Above the little wooden table, the light is burning, as always. As always, when I can't fall asleep I stare at the stovepipe, with its black knee joint, and at the two iron fir cones of the cuckoo clock. Then I see myself as a child.

I'm at home, standing at the veranda door, my hair is black and curly and I'm no taller than the door handle. I'm holding my stuffed animal in my arm, a brown dog named Mopi. My parents are coming back from town, along the uncovered wooden walkway. My mother has wound the chain of her red patent-leather purse around her hand so it won't rattle when she climbs the stairs. My father's carrying a white straw hat. He goes inside. My mother stops, brushes the hair off my forehead, and takes my stuffed animal, my *kuscheltier*—my cuddle toy. She places it on the veranda table, the chain of her purse rattles, and I say:

Give me my Mopi or else I'll be alone.

She laughs: But you have me.

I say: But you can die and Mopi can't.

Above the light snoring of the people who were too weak to go dancing I hear my voice from years ago. It's strange how velvety it sounds. KUSCHELTIER—what a soft name for a dog stuffed with sawdust. But here in the camp there's only KUSCHEN—knuckling under—because what else would you call the silence that comes from fear. And KUSHAT' means eat in Russian. But I don't want to think of eating now, in addition to everything else. I dive into sleep, and I dream.

I'm riding home through the sky on a white pig. From the air it's easy to make out the land below, the boundaries look right, the plots are even fenced in. But the land is dotted with ownerless suitcases, and ownerless sheep are grazing among the suitcases. Hanging from their necks are fir cones that ring like little bells. I say:

That's either a large sheep shed with suitcases or a large train station with sheep. But there's nobody there anymore, where am I supposed to go now.

The hunger angel looks at me from the sky and says: Ride back.

I say: But then I'll die.

If you die, I'll make everything orange, and it won't hurt, he says.

And I ride back, and he keeps his word. As I die, the sky over every watchtower turns orange, and it doesn't hurt.

Then I wake up and use my pillowcase to wipe the corners of my mouth. That's the bedbugs' favorite spot at night.

Cinder blocks

The cinder blocks used for walls are made of slag, cement, and lime slurry. They're mixed in a revolving drum and shaped in a block press with a hand lever. The brickworks were located behind the coke plant, near the slag heaps on the other side of the yama. That area had enough room for drying thousands of freshly pressed blocks. They were laid out on the ground in narrow rows, close together like gravestones in a military cemetery. Where the ground was swollen or pockmarked with holes, the rows were wavy. The wet blocks were carried there on little boards that were also swollen, cracked, and pockmarked with holes.

Carrying the blocks involved a long balancing act, forty meters from the press to the drying area. The rows were never even, because each person had his own way of balancing and positioning his block. Also because the blocks weren't set down in any order—some were placed in front, some in back, and some in the middle of a row, either to replace a ruined block or to use space that had been overlooked the previous day.

The freshly pressed mass weighed ten kilograms and was

crumbly like wet sand. Carrying the board in front of you required nimble footwork—you had to coordinate your shoulders, elbows, hips, stomach, and knees with every step. The ten kilos weren't yet a cinder block, and you couldn't let them know you were carrying them. You had to trick them by rocking evenly back and forth, so the material wouldn't wobble, and then let it slide off in one move at the drying area. Everything had to happen quickly and evenly, so that the new block made a smooth landing, scared but not jolted. For this you needed to squat, bending your knees until the board was under your chin, then spread your elbows like wings and let the block slip off just right. That was the only way you could place it close to the next block without damaging the edges of either. One false move and the block would collapse like so much dirt.

Carrying the blocks, and especially placing them, put a strain on your face as well. You had to keep your tongue straight and your eyes fixed squarely ahead. If anything went wrong you couldn't even curse in anger. After a cinder-block shift, our eyes and lips were as stiff and square as the blocks. And on top of this we had the cement to cope with. The cement ran away, it flew through the air. More cement stuck to our bodies and to the drum and to the press than got mixed into the bricks. To press the cinder blocks you first set your board in the mold. Then you shoveled some mix into the form and pulled the lever. Then you pulled the lever again to raise both the board and the new block. After that you took the board and carried it off to the drying area, with nimble footwork and without losing your balance.

Cinder blocks were pressed day and night. In the mornings the mold was still cool and moist from the dew, your feet were still light, the sun had yet to hit the drying area. But it was already blazing on the peaks of the slag heaps, and by midday the heat was overpowering. Your feet lost their even gait, your knees shook, every nerve in your calves simmered. Your fingers were numb. You could no longer keep your tongue straight while placing the blocks. There was a lot of waste, and a lot of beating. In the evening a spotlight cast a beam of harsh light on the scene. Moths twirled around, and the mixing drum and the press loomed in the light like machines covered with fur. The moths weren't drawn only to the light. The moist smell of the mix attracted them, like night-blooming flowers. They settled on the blocks that were drying, tapping with their threadlike legs and feeding tubes, even though much of the area was only half-lit. They also settled on the block you were carrying and distracted you from your balancing act. You could see the little hairs on their heads, the decorative rings on their abdomens, and you could hear their wings rustling, as though the block were alive. Occasionally two or three appeared at once and sat there as though they'd hatched out of the block itself. As though the wet mix on the board were not made of slag, cement, and lime slurry but was a square lump of larvae from which the moths emerged. They let themselves be carried from the press to the drying area, out of the spotlight into the layered shadows. The shadows were crooked and dangerous, they deformed the outlines of the blocks and distorted the rows. The block on its board no longer knew what it looked like. And you felt unsure, afraid you might mistake the edges of the shadows for the edges of the blocks. The flickering slag heaps a little way off added to the confusion. They glowed in countless places with yellow eyes, like nocturnal animals that create their own light, illuminating or burning off their lack of sleep. The slag heaps' glowing eyes smelled sharply of sulfur.

Toward morning it turned cool, a milk-glass sky. Your feet felt lighter, at least in your head, because the shift was near its end and you wanted to forget how tired you were. The flood-light was tired, too, overcast and pale. The blue air settled evenly on each row and every block of our surreal military cemetery. A quiet justice unfolded, the only one that existed here.

The cinder blocks had it good, our dead had neither rows nor stones. But you couldn't think about that, otherwise you wouldn't be able to balance your load for several days or nights. If you thought about that even a little there would be a lot of waste, and a lot of beating.

The gullible bottle
and the skeptical one

It was the skinandbones time, the eternity of cabbage soup. Kapusta when you get up in the morning, kapusta after roll call in the evening. KAPUSTA means cabbage in Russian, and cabbage soup in Russian means soup that often has no cabbage at all. If you take away the Russian and the soup, kapusta is just a word made of two things that have nothing in common—except this word. CAP is Romanian for head, and PUSTA is the Great Hungarian Plain. The camp is as Russian as the cabbage soup, but we think these things up in German. Nonsense like that is supposed to show we're still clever. But no matter what you do with it, KAPUSTA doesn't work as a hunger word. Hunger words make up a map, but instead of reciting countries in your head you list names of food. Wedding soup, mincemeat, spare ribs, pig's knuckles, roast hare, liver dumplings, haunch of venison, hasenpfeffer, and so on.

All hunger words are also eating words, you picture the food in front of your eyes and feel the taste in your mouth. Hunger words, or eating words, feed your imagination. They eat themselves, and they like what they eat. You never get full, but at least you're there for the meal. Every person with chronic hunger has his preferred eating words, some rare, some common, and some in constant use. Each person thinks a different word tastes best. Orach didn't work as an eating word any more than kapusta, because we actually ate it. Had to eat it.

I believe that in hunger there is no difference between blindness and sight, blind hunger sees food best. There are silent hunger words and loud ones, just as hunger has its secret side and its public side. Hunger words, or eating words, dominate every conversation, but even so, you're still alone. Everyone eats his words by himself although we're all eating together. There's no thought for the hunger of others, you can't hunger together. Cabbage soup was our main food, but it mainly took the meat from our bones and the sanity from our minds. The hunger angel ran around in hysterics. He lost all proportion, growing more in a single day than grass in an entire summer or snow in an entire winter. Perhaps as much as a tall, pointed tree grows in its entire life. It seems to me the hunger angel didn't just grow in size but also in number. He provided each of us with our own individual agony, and yet we were all alike. Because in the trinity of skin, bones, and brown water, men and women lose all difference, and lose all sexual drive. Of course you go on saying HE or SHE but that's merely a grammatical holdover. Half-starved humans are really neither masculine nor feminine but genderless, like objects.

No matter where I was, in my bunk or between the barracks, at the yama on a shift or with Kobelian on the steppe, near the cooling tower, or washing up in the banya, or going door-to-door—everything I did was hungry. Everything matched the magnitude of my hunger in length, width, height, and color. Between the sky overhead and the dust of the earth, every place smelled of a different food. The main street of the camp smelled like caramel, the entrance to the camp like freshly baked bread, crossing the street to the factory smelled like warm apricots, the wooden fence of the factory like candied nuts, the factory gate like scrambled eggs, the yama like stewed peppers, the slag heaps like tomato soup, the cooling tower like roasted eggplant, the labyrinth of steaming pipes like strudel with vanilla sauce. The lumps of tar in the weeds smelled like quince compote and the coke ovens like cantaloupe. It was magic and it was agony. Even the wind fed the hunger, spinning food we could literally see.

Because the skinandbones people were sexless to each other, the hunger angel coupled with everyone. He also betrayed the flesh he had just stolen from us, dragging more and more lice and bedbugs into our beds. The skinandbones time meant the weekly delousing parade in the yard after work. Every person and every thing had to be taken outside to be deloused—suitcases, clothes, bunks, and ourselves.

It was the third summer, the acacias were blooming, the evening breeze smelled like warm café au lait. I had taken everything outside. Then Tur Prikulitsch came over with the green-toothed Tovarishch Shishtvanyonov, who was carrying a freshly peeled willow cane, twice as long as a flute, flexible enough for beating, with a sharpened tip for rummaging around. Disgusted by our misery, he would skewer things in our suitcases and fling them out onto the ground.

I had positioned myself as close as possible to the middle of the delousing parade, because the searches at the front and near the end were merciless. But this time Shishtvanyonov decided he wanted to bring some rigor to the middle. His cane drilled through the clothes in my gramophone box and hit my toilet kit. He put down the cane, opened my toilet kit, and discovered my secret cabbage soup. For three weeks I'd been storing cabbage soup in the two beautiful bottles I couldn't throw away just because they were empty. And so, because they were empty I filled them with cabbage soup. One was a round-bellied bottle of rippled glass, with a screw top, the other had a flat belly and a wider neck, for which I'd even whittled a decent wooden stopper. To keep the cabbage soup from spoiling, I sealed it airtight the way we sealed stewed fruit at home. Trudi Pelikan lent me a candle from the sick barrack, and I dripped some stearine around the stopper.

Shto eto, asked Shishtvanyonov.

Cabbage soup.

What for.

He shook the little bottle so that the soup foamed up.

Na pamyat', I said.

Kobelian had taught me that Russians considered memento a good word, that's why I said it. But Shishtvanyonov was probably wondering what I needed this memento for. Who could be dumb enough to need little bottles of cabbage soup to remind him of cabbage soup when cabbage soup is served here twice a day.

For home, he asked.

I nodded. That was the worst thing possible, that I intended to take cabbage soup home in little bottles. He would have beaten me on the spot, and I could have put up with it, but he was only halfway through his parade and didn't want to fall behind. He confiscated my bottles and ordered me to report to him.

The next morning Tur Prikulitsch escorted me out of the mess hall to the officers' room. He marched down the camp street like a driven man, and I followed like a condemned man. I asked him what I should say. Without turning around he waved his hand dismissively as if to say, I'm not getting involved. Shishtvanyonov roared at me. Tur could have saved himself the trouble of translating, by now I knew it all by heart. I was a Fascist, a spy, a saboteur, and a pest, I had no culture, and by stealing cabbage soup I was committing treason against the camp, against Soviet authority, and against the Soviet people.

The cabbage soup was thin enough in the camp, but in these bottles with their narrow necks, it was almost completely clear. And as far as Shishtvanyonov was concerned, the few strands of cabbage floating in the bottles were a clear denunciation. My situation was precarious. Then Tur held up his finger, he had an idea: medicine. For the Russians, though, medicine was only a half-good word. Tur realized that just in time, so he twirled his index finger against his forehead as if he were drilling a hole and said, with a hint of meanness in his voice: Obscurantism.

That made sense. Tur explained that I'd only been in the camp for three years, that I wasn't yet reeducated, that I still believed in magic potions against disease, and so I kept the bottle with the screw top against diarrhea, and the one with the stopper against constipation. Shishtvanyonov pondered what Tur was saying, and not only believed him but even went so far as to note that while obscurantism was admittedly not good in the camp, it wasn't such a bad thing in life. He examined both bottles one more time, shook them until the foam rose in their necks, then moved the one with the screw top a little to the right and the one with the wooden stopper exactly the same distance to the left so that the two bottles were touching each other. By then Shishtvanyonov's mouth had softened and his gaze had mellowed, thanks to the bottles. Tur had another good idea and said:

Get lost. Now.

I suspect that Shishtvanyonov didn't simply throw the bottles away, for some inexplicable—or even explicable—reason.

But what are reasons, really. To this day I don't know why I filled the bottles with cabbage soup. Did it have something to do with my grandmother's sentence: I know you'll come back. Was I really so naïve as to think I'd come home and present the cabbage soup to my family as though I were bringing them two bottles of life in the camp. Or was I still clinging to the notion, despite the hunger angel, that whenever you go on a trip you bring back a souvenir. From her one and only voyage on a ship my grandmother had brought me a sky-blue, thumb-sized Turkish slipper from Constantinople. But that was my other grandmother, who hadn't said anything about coming back, who lived in a different house and hadn't even been at ours to say good-bye. Did I think the bottles would be some kind of witness for me at home. Or was one bottle gullible and the other skeptical. Was the screw-top bottle filled with my trip home and the stoppered bottle filled with my staying here forever. Could it be that they were opposites, just like diarrhea and constipation. Did Tur Prikulitsch know more about me than he should. Was talking to Bea Zakel doing me any good.

Was going home even the opposite of staying here. I probably wanted to be up to both possibilities, if it came to that. I probably wanted to make sure that my life here, my life in general, wouldn't stay trapped in yearning to go home every day and never being able to. The more I wanted to go home, the more I tried not to want it so much that I'd be destroyed if they never let me. I never lost my yearning to go home, but in order to have something besides that, I told myself that even if they kept us here forever, this would still be my life. After all, the Russians have their lives. I don't want to struggle so hard against settling here. All I have to do is stay the way the stoppered half of me already is. I can reeducate myself, I don't yet know how, but the steppe will see to it. The hunger angel had taken possession of me, my scalp was fluttering. My hair had just been clipped on account of lice.

Once during the previous summer, Kobelian had unbuttoned his shirt in the open air, and as it fluttered, he'd said something about the grassy soul of the steppe and his Ural heart. That could beat in my breast as well, I thought.

On daylight poisoning

That morning the sun rose very early like a red balloon, so big and round that it made the sky over the coke plant look flat.

Our shift had begun during the night. We were standing under the floodlight inside the *pek* basin, a settling tank two meters deep and two barracks long and wide. The basin was coated with an ancient, vitrified layer of pitch one meter thick. Our job was to clean out the basin with crowbars and pickaxes, chip away the pitch, and load it into wheelbarrows. Then push the wheelbarrows up a rickety plank that led out of the basin to the tracks, and up another plank to dump the pieces in the freight car.

We chipped away at the black glass: fluted, curved, and jagged shards whizzed by our heads. There was no sign of dust. But then, when I came back down the rickety plank, pushing my empty wheelbarrow out of the black night and into the white funnel of light, the air shimmered like an organza cape made of glass dust. As soon as the wind shook the floodlamp, the cape turned into a shiny chrome birdcage that hovered in the exact same spot.

At six a.m. the shift was over, it had been light outside for an hour. The sun was now shriveled but angry, its globe tight like a pumpkin. My eyes were on fire, every suture in my skull was throbbing. On the way home to the camp everything was glaring. The veins in my neck were ticking away, about to explode, my eyeballs were boiling inside my head, my heart was drumming in my chest, my ears were crackling. My neck swelled like hot dough and stiffened. Head and neck became one. The swelling spread to my shoulders, neck and upper body became one. The light drilled through me, I had to hurry into the darkness of the barrack. But it wasn't dark enough, even the light from the window was deadly. I covered my head with my pillow. Relief came toward evening, but so did the night shift, and I had to go back to the floodlight at the pitch basin. On the second night, the nachal'nik came by with a bucket of lumpy, gray-pink paste that we smeared on our faces and necks before entering the site. The paste dried right away and then flaked off.

When the sun rose the next morning, the tar was raging inside my head even worse than before. I lurched into camp like a cat on its last legs and went directly to the sick barrack. Trudi Pelikan stroked my forehead. The medic drew a head in the air that was even more swollen than mine and said SOLN-TSYE and SVYET and BOLIT. And Trudi Pelikan cried and explained something about photochemical mucosal reactions.

What's that.

Daylight poisoning, she said.

She handed me a horseradish leaf with a dollop of salve they'd concocted out of marigolds and lard, for rubbing into the raw skin so it wouldn't crack. The medic told me I was too sensitive to work at the pitch basin, she said she might talk to Tur Prikulitsch and that in the meantime she'd write a note saying I needed three days to recover.

I spent three days in bed. Half asleep, half awake, I floated back home on waves of fever, to summer mornings in the Wench. The sun rises very early behind the fir trees, like a red balloon. I peek through the crack of the door, my parents are still asleep. I go into the kitchen, on the kitchen table there's a shaving mirror propped against the milk can. My Aunt Fini, who's as thin as a nutcracker, is wearing a white organza dress. She's running with a curling iron back and forth between the gas stove and the mirror, putting a wave in her hair. Then she combs my hair with her fingers and uses her spit to slick down my cowlick. She takes me by the hand, we go outside to pick daisies for the breakfast table.

The dewy grass comes up to my shoulders, the meadow rustles and buzzes, it's full of white-fringed daisies and blue-bells. The only thing I pick is ribwort, we call it shoot-weed, because you can use the stem as a sling and shoot the seed spike pretty far. I shoot at the glaring white organza dress. All of a sudden a living chain of locusts appears between the organza and Aunt Fini's equally white slip, hooked claw to claw and wrapped around her lower body. She drops her daisies, holds out her arms, and freezes in place. And I slip under her dress and shovel away the locusts with my hands, faster and faster. They're cold and heavy like wet screws. They pinch, I feel afraid. I look up and, instead of Aunt Fini with her freshly waved hair, I see a locust colossus on two skinny legs.

Under the organza dress was the first time I ever had to shovel in desperation. Now I was lying in a barrack for three days, rubbing myself with marigold salve, while everyone else went on working at the pitch basin site. But because I was too sensitive, Tur Prikulitsch reassigned me to the slag cellar.

Which is where I stayed.

Every shift is a work of art

There are two of us, Albert Gion and myself, two cellar-people working below the boilers of the factory. In the barrack Albert Gion is quick-tempered. In the dark cellar he is deliberate but decisive, the way melancholy people are. Maybe he wasn't always like that, maybe he became like that in the cellar, the way cellars are. He's been working here a long time. We don't say much, only what's necessary.

Albert Gion says: I'll flip three carts, then you flip three.

I say: After that I'll straighten the mountain—as we called the pile of slag.

He says: Right, then you go push.

Between flipping and pushing, the shift goes back and forth, until we're halfway through, until Albert Gion says:

Let's sleep for thirty minutes under the board, below number seven, it's quiet there.

And then we start the second half.

Albert Gion says: I'll flip three carts, then you flip three.

I say: After that I'll straighten the mountain.

He says: Right, then you go push.

I say: I'll push when number nine is full.

He says: No, you flip now, I'll push, the bunker's already full.

At the end of the shift one of us says: Come on, let's make sure the cellar's nice and clean for the next shift.

After my first week in the cellar, Tur Prikulitsch was once again standing behind me in the barber's mirror. I was half-shaved, and he raised his oily eyes and spotless fingers and asked:

So how are things in the cellar.

Cozy, I said, every shift is a work of art.

He smiled over the barber's shoulder, but had no idea how true this really was. You could hear the thin hatred in his tone, his nostrils had a pink shine, his temples were veined with marble.

Your face was pretty filthy yesterday, he said, and your cap was so full of holes its guts were hanging out.

Doesn't matter, I said, the coal dust is finger-thick and furry. But after every shift the cellar's nice and clean, because every shift is a work of art.

When a swan sings

After my first day in the cellar, Trudi said in the mess hall: No more pitch—you're a lucky man. It's nicer below ground, isn't it.

Then she told me that when she was hauling the lime wagon during her first year in camp, she'd often close her eyes and dream. Now she takes naked corpses out of the dying room to the back of the courtyard and lays them on the ground like freshly stripped logs. She said that now, too, when she carries the corpses to the door, she often closes her eyes and has the same dream as when she was harnessed to the lime wagon.

What is it, I asked.

That a rich, handsome, young American—he doesn't really have to be handsome or young, an old canned-pork tycoon would do—that a rich American falls in love with me. Actually, he doesn't even have to fall in love, he just has to be rich enough to pay my way out of here and marry me. Now, that would be a stroke of luck, she said. And if on top of that he had a sister for you.

She doesn't really have to be beautiful or young, and she doesn't even have to fall in love, I echoed. At that Trudi Pelikan laughed hysterically. The right corner of her mouth started fluttering and left her face, as though the thread connecting laughter to skin had torn in two.

That's why I kept things short when I told Trudi Pelikan about my recurring dream of riding home on the white pig. Just one sentence, and without the white pig:

You know, I said, I often dream that I'm riding home through the sky on a gray dog.

She asked: Is it one of the guard dogs.

No, a village dog, I said.

Trudi said: Why ride, it's faster to fly. I only dream when I'm awake. When I'm taking the corpses out to the courtyard, I wish I could fly away to America, like a swan.

I wondered if she knew about the swan on the oval sign at the Neptune Baths. I didn't ask her, but I did say: You know why a swan sounds hoarse when it sings, because its throat is always hungry.

On slag

In the summer I saw an embankment of white slag in the middle of the steppe and thought about the snowy peaks of the Carpathians. Kobelian said the embankment was originally supposed to become a road. The white slag was baked solid, with a grainy composition, like you find in lime-sinks or shell-sand. Here and there the white was streaked with pink that was often so dark it turned gray at the edge. I don't know why pink aging into gray is so heart-stoppingly beautiful, no longer like a mineral, but weary-sad, like people. Does homesickness have a color.

The other white slag was deposited in a series of man-high heaps beside the yama. That slag wasn't baked solid, the piles were edged with grass. If it rained hard while we were shoveling coal we took shelter in these heaps. We burrowed into the white slag, and it trickled back on top of us, covering us up. In winter, steam rose off the snow on top of the pile, while we warmed ourselves in our holes and were three times hidden: under the snow blanket, inside the slag, and wrapped in our fufaikas. The steam passed through every layer, and there was a cozy, familiar smell of sulfur. We sat buried up to our noses, which stuck out of the ground and broke through the melting layer of snow like bulbs that have sprouted too early. When we crawled out of the slag heaps, our clothes were riddled with holes from the tiny embers, and the padding came spilling out of our jackets.

From all my loading and unloading I was well acquainted with the rust-colored, ground-up slag from the blast furnace. That slag has nothing to do with the white kind, it's composed of reddish-brown dust that ghosts through the air with every swing of the shovel and slowly settles like falling folds of cloth. Because it's as dry as the hot summer and thoroughly aseptic, the blast-furnace slag has no bearing on homesickness.

Then there's the solidly baked greenish-brown slag in the overgrown meadow, in the wasteland behind the factory. Under the weeds it looked like broken lumps of salt lick. That slag and I had nothing to do with each other, it let me pass without making me think of anything in particular.

But my one-and-only slag, my daily slag, the slag of my day and night shift was the clinker-slag from the boilers at the coal furnaces, the hot and cold cellar slag. The furnaces stood above us, in the world of the living, five to a row, each several stories tall. They provided heat to the boilers, producing steam for the entire plant and hot and cold slag for us in the cellar. They also provided all our work, the hot phase and the cold phase of every shift.

Cold slag can only come from hot slag, it's nothing more than the dusty residue left when hot slag cools. Cold slag only has to be emptied once per shift, but the hot clinker-slag requires constant removal, following the rhythm of the furnaces. It has to be shoveled onto countless little rail-carts, then pushed to the top of the mountain of slag at the end of the tracks and dumped.

The hot slag changes from day to day, depending on the mix of coal, which can be kind or malicious. If it's a good mix, the glowing slabs that drop onto the transfer grate are four to five centimeters thick. Having expended their heat, they are brittle and break into pieces that fall easily through the hatch, like toasted bread. The hunger angel is amazed to see how quickly the little carts get filled even when we're weak from shoveling. But if the mix is bad, then the slag doesn't form clinkers and comes out like sticky, white-hot lava. It doesn't fall through the grate on its own but gets clogged in the furnace hatches. You have to use a poker to tear off clumps that stretch like dough. You can't get the oven empty or the cart full. It's an agonizing, time-consuming job.

If the mix is catastrophic, then the furnace gets a real case of diarrhea. Diarrhea slag doesn't wait for the hatch to open, it spurts out of the half-opened doors like shitted-out corn kernels. This slag is dangerous, it glows red and white and shouldn't be looked at, and it can find its way through every hole in your clothes. The flow can't be stopped, so the cart gets buried underneath. Somehow—the devil only knows how—you have to close the hatch, protect your legs, galoshes, and footwraps from the blazing flood, douse the blaze with the hose, dig out the little cart, push it up the mountain, and clean up after the accident—all at the same time. And if on top of everything else, this happens toward the end of your shift, then it's an absolute disaster. You lose an endless amount of time, and the other furnaces aren't going to wait for you, they need emptying, too. The rhythm becomes frantic, your eyes are swimming, your hands are flying, your feet are shaking. To this day I hate the diarrhea slag.

But I love the once-per-shift slag, the cold slag. It treats you decently, patiently, and predictably. Albert Gion and I needed each other only for the hot slag. For the cold slag we each wanted to be by ourselves. The cold slag is tame and trusting, almost in need of affection—a violet sand-dust that you can easily be left alone with. The cold slag comes from the last row of furnaces at the very back of the cellar, it has its own special hatches and its own little tin-bellied cart without bars.

The hunger angel knew how happy I was to be left alone with the cold slag. That it wasn't really cold but lukewarm and smelled a little like lilacs or fuzzy mountain peaches and late-summer apricots. But mostly the cold slag smelled of quitting time, because the shift would be over in fifteen minutes and the danger of a disaster was past. The cold slag smelled of going home from the cellar, of mess-hall soup, and of rest. It even smelled of civilian life, and that made me cocky. I imagined that I wasn't going from the cellar to the barrack in a padded suit, but that I was all decked out in a Borsalino, a camel-hair coat, and a burgundy silk scarf, on my way to a café in Bucharest or Vienna where I was about to sit down at a little marble-top table. So easygoing was the cold slag that it helped feed the delusions you needed in order to steal your way back into life. Drunk on poison, you could find true happiness with the cold slag, dead-sure happiness.

Tur Prikulitsch had reason to think I would complain. That's why he asked me every few days at the barber's:

Well, how is it down there in the cellar.

How are things going in the cellar.

How's the cellar doing.

Are things all right in the cellar.

Or just: And in the cellar.

And because I wanted to beat him at his own game, I always stuck to the same answer: Every shift is a work of art.

If he'd had the slightest idea about the mix of hunger and coal gases, he would have asked me where I spent my time in the cellar. And I could have said, with the fly ash, because fly ash is another type of cold slag, it drifts everywhere and coats the entire cellar with fur. You can find true happiness with fly ash, too. It isn't poisonous, and it flutters about, mouse-gray and velvety. The fly ash doesn't smell. It's made up of minuscule pieces, tiny scales, that constantly flit around, attaching themselves to everything, like frost crystals. Every surface gets furred. The fly ash turns the wire mesh around the lightbulb into a circus cage complete with fleas, lice, bedbugs, and termites. Termites have wedding wings, I learned in school, and they live in camps. They have a king, a queen, and soldiers. And the soldiers have big heads. There are jaw soldiers, nozzle soldiers, and gland soldiers. And they're all fed by the workers. And the queen is thirty times bigger than the workers. I imagine that's also the difference between the hunger angel and me. Or Bea Zakel and me. Or Tur Prikulitsch and me.

On contact with water, it's not the water that flows but the fly ash, because it sucks up the water and swells into formations, like in a cave. The formations can look like stacks of dishes or, if they're very big, like cement children eating gray apples. Fly ash mixed with water can work magic.

But without light and water, the fly ash just sits there, dead. On the cellar walls it looks just like real fur, on your padded cap like artificial fur, in your nostrils like rubber plugs. Albert Gion's face is black, in the cellar it disappears, all I see are the whites of his eyes and his teeth swimming through the air. With Albert Gion I never know if he's sad or simply with-drawn. When I ask, he says: I don't give it any thought. We're just two pill bugs underground. Seriously.

After our shift is over we shower in the banya next to the factory gate. Head, neck, and hands are soaped up three times, but the fly ash stays gray and the cold slag stays violet. The cellar colors have eaten into our skin. That didn't bother me, though, in fact I was even a little proud, after all they were also the colors of my life-giving delusion.

Bea Zakel felt sorry for me, she paused to find a tactful way of putting it, but she knew it wasn't a compliment when she said: You look like you stepped out of a silent movie, like Val-entino.

She had just washed her hair, her silk braid was plaited smooth and still damp. Her cheeks were well nourished, they blushed red like strawberries.

One time, when I was a child, I ran rhrough the garden while Mother and Aunt Fini were drinking coffee. I found a thick ripe strawberry—the first I'd ever seen—and called out: Look at this, a frog's on fire and it's glowing.

I brought a little piece of hot glowing slag home from the camp, stuck to my right shin. It cooled off inside me and changed into a piece of cold slag that shimmers through my skin like a tattoo.

The burgundy silk scarf

Once on our way home from the night shift, my cellar companion Albert Gion said: Now that the days are getting warmer, even if we don't have any food we can always put our hunger in the sun and warm it up. I didn't have any food so I went into the camp yard to warm up my hunger. The grass was still brown, battered, and singed by the frost. The March sun had a pale fringe. It drifted across the rippled-water sky above the Russian village. And I drifted over to the garbage behind the mess hall, goaded by the hunger angel. Most of the others were still at work, so if no one else had been there yet, I might just find a few potato peels. But then I saw Fenya by the mess hall talking to Bea Zakel, so I pretended I was out on a walk, since I could no longer rummage through the garbage. Fenya was wearing her purple sweater, and that made me think of my burgundy silk scarf. After the fiasco with the gaiters I didn't want to go back to the market. But surely Bea Zakel could trade my scarf for sugar and salt, anyone who could talk the way she could had to be good at haggling. Fenya headed off to the mess hall and her bread, limping in agony. As soon as I caught up to Bea I asked her: When are you going to the market. She said: Maybe tomorrow.

Bea could leave whenever she wanted to, she could always get a pass from Tur, if she even needed one. She waited on the bench by the main street while I went to fetch my scarf. It was lying on the bottom of my suitcase next to my white batiste handkerchief. I hadn't touched it for months, it was as soft as skin. I felt a shiver down my spine, I was ashamed in front of the scarf with its flowing squares, because I was so ragged and it was still so soft and alluring, with its matte and shiny checks. It hadn't changed in the camp, the checked pattern had maintained the same quiet order as before. The scarf wasn't really right for me anymore, and I wasn't right for it.

As I handed it to Bea, her gaze again slid furtively off to the side. Her eyes were enigmatic, the only beautiful thing about her. She wrapped the scarf around her neck and couldn't resist crossing her arms and stroking it with both hands. Her shoulders were narrow, her arms thin as sticks. But her hips and backside were impressive, a powerful foundation of hefty bones. With her delicate torso and massive lower body, Bea Zakel looked as if she'd been put together out of two different women.

Bea took my burgundy scarf to trade. But the next day Tur Prikulitsch was wearing the scarf around his neck at roll call. And for the entire week that followed. He had transformed my burgundy silk scarf into a roll-call rag. After that, every roll call was a dumb show starring my scarf. And it looked good on him, too. My bones were heavy as lead, I lost my ability to breathe in and out at the same time, to roll my eyes back without lifting my head and find a hook in a corner of cloud. My scarf draped around Tur Prikulitsch's neck wouldn't let me do it.

Pulling myself together, I finally asked Tur Prikulitsch after roll call where the scarf had come from. He said, with no hesitation: From home, I've had it forever.

He didn't mention Bea. Two weeks had passed, and Bea hadn't given me so much as a crumb of sugar or salt. Did the two of them, well-foddered as they were, have any idea how deeply they were betraying my hunger. Wasn't it their fault that I'd sunk into such misery that my own scarf didn't suit me anymore. Didn't they realize that it was still my property as long as I hadn't received anything in exchange. A whole month passed, the sun lost its paleness. The orach came up again silver-green, the wild dill spread its feathers. On my way back from the cellar I picked greens for my pillowcase. When I bent down everything around me went dark, all I could see was the black sun. I cooked my orach and and it tasted like mud, since I still didn't have any salt. And Tur Prikulitsch was still wearing my scarf, and I was still going to the cellar for the night shift and afterward passing through the empty afternoons to the garbage behind the mess hall, because even that tasted better than mock spinach or orach soup with no salt.

On my way to the garbage I again ran into Bea Zakel, and once more she started talking about the Beskid Mountains that flow into the eastern Carpathians. When she reached the part about leaving her little village of Lugi and arriving in Prague, just as Tur was finally switching from becoming a missionary to business, I interrupted her and asked:

Bea, did you give Tur my scarf.

She said: He simply took it. That's how he is.

How, I said.

Well, just like that, she said. I'm sure he'll give you something in return, maybe a day off.

It wasn't the sun sparkling in her eyes, it was fear. It wasn't me she was afraid of, it was Tur.

Bea, what good is a day off, I said. What I need is sugar and salt.

On chemical substances

Chemical substances are just like slag. Who knows what's seeping out of the piles of waste, the rotting wood, the rusting iron, and the broken brick. Odors aren't the only problem. When we arrived in the camp, we were shocked at what we saw, the coke plant was utterly destroyed. It was hard to believe the damage was just from the war. The rotting, rusting, molding, crumbling were older than the war. As old as human indifference, as old as the poison found in chemical substances. Clearly the chemicals themselves had ganged up and forced the factory into ruin. There must have been breakdowns and explosions in the iron of the pipes and machines. The factory was once state-of-the-art, the latest technology from the twenties and thirties, German industry. You could still make out names like FOERSTER and MANNESMANN on pieces of scrap.

We looked for names in the scrap and searched our heads for pleasant words as an antidote to the poison, because we sensed that these chemicals were continuing their attacks, and now plotting against us as well. And against our forced labor. In fact, the Russians and the Romanians had already found a pleasant word for our forced labor, it was on the list they had back home: REBUILDING. That was a detoxified word. If they were going to talk about BUILDING they should have called it FORCED BUILDING.

Because I was completely at the mercy of the chemical substances—they corroded our shoes, clothes, hands, and mucous membranes—I decided to reinterpret their odors for my own benefit. I told myself there were fragrant lanes, and for every path on the compound I came up with something enticing: fir resin, lemon blossoms, naphthalene, shoe polish, furniture wax, chrysanthemums, glycerin soap, camphor, alum. I refused to let the chemicals have their poisonous way with me, and so I succeeded in creating a pleasant addiction for myself. Being pleasantly addicted didn't mean I had made my peace with the chemicals. It only meant that, just as there were hunger words and eating words, there were also words of escape from these poisonous substances. And for me these words were both a necessity and a torture, because I believed them, and at the same time I knew why I needed them.

On my way to the yama, I saw water running down the rectangular scrubbing tower. I christened it PAGODA. The water gathered in a tank around its base and even in summer smelled like winter coats, like naphthalene. A round white smell, like the mothballs in the wardrobe back home. Close to the pagoda the naphthalene had more of an angular black smell. After I passed the pagoda, it became round and white again. I saw myself as a child, on the train to the Wench, on our way to summer vacation. I'm looking out the window at the gas fields around Kleinkopisch and spot the burning well. The flame is fox red, and I'm amazed that a flame that small could cause the whole valley to dry up. All the cornfields are ash gray, like at the end of autumn, they're old and withered, and it's only the middle of summer. This is the fire that's been in the news, and WELL is a bad word in a headline because it means the gas field is on fire again and no one can put it out. My mother says the latest plan is to bring water buffalo blood from the slaughterhouse, five thousand liters. They hope the blood will quickly congeal and plug the well. The well smells like our winter coats in the wardrobe, I say. And my mother says: Yes, naphthalene.

Petroleum, the Russians call it NYEFT'. You sometimes see the word on the cistern cars. It means oil, but immediately makes me think of naphthalene. Nowhere does the sun sting the way it does here, at the corner of the moika, the eight-story ruin of the coal washer. The sun sucks the oil out of the asphalt, leaving a sharp, greasy smell, bitter and salty, like a giant box of shoe polish. On hot days at noontime, my father would lie down on the couch for an hour's nap while my mother polished his shoes. No matter when I pass the moika, it's always noontime back home.

The fifty-eight coke batteries are numbered and look like a long row of open coffins standing on end. Bricks on the outside and crumbling fireclay inside. I think about CRUMBLING FIRE COFFINS. Puddles of oil glisten on the ground, the chips of fireclay scab up with yellow crystals. The smell reminds me of the yellow chrysanthemum bushes in Herr Carp's garden, but the only thing that grows here is poisonously pale grass. Noontime lies down in the hot wind, the bit of grass is undernourished just like us, it drags itself along carrying wavy stalks.

Albert Gion and I have the night shift. On my way to the cellar in the evening I pass all the pipes, a few packed in fiberglass, others naked and rusted. Some are knee-high, others run over my head. I really ought to follow one of these pipes, I think, at least once. At least once I ought to know where it's coming from and where it's going. Of course I still wouldn't know what it's transporting, assuming it's transporting anything at all. But if I followed one that was letting off white steam, at least I'd know it was transporting something— naphthalene steam. Surely somebody could sit down with me at least once and explain the workings of the coke plant. I'd like to know what happens here. But I'm not sure that the technical procedures, which have their own words, won't interfere with my escape words. I don't even know if I could absorb all the names of the hulking skeletons in the open lanes and clearings. White steam hisses out of the valves, I sense the ground vibrating under my feet. On the other side of the plant, the quarter-hour bell tinkles at battery number one and soon afterward the bell rings at number two. The exhausters show their iron ribs of ladders and stairs. And beyond the exhausters, the moon wanders into the steppe. On nights like this I see Hermannstadt, the small-town gables from back home, the Bridge of Lies, the Fingerling Stairway, and next to it the pawnshop TREASURE CHEST. I also see Herr Muspilli, our chemistry teacher.

The valves in the thicket of pipes are NAPHTHALENE SPRINGS, they drip. At night you see how white the stopcocks are, different from snow, a flowing white. And the towers are a different black from the night, prickly black. And the moon has one life here and another life at home, over the small-town gables. In both places its light shines all night long, illuminating its ancient inventory—a plush chair and a sewing machine. The plush chair smells like lemon blossoms, the sewing machine like furniture wax.

The MATRON, the imposing hyperbolic cooling tower, has my full admiration, she must be a hundred meters tall. Her black impregnated corset smells like fir resin. Her unchanging white cooling-tower cloud is made of steam. The steam doesn't smell, but it does stimulate the membranes of the nose and intensifies all the smells present, as well as the urge to invent escape words. Only the hunger angel can deceive as well as the Matron. Near the tower there's a pile of artificial fertilizer, from before the war. Kobelian told me that the fertilizer was also a coal derivative. DERIVATIVE sounded comforting. From a distance, the prewar artificial fertilizer glinted like glycerin soap in cellophane. I saw myself as an eleven-year-old boy in Bucharest, in the summer of 1938, in the Calea Victoriei. My first visit to a modern department store, with a candy section a whole block long. Sweet breath in my nose, cellophane crackling in my fingers. Cold and hot shivers inside and out: my first erection. On top of that, the store was called *Sora*—sister.

The prewar artificial fertilizer has layers of transparent yellow, mustard green, and gray—all baked together and smelling bitter, like alum. I have to trust the alum stone, after all, it staunches bleeding. Some of the plants that grow here consume nothing but alum, they bloom purple like stanched blood and later have brown-lacquered berries, like the dried blood of the steppe-dogs.

Anthracene is another chemical substance. It lurks on every path and eats through your rubber galoshes. Anthracene is oily sand, or oil that has crystallized into sand. When you step on it, it instantly reverts to oil, inky blue, silver green like trampled mushrooms. Anthracene smells like camphor.

And now and then the odor of coal tar rises from the pitch basin despite all my fragrant paths and all my words of escape.

Ever since my daylight poisoning I am afraid of the pitch basin and happy to have the cellar.

But even in the cellar there must be substances that can't be seen or smelled or tasted. And they are the most devious. Since I can't spot them, I can't rename them with my escape words. They hide from me, but they also make sure I get the healthy milk. Once a month, after the shift, Albert Gion and I are given healthy milk against the invisible substances, so that we won't succumb to the poisons as fast as Yuri, the Russian who worked in the cellar with Albert Gion before my daylight poisoning. To help us last longer, once a month at the factory guard shack they pour half a liter of healthy milk into a tin bowl. It's a gift from another world. It tastes like the person you could have remained if you hadn't gone into the service of the hunger angel. I believe the milk. I believe that it helps my lungs. That every sip destroys the poison, that the milk is like the snow, whose purity surpasses all expectations.

All of them, all of them.

And every day I hope its effect will protect me for a full month. I don't dare say it but I say it nevertheless: I hope the fresh milk is the unknown sister of my white handkerchief. And the flowing version of my grandmother's wish. I know you'll come back.

Who switched my country

Three nights in a row I was haunted by the same dream. Once again I was riding home through the clouds on a white pig. But this time when I looked down, the land had a different appearance, there was no sea along its edge. And no mountains in the middle, no Carpathians. Only flat land, and not a single village. Nothing but wild oats everywhere, already autumn-yellow.

Who switched my country, I asked.

The hunger angel looked at me from the sky and said: America.

And where is Transylvania, I asked.

He said: In America.

Where did all the people go, I asked.

He said nothing.

On the second night he also refused to tell me where the people had gone, and on the third night as well. And that bothered me the whole next day. Albert Gion sent me straight from our shift to the other men's barrack to see Zither Lommer, who was known for interpreting dreams. He shook

179

thirteen big white beans into my padded cap, turned them out onto the lid of his suitcase, and studied how far apart each bean was from the others. Then he examined their wormholes, dents, and scratches. Between the third and the ninth bean he saw a street, and the seventh was my mother. Numbers two, four, six, and eight were wheels, but small. The vehicle was a baby carriage. A white baby carriage. I said that was impossible, we didn't have our baby carriage anymore, because my father had converted it into a shopping cart as soon as I learned to walk. Zither Lommer asked if the converted baby carriage was white, and showed me on bean number nine how there was even a head inside the carriage, with a blue bonnet, probably a boy. I put my cap back on and asked what else he saw. He said: Nothing else. I had a piece of saved bread in my jacket. He said I didn't owe him anything since it was my first time. But I think it was because I was so devastated.

I went back to my barrack. I'd learned nothing about Transylvania and America and where the people had gone. Or about myself, either. It was a pity about the beans, I thought, maybe they were just used up from all the dreams here in the camp. But they'd make a good soup.

I'm always telling myself I don't have many feelings. Even when something does affect me I'm only moderately moved. I almost never cry. It's not that I'm stronger than the ones with teary eyes, I'm weaker. They have courage. When all you are is skin and bones, feelings are a brave thing. I'm more of a coward. The difference is minimal, though, I just use my strength not to cry. When I do allow myself a feeling, I take the part that hurts and bandage it up with a story that doesn't cry, that doesn't dwell on homesickness. For instance one about chestnuts and how they smell—even though that really does have to do with homesickness. But I make sure I only think about the Austro-Hungarian chestnuts that Grandfather told me about, the ones that smelled of fresh leather, the ones he shelled and ate before setting off around the globe on the Austrian sailing frigate *Donau*. That way I use the homesickness from my grandfather's story to tame my own homesickness here, to make it disappear. So, when I do have a feeling, it's actually a smell. The word-smell from the chestnuts or from the sailor. Over time every word-smell withers and dries out, like Zither Lommer's beans. Of course you can become a monster if you give up crying. The only thing that keeps me from becoming a monster, assuming I haven't turned into one already, is the sentence: I know you'll come back.

I taught my homesickness to be dry-eyed a long time ago. Now I'd like it to become ownerless. Then it would no longer see my condition here and wouldn't ask about my family back home. Then my mind would no longer be home to people, only objects. Then I could simply shove them back and forth across the place where it hurts, the way we shove our feet when we dance the Paloma. Objects may be small or large, and some may be too heavy, but they are finite.

If I can manage all this, my homesickness will no longer be susceptible to yearning. It will merely be hunger for home as the place where I once was full.

Potato man

For two months in the camp I ate potatoes as a supplement to the mess-hall fodder. Two months of boiled potatoes, strictly rationed into three-day cycles of appetizer, entrée, and dessert.

The appetizers consisted of peeled potatoes, boiled with salt and sprinkled with wild dill. I saved the peels for the next day, when I treated myself to an entrée of diced potatoes with noodles. The saved peels mixed with the fresh peels were my noodles. Day three was dessert—unpeeled potatoes, cut into slices and grilled on the fire, then sprinkled with roasted wild oat kernels and a bit of sugar.

I had borrowed half a measure of sugar and half a measure of salt from Trudi Pelikan. Like all of us, after the third anniversary of the peace Trudi Pelikan had thought they'd soon let us go home, so she gave her bell-shaped coat with the beautiful fur cuffs to Bea Zakel, who traded it at the market for five measures of sugar and five measures of salt. That deal went better than the one with my silk scarf, which Tur Prikulitsch still wore to roll call. No longer all the time, though, and never in the heat of summer, just every few days, now that autumn was here. And every few days I asked Bea Zakel when I'd get something for my scarf, either from her or from Tur.

After one evening roll call without the silk scarf Tur Prikulitsch ordered me, my cellar companion Albert Gion, and Paul Gast the lawyer to his office. Tur reeked of sugar-beet liquor. Not only his eyes but his tongue seemed oiled. He crossed out some columns on his list and filled our names in elsewhere and explained that Albert Gion didn't have to go to the cellar tomorrow and that I didn't have to go to the cellar and the lawyer didn't have to go to the factory. But what he wrote down was different from what he said. We were all confused. So Tur Prikulitsch started over, and this time he explained that Albert Gion had to go the cellar tomorrow as always, but with the lawyer, not with me. When I asked why not with me, he half-closed his eyes and said: Because tomorrow morning at six o'clock sharp you're going to the kolkhoz. Don't take anything, you're coming back in the evening. When I asked how I was getting there, he said: What do you mean how, on foot. You pass three slag heaps on your right, then keep an eye out for the kolkhoz on your left.

I was convinced I was going for more than just one day. The people assigned to the kolkhoz died more quickly. They lived five or six steps below the earth, in holes they had dug out of the ground, with roofs made of twigs and grass. The rain dripped down from above, and the groundwater seeped up from below. They were given one liter of water daily for drinking and washing. They died of thirst in the heat instead of starving to death. And with all the filth and vermin, their wounds got infected with tetanus. Everyone in the camp was afraid of the kolkhoz. I was convinced that instead of paying me for the scarf, Tur Prikulitsch was sending me to the kolkhoz to die, and then he would have inherited the scarf from me.

At six o'clock I set off with my pillowcase in my jacket, in case there was something to steal at the kolkhoz. The wind whistled over the fields of cabbages and beets, the grasses swayed orange, the dew glistened in waves. I saw patches of fiery orach. The wind pushed against me, the entire steppe streamed into me, urging me to collapse because I was so thin and it was so greedy. I passed a cabbage field and a narrow swath of acacias and then the first slag heap, then grassland, and after that a cornfield. Then came the second slag heap. Steppe-dogs peered out over the grass. They stood on their hind legs, with brown furry backs and pale bellies and tails the length of a finger. They nodded and pressed their front paws together like human hands at prayer. Their ears were on the sides of their heads, like human ears. They nodded for one final second, then the empty grass rippled over their burrows, but very differently than in the wind.

Only then did it occur to me that the animals could sense I was walking through the steppe alone and unguarded. Steppe-dogs have keen instincts, I thought, what they're praying for is flight, for escape. And I could escape, but where to. Maybe they think I've already made my escape and they're trying to warn me. I looked back to see if I was being followed. Two figures were coming up far behind me, they appeared to be a man and a child, carrying two short-handled shovels, not rifles. The sky stretched out over the steppe like a blue net that seemed to grow out of the earth at the horizon, with no gap to slip through.

There had been three attempts to escape from the camp. All three men who tried came from the Carpatho-Ukraine, like Tur Prikulitsch. Despite the fact they spoke fluent Russian, all three were caught and paraded at roll call, their bodies disfigured from the beatings they'd received. After that they were never seen again, sent either to a penal camp or to their grave.

To my left I now saw a little hut made of boards, and a guard wearing a pistol on his belt, a thin young man, half a head shorter than me. He'd been waiting for me and waved me over. I didn't get a chance to catch my breath, he was in a rush, we hurried past the fields of cabbage. He was chewing sunflower seeds, popping two in his mouth at the same time. He bit down once, then spat both husks out of one corner of his mouth while snapping up the next seeds in the other, after which the empty husks went flying out again. We walked as quickly as he snapped. Maybe he's mute, I thought. He didn't speak, he didn't sweat, his mouth acrobatics never lost their rhythm. He walked as though the wind were pulling him forward, cracking his seeds like a husking machine, without saying a word. Then he grabbed my arm and we stopped. Scattered across the field were some twenty women. They had no tools, they were digging potatoes with their bare hands. The guard assigned me to a row. The sun was standing in the middle of the sky like a glowing ember. I shoveled with my hands, the ground was hard. My skin cracked, the dirt burned in the cuts. When I lifted my head, swarms of little specks flickered before my eyes. The blood froze inside my brain. Out here, this young man with the pistol was not only our guard but also nachal'nik, foreman, and inspector all in one. When he caught the women talking he whipped them in the face with a potato plant or stuffed a rotten potato in their mouths. And he wasn't mute. I couldn't understand what he was screaming, but it wasn't coal curses, construction-site commands, or cellar words.

It slowly dawned on me that Tur Prikulitsch had something

else in mind. That he had made an agreement with the young man, who was supposed to work me all day long and then shoot me in the evening, as I attempted to escape. Or else he was supposed to stick me in my own private hole for the night, since I was the only man here. And probably not just for tonight, but for every night from now on, and I'd never make it back to the camp.

When evening came, our guard, nachal'nik, foreman, and inspector also became camp commandant. The women lined up to be counted. They stated their names and numbers, opened their fufaikas to the left to show their pockets, and held out their hands with two potatoes in each. They were allowed to take four middle-sized ones. If a potato was too big it was exchanged. I was the last person in line and held out my pillowcase. It was filled with twenty-seven potatoes, seven middle-sized and twenty larger ones. I, too, was allowed to keep four middle-sized potatoes, the others I had to take out. The pistol man asked my name. I said: Leopold Auberg. As if in response to my name, he took a middle-sized potato and kicked it over my shoulder. I ducked. The next one he's not going to kick with his foot, I thought, he'll throw it at my head and shoot it in midair with his pistol and blow it to shreds along with my brains. He didn't take his eyes off me as I was thinking that, and when I stuck my pillowcase in my pants pocket he grabbed my arm, pulled me out of the line, and, as if he were once again mute, pointed me in the direction I had come from that morning, at the evening, and at the steppe. Then he left me standing there. He commanded the women to march and set off behind them, in the opposite direction. I stood at the edge of the field and watched him march away with the women. I was certain that he'd leave his brigade any minute and come back, that he'd fire his pistol just once, that there'd be no witnesses, only the verdict: Shot while attempting to escape.

The brigade moved off into the distance like a brown snake, smaller and smaller. I stood rooted in front of the big pile of potatoes and now began to think Tur Prikulitsch's agreement wasn't with the guard but with me. That this pile of potatoes was the agreement, and Tur wanted to pay for my scarf with potatoes.

I stuffed my clothes with potatoes of all sizes, all the way up to my cap. I counted 273. The hunger angel helped me—he was, after all, a notorious thief. But after he'd helped me, he was once again a notorious tormentor and left me to fend for myself on the long way home. The potatoes were heavier than I was.

I set off. Soon I was itching everywhere: the head louse, the neck-and-throat louse, the armpit louse, the chest louse, and the pubic louse. My toes already itched from the footwraps in the galoshes. To scratch anywhere I would have had to lift my arm, which I couldn't do with my overstuffed sleeves. To walk normally I would have had to bend my knees, which I couldn't do with my overstuffed pant legs. I shuffled past the first slag heap. The second heap didn't come and didn't come, or maybe I'd missed it, and now it was much too dark to make out the third slag heap. Stars were strung out across all parts of the sky. I knew the Milky Way ran north and south, because Oswald Enyeter the barber had explained it to me after the second one of his countrymen tried to escape and failed, and was put on display at the roll-call grounds. To travel west, he said, you have to cross the Milky Way and turn right, then go straight, always keeping the Big Dipper on your right. But I couldn't even find the second and third slag heaps that now, on my way back, should be coming up on my left. Better to be guarded all around than lost all around. The acacias, the corn, even my steps were cloaked in black. The cabbages followed me like human heads in a fantastic assortment of caps and hairstyles. The moon wore a white bonnet and touched my face like a nurse. Maybe I no longer need the potatoes at all, I thought, maybe I'm going to die from the poison in the cellar and just don't know it yet. I heard halting birdcalls from the trees and a sad, gurgling lament in the distance. The night silhouettes flowed around me. I can't allow myself to be afraid, I thought, or else I'll drown. I talked to myself, so as not to pray:

The things that last never squander themselves, they need only one unchanging connection to the world. The steppe connects to the world through lurking, the moon through giving light, the steppe-dogs through fleeing, and the grass through swaying. And my connection to the world is through eating.

The wind hummed, I heard my mother's voice. In that last summer at home my mother should not have said: Don't stab the potato with your fork because it will fall apart, use your spoon, the fork is for meat. But my mother couldn't have imagined that the steppe would know her voice, that one night on the steppe the potatoes would pull me into the earth and all the stars would stab me from above. No one could have guessed, back then at the table, that I would be hauling myself like a big trunk through fields and grassland all the way to the camp gate. That only three years later I would be alone in the night, a man made of potatoes, and that what I would call my way home was a road back to a camp.

At the gate, the dogs barked in their soprano night-voices that always sounded like crying. Perhaps Tur Prikulitsch had also made an agreement with the guards, because they waved me through with no inspection. I heard them laughing behind me, their shoes tapping on the ground. With my clothes stuffed so full, I couldn't turn around, presumably one of the guards was aping my stiff gait.

The next day I took three middle-sized potatoes to Albert Gion on our night shift, thinking he might want to roast them in peace and quiet over the fire in back, in the open iron basket. He didn't. He studied them one at a time and put them in his cap. He asked: Why exactly 273.

Because minus 273 degrees Celsius is absolute zero, I said, it doesn't get colder than that.

You're very scientific today, he said, but I'm sure you miscounted.

I couldn't have, I said, the number 273 watches out for itself, it's a given.

What's given, said Albert Gion, is that you should have thought of something else. My God, Leo, you could have run away.

I gave Trudi Pelikan twenty potatoes, to pay her back for the sugar and salt. Within two months, just before Christmas, all 273 potatoes were gone. The last ones sprouted blue-green sliding eyes like Bea Zakel's. I wondered whether I should tell her that someday.

Sky below earth above

Deep in the fruit garden, at our summerhouse in the Wench, stood a wooden bench without a back. We called it Uncle Hermann. We called it that because we didn't know anybody by that name. Uncle Hermann had two round feet made of tree trunks stuck into the earth. The top of his seat was smooth, but the underside was still rough timber, with bark. When the sun was blazing, Uncle Hermann sweated drops of resin. If you plucked them off they grew back the next day.

Higher up on the grass hill stood Aunt Luia. She had a back and four legs and was smaller and slimmer than Uncle Hermann. She was older as well, Uncle Hermann had come after her. I climbed up to Aunt Luia and rolled down the hill. Sky below earth above and grass in between. The grass always held me firmly by the feet so I wouldn't fall into the sky. And I always saw Aunt Luia's gray underbelly.

One evening my mother was sitting on Aunt Luia, and I was lying on my back in the grass at her feet. We were looking up at the stars, which were all out. And Mother pulled the collar of her jacket over her chin, until the collar had lips. Until not she, but the collar said:

Heaven and earth make up the world. The reason the sky's so big is because there's a coat hanging there for every human. And the reason the earth is so big is because the world's toes are so far away. So far away you have to stop thinking, because distances like that make you feel hollow and sick to your stomach.

I asked: Where is the farthest place in all the world.

At the end of the world.

At its toes.

Yes.

Does it also have ten.

I think so.

Do you know which coat is yours.

I'll know when I'm up in heaven.

But that's where the dead people are.

Yes.

How do they get there.

They travel there with the soul.

Does the soul have toes, too.

No, wings.

Do the coats have sleeves.

Yes.

Are the sleeves their wings.

Yes.

Are Uncle Hermann and Aunt Luia a couple.

If wood gets married, then yes.

Then Mother stood up and went into the house. And I sat down on Aunt Luia in the exact spot where she had been sitting. The wood was warm. The black wind quivered in the fruit garden.

On boredom

Today I don't have to work the early-morning shift, the after-noon shift, or the night shift. After the last night shift of a given rotation we have a free Wednesday, which counts as my Sunday, and lasts until two p.m. on Thursday. I'm drowning in all this free air, I ought to trim my nails, but last time it felt as though the nails I was trimming belonged to someone else. I don't know who.

From the barrack window I can see across the camp to the mess hall. The two Zirris are coming up the camp street carry-ing a heavy bucket, it must be coal. They pass the first bench and sit down on the second because it has a back. I could open the window and wave or else go out to them. I quickly slip into my galoshes but then I just stay there, sitting on my bed.

There's the boredom of the rubber worm with its delusions of grandeur, the black knee of the stovepipe, the shadow of the dilapidated little table—a new one appears every time the sun moves. There's the boredom of the water level in the bucket and the water in my swollen legs. There's the boredom of my frayed shirt seam and the borrowed sewing needle, and the shaky boredom of sewing, when my brain slides over my eyes, and there's the boredom of the bitten-off thread.

Among the men there's the boredom of vague depressions during grumpy card games that lack all passion. Someone with a good hand ought to want to win, but the men break off the game before anyone wins or loses. And among the women there's the boredom of singing homesick songs while picking nits in the boredom of solid lice combs made of horn and Bakelite. And there's the boredom of the jagged metal combs that are of no use. There's the boredom of having your head shaved and the boredom of skulls that look like porcelain jars decorated with pus blooms and garlands of lice bites, both fresh and fading. There's also the mute boredom of Kati Sentry. Kati Sentry never sings. I asked her: Kati, can't you sing. She said: I've already combed my hair. See, the comb scratches when there isn't any hair.

The camp yard is an empty village in the sun, the sharp tips of the clouds are fire. On the mountain meadow my Aunt Fini pointed to the evening sun. A gust of wind had lifted her hair like a bird's nest and parted it in back with a slashing white line. And she said: The Christ child is baking cake. I asked: Already. She said: Already.

There's the boredom of wasted conversations, not to mention opportunities. Even the simplest request takes many words, and there's no guarantee that any one of them will do the trick. I often avoid conversations, and when I seek them out, I am afraid of them, most of all of the ones with Bea Zakel. Maybe the reason I dive into her sidelong gaze is not because I want something from her but because I want to beg mercy from Tur. The truth is I speak with everyone more than I want to, simply to be less alone. As if anyone could be alone in the camp. No one can be alone here, even if the camp is an empty village in the sun.

It's always the same, I lie down to sleep, because it won't get any quieter later on, since the others will be coming off work. But night-shift workers don't sleep for long stretches, and I'm awake after four hours of obligatory rest. I could try to calculate how long it is until the next boring spring in the camp with the next senseless peace anniversary and the rumor that we'll soon be sent home. And then there I am, lying in the new grass for the new anniversary, and I have the whole earth strapped onto my back. But they ship us farther east, to another camp, where we're supposed to chop down trees. I pack my cellar-things into my gramophone suitcase, I pack and pack and never finish. The others are already waiting. The train is whistling, I jump onto the step at the last moment. We ride from one fir forest to the next. The firs leap out of the way and yield to the tracks and then hop back in place after the train has passed. We arrive and climb off the train, the first one out is Commandant Shishtvanyonov. I take my time, hoping that no one notices I don't have a saw or an axe in my gramophone suitcase, just my cellar-things and my white handkerchief. Immediately after stepping off the train the commandant changes clothes, now his uniform has horn buttons and oak-leaf epaulettes, even though we're in a fir forest. He's impatient—*Davay*, come on, move it, he tells me, we have more than enough saws and axes. I climb out, and he hands me a brown paper sack. Not more cement, I think. But one corner of the sack is torn and it's leaking white flour. I thank him for the present, I carry the sack under my left arm and salute with my right. Shishtvanyonov says: Get a move on, here in the mountains we sometimes have to blow things up. Then I understand, the white flour is blasting powder.

Instead of having thoughts like that, I could read. But I've long since sold the terrible *Zarathustra*, the thick *Faust*, and the onionskin edition of Weinheber as cigarette paper to still my hunger for a little while. On my last free Wednesday I also imagined being shipped farther east, but that time we didn't even need a train. We traveled in our barrack, which stretched out like an accordion, without any tracks or wheels. The ride was smooth, the acacias rushed by, scratching the windows with their branches, and I sat next to Kobelian and asked: How can it be that we're riding, when we don't have any wheels. And he said: That's because the camp is always on track.

I'm tired and don't want to yearn so much for anything. There are all kinds of boredom, some that go running ahead and others that come limping behind. If I treat them well they won't hurt me and they'll be mine to have. All year long, over the Russian village, there's the boredom of the moon— the thin moon whose neck resembles a cucumber flower, or a trumpet with gray valves. Then a few days later the half-moon that hangs in the sky like a cap. And then the boredom of a full moon, full to the point of overflowing. Every day there's the boredom of the barbed wire on the camp wall, the boredom of the guards in the towers, Tur Prikulitsch's shiny toecaps, and the boredom of my own torn galoshes. There's the boredom of the cooling-tower cloud as well as the boredom of the white bread linens. And there's the boredom of the corrugated asbestos sheets, the streaks of tar, and the old puddles of oil.

There's the boredom of the sun, when the wood shrivels and the earth gets thinner than reason in your head, when the guard dogs doze instead of bark. Before the grass has entirely withered, the sky closes in, and then there's the boredom when the ropes of rain fall, when the wood swells and your shoes stick in the mud and your clothes stick to your skin. The summer is cruel to its leaves, the fall to its colors, the winter to us.

There's the boredom of freshly fallen snow with coal dust and old snow with coal dust, the boredom of old snow with potato peels and freshly fallen snow without potato peels. The boredom of snow with cement creases and tar stains, the floury wool on the guard dogs, and their different barks, either metallic-deep or soprano-high. There's the boredom of dripping pipes, with icicles like glass radishes, and the boredom of plushly upholstered snow on the steps to the cellar. And the hairnet of icy threads melting on the chipped fireclay of the coke ovens. And the sticky snow that's so fond of humans, which glazes our eyes and burns our cheeks.

On the wide Russian train tracks there's the snow on the wooden cross ties and the rust on the wreaths of densely set screws that come in sets of two, three, or even five, like epaulettes for different ranks. And on the train embankment, if someone falls over, there's the boredom of the snow with the corpse and the shovel. Scarcely has the corpse been cleared away than it's already forgotten, because bodies that thin hardly leave any trace in snow that thick. All you can see is the boredom of an abandoned shovel. It's best not to go near the shovel. When the wind is weak, a soul flies up, adorned with feathers. When the wind is strong, the soul is carried off in waves. And not just the soul, since presumably every corpse also releases a hunger angel who goes looking for a new host. But none of us can nourish two hunger angels.

Trudi Pelikan told me that she and the Russian medic drove with Kobelian to the train embankment and loaded Corina Marcu's frozen body onto the truck. That Trudi climbed into the truck bed to undress the body before it was buried, but that the medic said: We'll take care of that later. That the medic sat with Kobelian in the cab and Trudi sat in the truck bed with the body. That Kobelian didn't drive to the cemetery but to the camp, where Bea Zakel was waiting in the sick barrack and that she stepped outside carrying her baby when she heard the rumble of the truck. That Kobelian hoisted Corina Marcu onto his shoulder and didn't carry her to the dying room or to the surgery but to the medic's own room, as the medic told him to do. That he didn't know where to put the body, because the medic said: Wait. That the dead woman grew too heavy and he let her slide down his side and stood her on the ground. That he propped up the body until the medic had stashed her canned goods in a bucket and the table was free. That Kobelian laid the dead woman on the table without saying another word. That Trudi Pelikan started to unbutton Corina Marcu's jacket, because she thought Bea Zakel was waiting for her clothes. That the medic said: First the hair. That Bea Zakel locked her child up with the other children behind the wooden screen. That her child kept kicking the wooden screen and screaming until the other children joined in even more shrilly, the way dogs bark more shrilly after one has already started. That Bea Zakel pulled the dead woman's head over the edge of the table so that her hair hung down. That as if by some miracle Corina Marcu's head had never been shaved and the medic then cut her hair with the clippers. That Bea Zakel placed the hair neatly inside a little wooden box. That Trudi wanted to know what that was good for and the medic said: For window cushions. That Trudi asked: For whom, and Bea Zakel said: For the tailor shop, Herr Reusch sews window cushions for us, the hair stops the draft. That the medic washed her hands with soap and said: You know what I'm afraid of, that it's so boring when you're dead. That Bea Zakel said, with an unusually high-pitched voice: You're right to be afraid. That Bea Zakel then tore two empty pages out of the sick register and covered the little wooden box. That with the box tucked under her arm like that she looked like she'd just been to the store in the Russian village and had bought something perishable. That Bea didn't wait for the clothes but disappeared with the little box before the dead woman was completely undressed. That Kobelian went to his truck. That it took some time to undress Corina Marcu, because Trudi didn't want to ruin the good fufaika by cutting it off the body. That with all the tugging a cat brooch fell out of the dead woman's pocket and landed on the floor next to the bucket. That when Trudi Pelikan bent down to pick it up she read the printed label off one of the shiny tins in the bucket: CORNED BEEF. That she couldn't believe her eyes. That meanwhile the medic picked up the brooch. That the truck was rumbling outside the whole time and didn't drive off. That the medic went out holding the cat brooch and came back empty-handed and said: Kobelian's sitting at the steering wheel, bawling, and saying My God My God over and over.

Boredom is fear's patience. Fear doesn't want to exaggerate. Only on occasion—and fear considers this very important—does it want to know how things stand with me.

I could eat a piece of saved bread from my pillowcase, with a pinch of sugar or salt. Or dry my wet footwraps on the chair next to the stove. The little wooden table casts a longer shadow, the sun has moved. In the spring, next spring, maybe I'll finagle two pieces of rubber from the conveyor belt in the factory or from a tire in the garage. Then I'll take them to the cobbler.

Bea Zakel was the first in the camp to wear the shoes we called *balletki*. She'd had them since the previous summer. I'd gone to see her in the clothes room, I needed new wooden shoes. I rummaged through the pile, and Bea Zakel said: The only shoes I have left are either too big or too small, nothing but thimbles or ships, the medium-sized shoes are all gone. Because I wanted to stay there longer, I tried on several pairs. At first I decided on a small pair, then I asked when some medium shoes would be coming in. In the end I took two large ones. Bea Zakel said: Put them on right now, leave the old ones here. Look what I have: ballet shoes.

I asked: Where from?

She said: From the cobbler. See how they bend, just like barefoot.

How much do they cost, I asked.

She said: You have to ask Tur.

Kobelian might give me the pieces of rubber for free. They have to be at least as big as two shovel blades. But I'll need money for the cobbler. I'll have to sell some coal now while it's still cold out. In the summer, next summer, the boredom may take off its footwraps and wear ballet shoes. Then it will walk around just like barefoot.

The ersatz-brother

At the beginning of November, Tur Prikulitsch summons me to his office.

I have a letter from home.

My mouth is smacking with joy so much I can't close it. Tur opens one half of a cabinet and searches through a box. The closed half has a picture of Stalin pasted on the door: his cheekbones are high and gray like two slag heaps, his nose is as impressive as an iron bridge, his mustache looks like a swallow. The coal stove next to the table is clanging away, a tin pot of black tea is humming on top. Next to the stove is the bucket with anthracite. Tur says: Put in a little more coal while I look for your letter.

I pick through the bucket for three suitable chunks, the flame shoots up like a white hare jumping through a yellow hare. Then the yellow one jumps through the white one, the hares tear each other apart and whistle in two-part harmony: Hasevey. The fire blows heat into my face and the waiting blows fear. I close the little feed door and Tur closes the cabinet. He hands me a Red Cross postcard.

The postcard has a photo that's been sewn on with white thread, evenly stitched by machine. The photo is of a baby. Tur looks me in the face, and I look at the card, and the child sewn onto the card looks me in the face, and from the door of the cabinet Stalin looks all of us in the face.

Underneath the photo is written:

Robert, b. April 17, 1947.

My mother's handwriting. The baby is wearing a crocheted bonnet with a bow under his chin. I read once again: Robert, b. April 17, 1947. Nothing else. The handwriting is like a stab, my mother's practical thinking, saving space by abbreviating born with b. My pulse is throbbing in the card and not in the hand that's holding it. Tur places the mail register and a pencil on the table, I'm supposed to find my name and sign. He goes to the stove, spreads out his hands, and listens to the tea water humming and the hares whistling in the fire. First the columns start to swim before my eyes, then the letters. Then I kneel at the edge of the table, drop my hands on the table and my face in my hands, and sob.

Do you want some tea, asks Tur. Do you want brandy. I thought you'd be happy.

Yes, I say, I'm happy, because we still have our old sewing machine at home.

I drink a glass of brandy with Tur Prikulitsch, and then another. Much too much for skinandbones people. The brandy burns in my stomach and the tears burn in my face. It's been forever since I cried, I've taught my homesickness to be dry-eyed. I've even managed to make it ownerless. Tur presses a pencil into my hand and points to the proper column. My hand shakes as I write: Leopold. I need your full name, says Tur. You write the rest, I say, I can't.

Then I step out into the snow, the sewn-on child tucked away in the pocket of my fufaika. Looking in at the office window, I can see the cushion used to stop the draft, the one Trudi Pelikan told me about. It's very evenly stitched and stuffed. Corina Marcu's hair couldn't have been enough, there has to be other hair inside the cushion as well. Funnels of white start flowing from the lightbulbs, the rear watchtower is swinging back and forth in the sky. Zither Lommer's white beans are strewn all across the snowyard. The snow slips farther and farther away, along with the camp wall. But on the path where I am walking, it rises up to my neck. The wind has a sharp scythe. I have no feet, I'm walking on my cheeks, and soon I have no cheeks. I have nothing but the sewn-on child, my ersatz-brother. My parents had a baby because they've given up on me. Just as my mother abbreviated born with b., she'll abbreviate died with d. She's already done so. Isn't my mother ashamed of the space below the precisely stitched white thread, below the handwritten line, the space in which I can't help but read:

As far as I'm concerned you can die where you are, we'll have more room at home.

The white space below the line

My mother's Red Cross postcard came in November. It had taken seven months to get to the camp. She'd sent it from home in April. By then the sewn-on child was already nine months old.

I stowed the postcard with my ersatz-brother in the bottom of my suitcase, next to the white handkerchief. My mother had written only one line on the card, and not a word in that line was about me. I didn't even appear in the white space below the line.

In the Russian village I'd learned to beg for food. But I wasn't going to beg my mother to mention my name. For the two years that followed I forced myself not to answer her card. Over the past two years the hunger angel had taught me how to beg, and in the two that followed he taught me tough pride, as rough and raw as being steadfast with bread. He tormented me cruelly. Day after day he showed me my mother forgetting all about me so that she could feed her ersatz-child. Tidy and well nourished, she pushed her white baby carriage back and forth inside my head. And I watched her from all sides, from every place I didn't appear, including the white space below the line.

Minkowski's wire

Everyone in the camp has his own here and now. Everyone touches the ground in rubber galoshes or wooden shoes, even if he's twelve meters below the earth, sitting on the board of silence.

When Albert Gion and I aren't working, we sit on a bench made of two stones and a board. The lightbulb burns in its wire cage, and a coke fire burns in the iron basket. We rest and don't speak. I often ask myself, Can I still do arithmetic. Given that we're now in our fourth year of camp, and our third year of peace, there must have also been a first and second peace year here in the cellar, just like there must have been a time before the peace, without me. And the number of day and night shifts must correspond to the number of layers in the earth. I should have counted my shifts with Albert Gion, but can I still do arithmetic.

Can I still read. My father gave me a book for Christmas: *Physics and You*. According to the book, each and every thing— every person and every event—has its own place and its own time. This is a law of nature. It follows that each and every thing has its reason for being in the world, and also a wire that connects it to everything else that exists, the MINKOWSKI-WIRE. As I sit here, I have a Minkowski-wire running straight up from my head. When I bend, it bends, and when I move, it moves with me. So I'm not alone. Every corner in the cellar also has its wire, as does every person in the camp. And no wire touches another. Above all our heads is a strictly ordered forest of wires. Every person is in his place and breathes with his wire. The cooling tower breathes double, since the cooling-tower cloud likely has a wire of its own. But the book doesn't account for all the things inside a labor camp. For instance, the hunger angel must have a Minkowski-wire of his own, only it's not clear from the book if the hunger angel's wire always stays attached to us, which is why he never really goes away when he says he's coming back. Maybe the book would have impressed the hunger angel. I should have brought it along.

I almost always sit in silence on the cellar bench and peer into my head as if through a bright crack in a door. The book also said that every person is moving through his own film at every moment and in every place, and that the reels all spin at sixteen frames per second. PROBABILITY OF PRESENCE was another memorable phrase in *Physics and You*. As if there were a chance I might not really be here. Then I could be elsewhere without even having to want to leave here. And that's because as a body in a specific place, in this case the cellar, I am a particle, but because of my Minkowski-wire I am also a wave. And as a wave I can also be in another place, and someone who isn't here can be here with me. I can pick out anyone I want. But instead of a person I'd rather it be an object, that would go better with the layers of earth in the cellar. For instance, the DINO-SAUR, which was the name of the long-distance bus that ran between Hermannstadt and the spa town ten kilometers away: very elegant, dark red, with chrome bumpers. My mother and Aunt Fini used to take the DINOSAUR to the baths. When they came back they let me lick their bare arms to taste the salt from the baths. And they told me how the salt collected in pearly scales on the grass stalks in the meadow. Through the bright door-crack in my head I cause the DINOSAUR to run between me and the cellar. It has its own bright door-crack and its own Minkowski-wire. Our wires never touch, but our bright door-cracks join below the lightbulb, where the fly ash is swirling around with its Minkowski-wire. And on the bench beside me Albert Gion sits quietly with his Minkowski-wire. The bench is the board of silence, because Albert Gion can't tell me which film he's in at the moment, just like I can't tell him that I have a dark-red long-distance bus with chrome bumpers right here in the cellar. Every shift is a work of art. But its Minkowski-wire is nothing but a steel cable with little carts moving up and down. And every cart with its wire is nothing but a load of slag twelve meters below the earth.

Sometimes I'm convinced I died a hundred years ago, and that the soles of my feet are transparent. When I look through the bright crack in my head, what I'm really searching for is this stubborn shy hope that at some time and in some place someone is thinking of me. Even if that person cannot know where I am at any given moment. It may be that I'm the old gap-toothed man in the upper-left corner of a wedding photo that doesn't exist, and simultaneously a skinny child in a schoolyard that also doesn't exist. Likewise, I am both the rival and the brother of my ersatz-brother, and he is also my rival because we both exist at the same moment. But we exist at different moments, too, since we have not seen each other ever, that is, at any one point in time.

And at the same moment I know that the hunger angel sees me dead, but the death that he sees has not happened to me, not yet.

Black dogs

I step out of the cellar into the blinding morning snow. Four statues made of black slag are standing on the watchtowers. They're not soldiers, but four black dogs. The first and the third statues move their heads, while the second and fourth stay frozen. Then the first dog moves its legs, the fourth moves its rifle, and the second and third stay frozen.

The snow on the roof of the mess hall is a white linen sheet. Why did Fenya put the bread cloth on the roof.

The cooling-tower cloud is a white baby carriage rolling toward the white birches in the Russian village. One day, when the white batiste handkerchief was in its third winter inside my suitcase, I went out begging again. I knocked on the door of the old Russian woman. A man my age opened. I asked if his name was Boris. He said NYET. I asked if an old lady lived here. He said NYET.

In the mess hall the bread is on its way. Someday when I'm alone at the bread counter, I'll screw up my courage and ask Fenya: When am I going home, I'm practically a statue made of black slag. Fenya will say: Well, you have tracks in the cellar, and you have a mountain. The little carts are always going home, you should go with them. You used to like taking the train into the mountains. And I'll say: But that was when I was still at home. Well, she'll say, so everything will be just like it was at home.

But then I enter the mess hall and take my place in line. The bread is covered with white snow from the roof. I could work things out so I'm the last one in line, so I could be alone with Fenya when she administers my bread. But I don't dare, her saintliness is too cold, and her face has the same three noses it always does—two of them being the beaks of her scales.

A spoon here, a spoon there

It was Advent once again, and I was amazed to see my little wire tree with the green fir-wool set up on the table in the barrack. Paul Gast the lawyer had kept it in his suitcase, and this year he decorated it with three bread-ball ornaments. Because we've been here three years, he said. He could afford to treat us to the bread ornaments because he stole the bread from his wife, but he didn't think we knew that.

Heidrun Gast lived in one of the women's barracks, as married couples weren't allowed to live together. She already had the dead-monkey face, the slit mouth running from one ear to the other, swollen eyes, and the white hare in the hollows of her cheeks. Since summer she'd been working in the garage, where she had to fill the truck batteries. Her face was more pockmarked than her fufaika, from all the sulfuric acid.

Every day in the mess hall we saw what the hunger angel could do to a marriage. The lawyer searched for his wife like a watchdog. If she was sitting at a table between other people, he gave her arm a tug, then squeezed in close to her so that her soup was next to his. When she looked away for a second he dipped his spoon in her bowl. If she noticed what he was doing he said: A spoon here, a spoon there.

January had barely begun. The little tree with the bread ornaments was still on the table in our barrack when Heidrun Gast died. And the bread ornaments were still hanging on the little tree when Paul Gast started wearing his wife's coat with the small rounded collar and the tattered pocket flaps made of rabbit fur. He also started to get shaved more often than he used to.

By the middle of January our singer Loni Mich was wearing the coat. And the lawyer was allowed behind her blanket. Around this time the barber asked: Anyone here have children back home.

The lawyer said: I do.

How many, asked the barber.

Three, said the lawyer.

His eyes stared out of the shaving lather and fixed on the door, where my padded cap with the earflaps hung on a hook like a duck that had been shot out of the sky. The lawyer heaved a deep sigh, blowing a gob of foam off the back of the barber's hand onto the ground. It landed between the chair legs, right next to the lawyer's rubber galoshes. Wrapped around the soles of his galoshes and tied off at the ankles were two brand-new, glistening pieces of copper wire.

Once my hunger
angel was a lawyer

Don't ever tell this to my husband, said Heidrun Gast. She was sitting between Trudi Pelikan and me, because Paul Gast the lawyer hadn't come to eat that day, he had an abscessed tooth. So Heidrun Gast was able to talk.

And what she told us was this: The garage where she worked was housed in a bombed-out factory. The ceiling over the repair bay had a hole as big as a tree canopy. She could look up through the hole and see people clearing rubble from the next level of the factory. Now and then a potato was lying on the floor of the repair bay, which a man had tossed down especially for Heidrun Gast. Always the same man. Heidrun Gast looked up at him, and he looked down at her. They couldn't talk, he was surrounded by guards up in the factory just as she was down in the garage. The man wore a striped fufaika, he was a German prisoner of war. The last potato was a very small one, Heidrun Gast found it lying among the toolboxes. It's possible that the potato had been there one or two days and she just hadn't seen it. Either the man had tossed it down in more of a hurry than usual or else the potato had rolled farther than usual because it was so small. Or he had deliberately tossed it in a different spot. At first Heidrun Gast wasn't sure the potato had really come from the man above and hadn't been placed there by the nachal'nik as a trap. She nudged it halfway under the stairs with the tip of her shoe, so the potato couldn't be seen unless you knew it was there. She wanted to make sure the nachal'nik wasn't spying on her. She waited until just before quitting time, and when she picked up the potato she noticed there was a thread tied around it. As always, Heidrun Gast had looked up through the hole as often as she could that day, but there was no sign of the man. Back in her barrack that evening she bit off the thread. The potato had been sliced in two, and a scrap of cloth placed between the two halves. She could make out some writing: ELFRIEDE RO, ERSTRASS, ENSBU, and, on the bottom, ERMAN. The other letters had been eaten away by the potato starch. After the lawyer had finished his soup in the mess hall and returned to his barracks, Heidrun Gast went out to the yard, found a late fire, tossed in the scrap of cloth, and roasted the two potato halves. I realize that I ate a message, she told us, and that was sixty-one days ago. I know he didn't go home, and I'm sure he didn't die, he was still healthy. He just vanished from the face of the earth, she said, like the potato in my mouth. I miss him.

A thin film of ice quivered in her eyes. The hollows of her cheeks were furred in white and clinging to her bones. Her hunger angel had to see there was nothing more to be gotten from her. I felt queasy, it seemed that the more Heidrun Gast confided in me, the sooner her hunger angel was likely to leave her. As if her hunger angel were looking to move in with me.

Only the hunger angel could forbid Paul Gast from eating his wife's food. But the hunger angel is a thief himself. All the hunger angels know each other, I thought, just as we all know each other. And they have the same professions we do. Paul Gast's hunger angel is a lawyer just like he is. And Heidrun Gast's hunger angel fetches and carries for her husband's. Mine also fetches and carries, but I have no idea for whom.

I said: Heidrun, eat your soup.

I can't, she said.

I reached for her soup. Trudi Pelikan was also eyeing it furtively. And Albert Gion from across the table. I began spooning away, without counting. I didn't slurp, because slurping takes longer. I ate for myself, without Heidrun Gast or Trudi Pelikan or Albert Gion. I forgot everything around me, the entire mess hall. I sucked the soup into my heart. Faced with this bowl of soup, my hunger angel ceased being a servant and became a lawyer.

I shoved the empty dish over to Heidrun Gast, until it touched the little finger of her left hand. She licked her unused spoon and wiped it dry on her jacket, as if she and not I had eaten the soup. Either she could no longer tell whether she was eating or watching, or she was acting as though she had eaten. One way or the other, you could see her hunger angel stretched out inside her slit mouth, mercifully pale on the outside and dark blue inside. He may have even been able to stand in a horizontal position. And it was clear that he was counting her days in the thin cabbage soup. But it's also possible that he had forgotten Heidrun Gast and was calibrating the scale in the back of my throat. Or that as we were eating he was figuring out how much he could get from me and how long it would be before he got it.

I have a plan

When the hunger angel weighs me, I will deceive his scales.

I will be just as light as my saved bread. And just as hard to bite.

You'll see, I tell myself, it's a short plan with a long life.

The tin kiss

After supper I went to the cellar for the night shift. There was a brightness in the sky. A flock of birds was flying like a gray necklace from the Russian village toward the camp. I don't know if the birds were screeching in the brightness or in the roof of my mouth. I also don't know if they were screeching with their beaks or rubbing their feet together or if their wings had old bones with no cartilage.

Suddenly a piece of the necklace broke away and split into mustaches. Three of them flew right into the soldier in the rear watchtower, just under the brim of his cap. They stayed there a long time, and didn't fly out again until I'd reached the factory gate and turned around one more time. The soldier's rifle was shaking, but he stayed frozen. I thought, The man is made of wood, and the rifle of flesh.

I didn't want to trade places with the guard in the tower or with the bird necklace. Nor did I want to be the slag worker who has to climb down the same sixty-four steps into the cellar every evening. But I did want to trade places. I think I wanted to be the rifle.

During the night shift I flipped one cart after the next, as always, and Albert Gion did the pushing. Then we switched. The hot slag cloaked us in fog. The pieces of ember smelled like fir resin and my sweaty neck like honey tea. The whites of Albert Gion's eyes swung back and forth like two peeled eggs, his teeth like a lice comb. In the cellar his black face had disappeared.

During the break, sitting on the board of silence, the little coke fire lit up our legs all the way to our knees. Albert Gion unbuttoned his jacket and asked: What does Heidrun Gast miss more, the German or the potatoes. That wasn't the first time she's untied a potato, who knows what was written on the other scraps. The lawyer's right to steal her food. An old marriage makes you hungry, infidelity makes you full. Albert Gion tapped me on the knee, as a sign the break was over, I thought. But then he said: Tomorrow I'm taking the soup, what does your Minkowski-wire say to that. My Minkowski-wire said nothing. We sat there a while in silence. My black hand disappeared on the bench. Just like his.

The next day Paul Gast was again sitting next to his wife in the mess hall, despite his abscessed teeth. He was back to eating, and Heidrun Gast was back to keeping quiet. What my Minkowski-wire said to that was that I was disappointed, as so often. And that Albert Gion was being spiteful in a way I'd never seen. He was out to spoil the lawyer's meal and tried to pick a fight. He accused the lawyer of snoring so loud it was unbearable. Then I turned spiteful too and told Albert Gion that his snoring was even worse than the lawyer's. Albert Gion was furious that I'd spoiled his fight. He raised his hand to strike me, and his bony face was like a horse's head. By that time the lawyer's spoon was already well into his wife's soup.

She dipped her spoon less and less and he dipped his more and more. He slurped, and his wife began to cough, just to do something with her mouth. And when she coughed she covered her mouth, daintily holding out her little finger that was corroded by the sulfuric acid and grimy from the lubricating oil. Here in the mess hall all of us had dirty fingers, the only one with clean hands was Oswald Enyeter the barber, but the hair on his hands was as dark as the filth on ours, and looked as though he'd borrowed some fur from the steppe-dogs. Trudi Pelikan also had clean hands, ever since she became a nurse. Clean, but colored yellowish brown from rubbing ichthyol on all the sick people.

While I was thinking about Heidrun Gast's little finger and the condition of our hands, Karli Halmen came up to me and wanted to swap bread. My mind wasn't clear enough for swapping bread, so I fended him off and stuck with my own portion. Then he traded with Albert Gion. That pained me, because the piece of bread that Albert Gion then bit into seemed bigger than mine by a third.

From all around the mess hall came the clatter of tin. Every spoonful of soup is a tin kiss, I thought. And every one of us is ruled by our hunger, as though by an alien power. But no matter how well I knew that in the moment, I forgot it right away.

The way of the world

The naked truth is that Paul Gast the lawyer stole his wife's soup right out of her bowl until she could no longer get out of bed and died because she couldn't help it, just like he stole her soup because his hunger couldn't help it, just like he wore her coat with the rabbit-fur pocket flaps and couldn't help it that she had died, just like our singer Loni Mich wore the coat and couldn't help it that a coat was free because the lawyer's wife had died, just like the lawyer couldn't help it that he was also free because his wife had died, just like he couldn't help wanting to replace her with Loni Mich, and Loni Mich couldn't help wanting a man behind the blanket, or wanting a coat, or that the two things were tied together, just like the winter couldn't help being icy cold and the coat couldn't help being so warm, and the days couldn't help being a chain of causes and effects, just like all causes and effects couldn't help it that they were the naked truth, even though this was all about a coat.

That was the way of the world: because each person couldn't help it, no one could.

White hare

Father, the white hare is hunting us down, chasing us out of life. He's growing in the hollows of more and more cheeks.

He hasn't crawled out of my face yet, he's just been looking at my flesh from the inside, because it is also his. Hase-veh.

His eyes are coals, his muzzle is a tin dish, his legs are pokers, his stomach is a little cart in the cellar, his path is a set of tracks rising steeply up the mountain.

He's still sitting inside me, pink-skinned, waiting with his own knife, which is also Fenya's, the knife for cutting bread.

Homesickness. That's the
last thing I need

The seven years after my return home were seven years without homesickness, without *Heimweh*. But when I looked in the display window of the bookstore on the main square and saw *The Sun Also Rises* by Hemingway, I read *The Sun Also Rises* by Heimweh. And so I bought the book and set off on my home-weh, I mean my way home.

There are words that do whatever they want with me. They're completely different from me and they think differently than what they really are. They deliberately pop into my mind so I'll think there's one thing that intends a different thing, even though I may not want that second thing at all. Hemingway. Heimweh. Homesickness. That's the last thing I need.

There are words that have me as their target, that seem created solely for my re-deportation—not counting the word RE-DEPORTATION. That word would be of no use if I were re-deported. Another useless word is MEMORY. The word HARM won't help if I'm re-deported, either. Nor the word EXPERIENCE. Whenever I have to deal with these useless words, I have to pretend I'm dumber than I am. But they're harder on me with each new encounter.

In the camp we had lice on our heads, in our eyebrows, on our necks, in our armpits, and in our pubic hair. We had bedbugs in our bunks. We were hungry. But we didn't say: I have lice and bedbugs or I'm hungry. We said: I'm homesick. Which was the last thing we needed.

Some people speak and sing and walk and sit and sleep and silence their homesickness, for a long time, and to no avail. Some say that over time homesickness loses its specific content, that it starts to smolder and only then becomes all-consuming, because it's no longer focused on a concrete home. I am one of the people who say that.

I know that even lice can yearn for home, in three different places: there's the head louse, the clothes louse, and the crab louse. The head louse crawls on your scalp, behind your ears, in your eyebrows, along the hairline on your neck. If your neck itches, it could also be a clothes louse in your shirt collar. The clothes louse doesn't crawl. It sits in the stitches of whatever you're wearing. It's called a clothes louse but it doesn't live off threads. The crab louse crawls and itches inside your pubic hair. We didn't say: Pubic hair. We said: I've got an itch down there.

Lice come in different sizes, but they're all white and look like little crabs. When you squeeze them between your thumbnails you hear a dry crack. They leave behind a watery speck on one nail and a sticky speck of blood on the other. The colorless eggs are strung together like a glass rosary or transparent peas in a pod. Lice are only dangerous if they're carrying typhus or typhoid fever. Otherwise you can live with them. You get used to itching all over.

You might think that the camp lice got transferred from head to head at the barber's, by comb. But they had no need of that, they were able to crawl from bed to bed inside the barrack. We set the feet of our bunks in tin cans filled with water so as to block their path, but they were as hungry as we were and found other ways. We shared lice during roll call, in line at the food counter, at the long tables in the mess hall, at work loading and unloading, while squatting during a cigarette break, while dancing the Paloma.

Our heads were shorn with a special clipper, the men by Oswald Enyeter in his barber room, the women by the Russian medic in a wooden shack next to the sick barrack. When their hair was first cut off, the women were allowed to take their braids and keep them in their suitcases as souvenirs of themselves.

I don't know why the men didn't help each other pick lice. The women put their heads together every day, told stories and sang and picked the lice off one another.

In the very first winter, Zither Lommer taught us how to remove the lice from wool sweaters. At sunset, when it's well below freezing, you dig a hole in the ground thirty centimeters deep, stick the sweater in the hole, and loosely cover the hole, leaving just a little bit of wool sticking out, the length of a finger. During the night all the lice crawl out of the sweater. By sunrise they've gathered in white clumps on the little tip of wool. Then you can squash them all at once with your shoe.

Once March came and we could work the earth, we dug holes between the barracks. Each evening the sweater tips stuck out of the ground, like a knitted garden that bloomed at dawn with white foam, like cauliflower. We squashed the lice and pulled the sweaters out of the ground. The sweaters again kept us warm, and Zither Lommer said: Clothes don't die even when you bury them.

The seven years after my return home were seven years without lice. But for sixty years, whenever there's cauliflower on my plate, I'm eating lice from the sweater tips at sunrise. And to this day whipped cream is never just a topping on the cake.

In the camp, from the second year on, we had a new method of getting rid of lice—the ETUBA, a hot-air chamber over a hundred degrees Celsius set up next to the showers. Every Saturday we hung our clothes on iron hooks which circled around on rollers like the little trolleys in the cooling room of a slaughterhouse. The clothes took much longer to roast than we did to shower, about one and a half hours—we quickly ran out of time, as well as hot water. So we stood in the entrance area and waited. Bent, mangy figures, in our nakedness we looked like worn-out draft animals. But no one was ashamed. What is there to be ashamed of when you no longer have a body. Yet our bodies were the reason we were in the camp, to perform bodily labor. The less of a body we had, the more it punished us. The shell that was left belonged to the Russians. I was never ashamed in front of the others, only in front of my earlier self, remembering my days in the Neptune baths, when my skin was smooth and I was giddy from the lavender steam and the gasping delight. When I never thought about worn-out draft animals on two legs.

After the clothes came out of the etuba, they stank of heat and salt. The fabric was singed and brittle. But two or three passes through the etuba turned smuggled sugar beets into candied fruit. I never had any sugar beets to bring to the etuba. I had a heart-shovel, coal, cement, sand, cinder blocks, and cellar slag. I had spent one terrifying day with the potatoes, but not a single day in the field with the sugar beets. Only the men who loaded and unloaded sugar beets at the kolkhoz had candied fruit in the etuba. I knew what candied fruit looked like from home: glass green, raspberry red, lemon yellow—little gemstones sprinkled inside a cake that got stuck between your teeth. The candied sugar beets were earthy brown, once peeled they looked like sugar-glazed fists. When I saw the others eating them, my homesickness ate cake, and my stomach contracted.

In the women's barrack on New Year's Eve in our fourth year, I, too, ate candied beets—in a cake that Trudi Pelikan hadn't so much baked as built. Instead of candied fruit there were candied beets, instead of nuts, sunflower seeds—instead of flour, corn bran—instead of dessert plates, faience tiles from the dying room in the sick barrack. Along with that, each of us received one cigarette from the market—LUCKY STRIKE. I took two puffs and was drunk. My head floated off my shoulders and merged with the other faces, the bunks started spinning in circles. We sang and locked arms and swayed to the Cattle Car Blues:

> The daphne's blooming in the wood
> The ditches still have snow
> The letter that you sent to me
> Has filled my heart with woe

Kati Sentry sat with her piece of cake at the little table under the barrack light. She watched us impassively. But when the song was over she rocked on her chair and said: UUUH, UUUH.

She had made this same deep uuuh, the dull sound of the deportation train, at our last stop during the snow-night four years ago. I froze, others cried. Trudi Pelikan also broke down. And Kati Sentry watched us cry and ate her cake. You could see that she liked it.

There are words that do whatever they want with me. I no longer know if the Russian word VOSH' means the bedbugs or the lice. With my word VOSH' I mean both. Maybe the word can't tell one from the other. But I can.

The bedbugs climbed up the walls, and during the night they dropped from the ceiling onto our beds. I don't know if they dropped during the day as well and we just didn't see them. But they were another reason the light in the barrack was kept on all night long.

Our bed frames were made of iron. Rusty bars with raw welded seams. The bedbugs reproduced there as well as in the unplaned boards under the straw sacks. Whenever the bedbugs gained the upper hand, we had to take our beds out into the yard—that mostly happened on weekends. We had wire brushes made by the men in the factory that we used on the bedbugs, brushing the bed frames and the boards so hard that they turned red with blood. Exterminating bedbugs was one order we were eager to carry out. We wanted to clean our beds and have a few nights' peace. We were happy to see the blood of the bedbugs, because it was our own. The more blood we saw, the more determined we were to brush down the bed. All the hate was drawn out of us. We brushed the bedbugs to death and felt a kind of pride, as if they were the Russians.

Then exhaustion hit us like a blow to the head. Pride that is tired makes you sad. Our pride brushed itself down to size until the next time. Knowing that all our work was ultimately in vain, we carried the beds, temporarily free of bedbugs, back to the barracks. And with pitiful humility, we told ourselves: At least now night can come.

And sixty years later I dream: I've been deported for the second, third, or sometimes even the seventh time. I set down my gramophone suitcase by the well and wander around the Appellplatz. There are no brigades here, no nachal'niks. I have no work. The world has forgotten me, and so has the new camp administration. I mention my experience as a camp veteran. I explain that I have my heart-shovel, and that my day and night shifts were always works of art. I'm not some Johnny-come-lately, I know how to do things. I know about cellars and slag. I have a blue-black, beetle-sized piece of slag grown into my shin from the first time I was deported. I show it off like a hero's medal. I don't know where I'm supposed to sleep, everything here is new. Where are the barracks, I ask. Where is Bea Zakel, where is Tur Prikulitsch. Limping Fenya has a different crocheted sweater in every dream, but she always has the same sash made of white bread cloth. She says there isn't any camp administration. I feel neglected. Nobody wants me here, but under no circumstances am I allowed to leave.

In which camp did my dream end up. Does my dream even care that the heart-shovel and the slag cellar really existed. That the five imprisoned years are more than enough for me. Does my dream want to go on deporting me and then refuse to let me work when I reach the seventh camp. That really hurts. I have nothing to counter with, no matter how many times the dream deports me and no matter which camp I end up in.

If I'm ever to be deported again in this life, I'll know: there are things that intend a different thing, even if you may not want that second thing at all.

What's driving me to stay so attached. Why do I insist on being miserable at night. Why can't I be free. Why am I forcing the camp to belong to me. Homesickness. That's the last thing I need.

A bright moment

One afternoon I found Kati Sentry sitting at the little wooden table in the barrack, probably because of the cuckoo clock. Who knows how long she'd been there. When I came in she asked me: Do you live here.

I said: Yes.

I do, too, she said, but behind the church. We moved into the new house last spring. Then my little brother died. He was old.

I said: But he was younger than you.

He was sick, that makes you old, she said. Then I put on his suede shoes and went back to the old house. There was a man in the courtyard. Then the man asked me, how did you get here. I showed him the suede shoes. Then he said, next time bring your head.

Then what did you do, I asked.

Then I went inside the church, she said.

I asked: What was your little brother's name.

She said: Latzi, just like you.

But my name is Leo, I said.

Maybe when you're at home, but here your name is Latzi, she said.

Such a bright moment, I thought, there's even a louse—a *Laus*—inside the name, since Latzi comes from Ladislaus.

Kati Sentry stood up, hunched over, and glanced at the cuckoo clock one more time from the door. But her right eye shimmered at me like old silk. She raised her index finger and said:

You know, you better stop waving to me in church.

Carelessness spread like hay

In the summer we were allowed to dance outside on the Appell-platz. Just before nightfall the swallows flew in pursuit of their hunger, the trees turned darkly jagged, and the clouds were tinged with red. Later a finger-thin moon hung over the mess hall. Anton Kowatsch's drumming drifted on the wind, the dancing couples swayed like bushes. The little bells of the coke batteries chimed, and the glow that followed every wave of tinkling lit up the sky over our heads. Before the brightness faded you could see Singing Loni's trembling goiter and the heavy eyes of Konrad Fonn the accordionist, always staring off to where there was nothing and nobody.

There was something bestial in the way Konrad Fonn pulled the ribs of the accordion apart and squeezed them together. His drooping eyelids hinted at a lascivious nature, but his eyes were too hollow and cold for that. The music didn't enter his soul—he just shooed the songs away, and they crawled into us. His accordion shuffled along, hollow and dull. Ever since Zither Lommer had supposedly boarded a ship in Odessa, to head somewhere in the direction of home, the orchestra was missing its warm bright tones. Maybe the accordion was as out of tune as the musician, maybe it questioned whether deportees pairing off and swaying on the Appellplatz like bushes really counted as dancing.

Kati Sentry was sitting on the bench, swinging her feet in time to the music. If a man asked her to dance she would run off into the darkness. Now and then she danced with one of the women, craning her neck and gazing at the sky. She must have danced often in the past since she was able to follow changes of rhythm. When she sat on the bench she would throw pebbles if she saw the couples come too close together. It wasn't a game, either, her face remained serious. Albert Gion told me that most people forget all about the Appellplatz on those nights, that they go so far as to say they're dancing on the plaza. He also told me he was never going to dance with Zirri Wandschneider again, she was clinging to him like a leech and hell-bent on giving herself to him. Besides, it wasn't him, it was the music doing the seducing, here in the darkness, he told me. During the winter Paloma, emotions stayed pleated like the ribs of the accordion, and locked up in the mess hall. The summer dance stirred up carelessness and spread it over our melancholy like hay. The barrack windows shimmered weakly, people felt rather than saw one another. Trudi Pelikan was of the opinion that homesickness trickled from the head to the belly when we were outside on the plaza. She saw the patterns of the couples shifting from one hour to the next— homesickness in pairs, was how she put it.

I think the mixture of goodwill and guile that these couplings revealed was probably as varied and possibly as wretched as the different mixes of coal. You couldn't mix what wasn't there. You had to mix what you had. And I had to keep out of all the mixes and make sure no one had any idea why.

The accordion player probably sensed why, there was something disdainful in his manner. I felt hurt even if I did find him repulsive. I couldn't resist looking at his face each time the glow from the factory lit up the sky and for as long as the light lasted. Every quarter hour I saw his neck above the accordion and his doglike head and his frightening eyes, white and stony, staring off to the side. Then the sky was black night once again. And I waited a quarter hour until the dog's head reappeared, as ugly as before. The summer Paloma on the Appellplatz always went like that. Only once did something different happen.

It was late September, on one of our last dance nights outside. I was sitting the way I so often did, with my feet on the wooden bench and both knees tucked under my chin. Paul Gast the lawyer took a break from the dancing and sat down next to my feet and said nothing. Perhaps he really did think about his dead wife Heidrun Gast every now and then. Because the moment he leaned back, a star fell over the Russian village. He said:

Leo, you have to wish for something, fast.

The Russian village swallowed the falling star, and all the others glittered like coarse salt.

I couldn't think of anything, he said, how about you.

I said: That we'll come out alive.

That was a lie, spread as carelessly as hay. I had wished that my ersatz-brother was no longer alive. I wanted to hurt my mother. After all, I didn't even know him.

On camp happiness

Happiness is something sudden.

I know mouth happiness and head happiness.

Mouth happiness comes with eating and is shorter than your mouth, even shorter than the word mouth. It doesn't even have time to climb into your head when you pronounce the word. Mouth happiness doesn't want to be talked about. If I were to talk about mouth happiness I'd have to add SUDDENLY before each sentence. And after each sentence: DON'T TELL ANYONE, BECAUSE EVERYONE IS HUNGRY.

I'll say it just this once: Suddenly you pull down the acacia branch, pick flowers and eat. You don't tell anyone, because everyone is hungry. You pick sorrel on the side of the path and eat. You pick wild thyme between the pipes and eat. You pick chamomile by the door to the cellar and eat. You pick wild garlic by the fence and eat. You pull down the branch and pick black mulberries and eat. You pick wild oats in the empty fields and eat. You don't find a single potato peel behind the mess hall, but you do find a cabbage stalk, and eat.

In winter you don't pick a thing. You leave your shift and

head home to the barrack and don't know where the snow will taste best. Should you take a handful right from the stairs to the cellar or hold off for the coal heap that's snowed under or wait until you're at the camp gate. Without deciding, you take a handful off the white cap on the fencepost and freshen up your pulse and your mouth and your throat down to your heart. Suddenly you no longer feel tired. You don't tell anyone, because everyone is tired.

Barring disaster, each day is like the next. You want each day to be like the next. But with happiness it's a little different, it's a matter of luck. Five comes after nine, says Oswald Enyeter the barber, and if you think of it that way, luck is always a little balamuc. I must be lucky because my grandmother said: I know you'll come back. I don't tell anyone, either, because everyone wants to come back. To be happy you need a goal. I have to find a goal, even if it's nothing more than the snow on the fencepost.

Head happiness is easier to talk about than mouth happiness.

Mouth happiness wants to be alone. It's mute and introverted. But head happiness is gregarious and craves other people. It's a happiness that wanders around, even if it's limping along behind. It lasts longer than you can bear. Head happiness is fragmented and difficult to sort out, it mixes itself whatever way it wants and changes quickly from bright to

dark
blurred
blind
resentful
hidden

fluttering
hesitant
impetuous
pushy
unsteady
fallen
dropped
stacked
threaded
deceived
threadbare
crumbled
confused
lurking
prickly
uneasy
repeated
cheeky
stolen
thrown away
left over
missed by just a hair.

Head happiness can have wet eyes, a craned neck, or shaky fingers. But it always bangs around in your forehead like a frog in a tin can.

The very last happiness is the onedroptoomuchhappiness. That comes when you die. I still remember that when Irma Pfeifer died in the mortar pit, Trudi Pelikan opened her mouth like a great big zero, made a clicking sound, and said in one word:

Onedroptoomuchhappiness.

She was right, because whenever we cleared away the dead we could see the relief, we could tell that the tangled nest inside the skull, the dizzying swing in the breath, the rhythm-crazed pump in the breast, the empty waiting room in the stomach were finally leaving them in peace.

There was never such a thing as pure head happiness, because hunger was in the mouths of everyone.

Even sixty years after the camp, eating still excites me greatly. I eat with every pore of my body. When I eat with other people I become unpleasant. I behave as though my way of eating were the only way. The others don't know mouth happiness, they eat sociably and politely. But when I eat, I think about the onedroptoomuchhappiness and how it will come to everyone as sure as we're sitting there, and that we'll have to give up the nest in our skull, the swing in our breath, the pump in our chest, the waiting room in our stomach. I love eating so much that I don't want to die, because then I couldn't eat anymore. For sixty years I have known that returning home was not enough to subdue my camp happiness. To this day its hunger bites the middle out of every other feeling. And what's left in the middle of me is emptiness.

Every day since I came back home, each feeling has a hunger of its own and expects me to reciprocate, but I don't. I won't ever let anyone cling to me again. I've been taught by hunger and am unreachable out of humility, not pride.

We're alive.
We only live once

During the skinandbones time, all I had inside my brain was a hurdy-gurdy droning day and night: hunger deceives, cold slashes, tiredness burdens, homesickness devours, bedbugs and lice bite. I wanted to work out a trade with things that aren't alive but aren't dead either. I wanted to make an emergency exchange, trading my body for the horizon line above and the dusty roads on the earth below. I wanted to borrow their endurance, exist without my body, and when the worst was over, slip back into my body and reappear in my fufaika. This had nothing to do with dying, quite the opposite.

Absolute zero is that which cannot be expressed. And we agree, absolute zero and I, that absolute zero itself is beyond discussion, except in the most roundabout way. The zero's wide-open mouth can eat but not speak. The zero encircles you with its strangling tenderness. An emergency exchange has no tolerance for compromise. It is urgent and direct, like:

1 shovel load = 1 gram bread.

During the skinandbones time my emergency exchange must have worked. Now and then I must have had the endurance of the horizon and the dusty roads. Otherwise with nothing but my skin and bones in the fufaika I wouldn't have survived.

Even now it's a mystery to me how our bodies get nourished. Things are torn down and built up inside the body just like at a construction site. You see yourself along with all the others day in and day out, but you never know how much inside you is breaking apart or coming together. How the calories give and take remains a riddle. How they erase all traces when they take, and put them back, when they give. You can't say exactly when things started to get better, but you know your strength has returned.

In our last year of camp we were given cash for our work. We could buy things at the market. We ate dried prunes, fish, Russian pancakes with sweet or salty cheese, bacon and lard, corn-flour cakes with sugar-beet paste, oily sunflower halva. Within a few weeks we were completely renourished. Fat and full as a sponge—BAMSTI was the word in the camp. We became men and women again, as though we were experiencing a second puberty.

The new vanity began with the women. The men went on shuffling into the day wearing their quilted work clothes, still content with how they looked, and pleased merely to supply the women with material for their vanity. The hunger angel developed a taste for clothes, for the new camp fashion. The men brought one-meter lengths of snow-white cotton rope from the factory. The women unraveled the rope, knotted the threads together, and used iron hooks to crochet bras, stockings, blouses, and vests. The stitches were always pulled to the inside, so you didn't see a single knot on the finished product. The women even fashioned hair ribbons and brooches out of the cotton threads. Trudy Pelikan wore a crocheted water-lily brooch like a demitasse pinned to her breast. One of the Zirris wore a lily-of-the-valley brooch with white thimbles affixed with wire, Loni Mich wore a dahlia dyed with red brick dust. During the first phase of this cotton transfer, I, too, was still content with how I looked. But I soon wanted to spruce myself up. I spent several long hours painstakingly sewing a newsboy cap out of my torn coat with the velvet collar. I had worked out the pattern in my head, a difficult, sophisticated construction. I took a band of tire rubber big enough so that the cap could be raked over the ear, and wrapped it in material. I used roofing felt for the bill, stiffened the oval upper part with cement-sack paper, and lined the whole cap with usable remnants from a tattered undershirt. The inner lining mattered to me, I felt my old vanity resurfacing, my need to look good even in places other people never see. It was a cap of expectation, a cap for better times.

A store in the Russian village further enhanced the women's crocheted camp fashion with toilet soap, powder, and rouge. All were the same brand: KRASNIY MAK—Red Poppy. The powder was pink and had a sharp, sweet aroma. The hunger angel was amazed.

The BALLETKI were the first fashion craze that caught on with men as well as women. I took half a rubber tire to the cobbler, others managed to get some rubberized material from the conveyor belt in the factory. The cobbler fashioned light summer shoes with very thin pliable soles, perfectly fitted to every foot. Handmade on the last, very elegant, good for stepping out. The hunger angel became light-footed. The Paloma grew giddy with excitement, everyone went to the plaza and danced until shortly before midnight, when the anthem sounded.

The women wanted to look nice for themselves and for the other women, but they also wanted to appeal to the men. And the men, eager to get at the crocheted underwear behind the blankets, worked a little harder on their own appearance. So in the wake of the balletki, men's fashion moved beyond the shoe. New fashions, new loves, mating season at the animal crossing, pregnancies, abortions in the local hospital. But also more and more babies behind the wooden screen in the sick barrack.

I paid a visit to Herr Reusch, who came from Guttenbrunn in the Banat. I only knew him from the Appell. By day he cleaned rubble out of the bombed-out factory. In the evening he repaired torn fufaikas in exchange for tobacco. He was a master tailor, and when the hunger angel started running around so recklessly, Herr Reusch's expertise was very much in demand. He rolled out a thin scrap of ribbon marked with centimeters, and measured me from my neck to my ankles. Then he said, one and a half meters of material for the pants and three meters for the jacket. Plus three big buttons and six small ones. He said he'd take care of the jacket lining himself. For the jacket I also wanted a belt with a buckle. He suggested a buckle with two metal rings and an inverted box pleat for the back of the jacket. He said that was the latest thing in America.

I ordered two metal rings from Anton Kowatsch and took all my cash to the store in the Russian village. The material for the pants was a muted blue with a bright-gray nap. The material for the jacket was a plaid of sandy beige and cement-sack brown, the squares stood out as if in relief. I also bought a ready-made tie, moss green with slanted diamonds. And three meters of repp fabric for a shirt, in light gray-green. Then some larger buttons for the pants and jacket and twelve very small ones for the shirt. That was in April 1949.

Three weeks later I had the shirt and the suit with the inverted box pleat and the iron buckle. Now at last the burgundy silk scarf with its matte and shiny checked pattern would have suited me perfectly. Tur Prikulitsch hadn't worn it for a long time, he'd probably thrown it away. The hunger angel was no longer inside our brains, but he was still perched on our necks. And he had a good memory, though he didn't need it, since our camp fashion was just another kind of hunger—eye hunger. The hunger angel said: Don't waste all your money, who knows what's yet to come. And I thought: Everything that's yet to come is already here.

I wanted some fancy clothes for going out, for the camp street, for the Paloma plaza, and even for the path to my cellar through the weeds, rust, and rubble. I changed clothes in the cellar before my shift. The hunger angel warned: Pride comes before a fall. But I told him: We're alive. We only live once. The orach never leaves here either, and yet it puts on red jewelry and tailors itself a new glove with a different thumb for every leaf.

Meanwhile my gramophone box had its new key, but was gradually becoming too small. I had the carpenter build me a solid wooden trunk for my new clothes. And I commissioned a substantial lock for the trunk from Paul Gast in the metal shop.

When I presented my new clothes on the plaza for the first time, I thought: Everything that's yet to come is already here. If only everything would stay the way it is.

Someday I'll stroll down
elegant lanes

The orach still grew whistling-green in the fourth year of peace, but we didn't pick it, we no longer felt the savage hunger. After four years of being starved, we were convinced that we were now being fattened up, not to go home but to stay here and work. Every year, the Russians waited expectantly for what was coming, while we were afraid of what might be in store. To us, the old time was a hurdle to overcome, for them a new time was flowing into their giant land.

There was a rumor that for years Tur Prikulitsch and Bea Zakel had been hoarding clothes meant for us, that they'd sold them at the market and divided the money with Shishtvan-yonov. As a result, many people had to freeze to death who, even according to the rules of the camp, had a right to under-wear, fufaikas, and shoes. We no longer counted how many. But I knew that 334 dead internees were resting in peace according to the registry Trudi Pelikan kept in the sick barrack, and I knew which peace they were resting in—the first, second, third, or fourth. For weeks I wouldn't think about them, but then they'd pop up like a rattle inside my brain and stay with me all day long.

Often, when I heard the little bells from the coke batteries, I had the sense they were ringing in a new year. And I thought: Someday I'd like to see a bench in a park instead of on the camp street, a bench with someone on it who's footloose and free, who's never been in a camp. On the plaza one evening the words CREPE SOLES made the rounds. Our singer Loni Mich asked what crepe was. And Karli Halmen winked at Paul Gast the lawyer and said, crepe comes from *krepieren*, to kick the bucket, we'll all be wearing crepe soles when we kick the bucket and go to the great sky over the steppe. After crepe soles the talk was of MUTTON CHOPS, which were supposed to be the latest thing in America. Loni Mich now asked what mutton chops were. The accordion player Konrad Fonn told her it meant hair cut like shaggy wool around your ears.

Every two weeks the cinema in the Russian village showed films and newsreels for us, the people from the camp. Mostly Russian films, but also some from America and even requisitioned German films from Berlin. In one of the American newsreels we saw confetti flying between the skyscrapers like snow and singing men with crepe soles and sideburns down to their chin. After the film the barber Oswald Enyeter said that these sideburns were the mutton chops. See, here we've gone completely Russian and it turns out we're following the latest American fashion, he said.

I didn't know what mutton chops were, either. I seldom went to the cinema. Because of my shift I was always working in the cellar or else too tired from working in the cellar when they showed the films. But I had my balletki for the summer, Kobelian had given me half a tire. And I could lock my gramophone suitcase, Paul Gast had made me a key with three fine bits like mouse teeth. From the carpenter I had a new wooden trunk with a good lock. I was outfitted with new clothes. I had no need of crepe soles in the cellar, and while I could grow mutton chops if I wanted to, they sounded more like something for Tur Prikulitsch. To me they looked downright apish.

Now it was easy for me to imagine running into Bea Zakel or Tur Prikulitsch in some other place, where we'd be on equal terms, perhaps at a train station with cast-iron pilasters and hanging baskets of petunias like at a spa. For instance: I'll climb aboard the train and Tur Prikulitsch will be sitting in the same compartment. I'll say a brief hello and sit diagonally across from him, that's all. At least I'll act as if that's all, I won't ask if he married Bea Zakel, even though I'll see his wedding ring. I'll unpack my sandwich and set it on the little folding table. White bread thickly spread with butter and slices of pink boiled ham. I won't enjoy the sandwich, but I'll make sure he doesn't notice that. Or perhaps I'll run into Zither Lommer and he'll be with the singer Loni Mich. Neither will recognize me, but I'll notice that her goiter has gotten bigger. The two of them will offer to take me to a concert in the Athenaeum. I'll decline and let them go their way. Then I'll appear as an usher in the Athenaeum and stop them at the entrance and point and say: Let's see your tickets, even-numbered seats on the right and odd on the left, I see you have 113 and 114 so you're sitting apart. And only when I laugh will they recognize me. But maybe I won't laugh.

I imagined a second meeting with Tur Prikulitsch, in a big city in America. This time he doesn't have a wedding ring, he's coming up the stairs with one of the Zirris on his arm. The Zirri won't recognize me but Tur will wink like Uncle Edwin the time he said: Quite the ladies' man, aren't I. But I'll just go on my way and that will be that.

Maybe I'll still be relatively young when I get out of the camp, in the prime of my life, as they say, like in Loni Mich's song: I WAS SCARCELY THIRTY. Maybe I'll meet Tur Prikulitsch a third and fourth time and on numerous occasions after that, in a third, fourth, sixth, or even eighth future. One day I'll look out of a third-floor hotel window and it will be raining. And on the street below a man will be opening his umbrella. He'll take a long time and will get wet because his umbrella won't open. I'll see that his hands are Tur's hands, but he won't know that. If he realized that, I'll think to myself, he wouldn't take so long trying to open his umbrella, or else he'd put on gloves, or else he wouldn't venture out on this street in the first place. If it weren't Tur Prikulitsch but just a man with Tur's hands, I'd call out from my window: Hey, why don't you go across the street, you won't get wet under the marquee. If the man looks up he might say: Do we know each other. And I would say: I don't know your face but I know your hands.

Someday, I thought, I'll stroll down elegant lanes, where people have a different way of life than in the small town where I was born. The elegant lane will be a promenade by the Black Sea. The water will be white with foam, with rocking waves like I've never seen. Neon signs will light up the promenade, saxophones will play. I'll run into Bea Zakel and recognize her by her slowly drifting eyes. I won't have a face, because she won't recognize me. She'll still have her heavy hair, but it won't be braided, it will flutter around her temples, bleached flour-white, like seagull wings. She'll also still have her high cheekbones, which will cast two hard-edged shadows, the way buildings do at high noon. The right angles of the shadows will make me think about the settlement behind the camp.

A new Russian settlement had gone up behind the camp in the third fall—rows of little houses known as Finnish cabins because they were built from prefabricated wooden parts that came from Finland. Karli Halmen told me that the parts had been precisely cut and that they came with detailed construction plans. And that all the parts got mixed up when they were unloaded, so that no one knew what went where. The construction was a disaster, with too few parts here and too many there, and sometimes the wrong parts altogether. In all my years in the camp, the construction supervisor was the only person who saw the deportees as people from civilized countries, where a right angle really did have ninety degrees. He considered us thinking human beings and not just forced laborers, which is why I remember him so well. Once during a cigarette break at the construction site he gave a speech about socialism and its good intentions being wrecked by people who didn't know what they were doing. He concluded with the remark: The Russians know what a right angle is, but they can't manage to build one.

Someday, I thought to myself, who knows in which year of peace and in which future, I'll come to the land with the mountain ridges, the place I travel to in my dreams when I ride through the sky on the white pig, the place people say is my homeland.

There were many variations on the theme of going home, different scenarios circulated through the camp. According to one, our best years would be behind us by the time we made it back, and we'd suffer the same fate as the prisoners of war from the

First World War—a return journey lasting decades. Shishtvanyonov orders us to our last and shortest roll call and proclaims:

I hereby disband the camp. Get lost.

And everyone heads out on his own, farther east, in the wrong
direction, because all roads west are closed. Over the Urals, all
the way across Siberia, past Alaska, America, and then Gibraltar
and the Mediterranean. Then, twenty-five years later, we'll
arrive at our home in the west, assuming it's still there and not
already part of Russia.

In other versions we never even leave, they keep us here so
long that the camp turns into a village without watchtowers,
and we simply become villagers out of habit, though we still
won't be Russians or Ukrainians. Or they keep us here until
we no longer want to leave, because we're convinced that no
one is waiting for us at home, that other people are living
in our houses, and that our families have long since been driven
out to who knows where, and no longer have a home of their
own either. Or we wind up wanting to stay here because we no
longer know what to make of our home and our home no longer
knows what to make of us.

When you haven't heard from that other world you know as
home for so long, you wonder if you should even want to go
back, or what you should wish for once you're there. In the
camp, all wishing was taken away from us. We didn't have to
decide anything, nor did we want to. It's true, we wanted to go
home, but we contented ourselves with looking back, and
didn't dare yearn ahead. People mistook memory for yearning.
How can you tell the difference, if the same thing keeps churn-
ing in your head over and over and your world is so lost to you
that you don't even miss it.

What will become of me at home, I thought. Wandering

in the valley between the mountain ridges, I'll always be a returnee, wherever I go I'll always be preceded by a tch-tch-tch, as though a train were pulling in. I'll fall into my own trap, into a horrible intimacy. That's my family, I'll say, and I will mean the people from the camp. My mother will tell me I should become a librarian, because then I'd never be out in the cold. And you always wanted to read, she'll say. My grandfather will tell me I should consider becoming a traveling salesman. Since you always wanted to travel, he'll say. My mother may say this, and my grandfather may say that, but here it was the fourth year of peace and despite the new ersatz-brother, I had no idea whether they were still alive. In the camp, professions like traveling salesman were good for head happiness, because they gave you something to talk about.

Once on the board of silence in the cellar I talked about it with Albert Gion and even managed to coax him into speaking. Maybe I'll become a traveling salesman later on, I said, with all kinds of stuff in my suitcase, silk scarves and pencils, colored chalk, salves, and stain-remover. I remember a shell from Hawaii that my grandfather brought my grandmother, as big as a gramophone funnel, with bluish mother-of-pearl on the inside. Or maybe I'll become a builder, a master of blueprints, I said on the board of silence in the cellar, an ozalid-blue master. Then I'll have my own office. I'll build houses for people with money, and one of them will be completely round like this iron basket. First I'll draw the plans on sandwich paper. In the center there'll be a pole running from the cellar up to the cupola. The rooms will be like slices of a cake—four, six, or eight sections of a circle. I'll set the sandwich paper in a frame on top of the blueprint paper and set the frame in the sun to be exposed for five to ten minutes. Then I'll roll the blueprint paper into a tube and run some ammonia steam inside and just a few minutes later my plans will come out beautifully: pink, purple, cinnamon-brown.

Albert Gion listened to me and said: Blueprints, haven't you had enough of steam by now, I think you're overtired. The reason we're in the cellar in the first place is because we don't have a profession, much less a good one. Barber, cobbler, tailor—those are good professions. The best, at least here in the camp. But either you brought them from home or you didn't. Those are professions that decide your fate. If we'd known we'd be sent to a camp someday we would all have become barbers or cobblers or tailors. Never traveling salesmen or master builders or master blueprinters.

Albert Gion was right. Is hauling mortar a profession. If you spend years carrying mortar or cinder blocks or shoveling coal or scratching potatoes out of the earth with your hands or cleaning up the cellar, you know how to do something, but that doesn't count. Hard labor is not a profession. And labor was all what was demanded of us, never a profession. Fetch and carry is all we did, and that's no profession.

We no longer felt the savage hunger, and the orach still grew silver-green. Soon it would turn woody and flaming red. But because we knew what hunger was, we didn't pick it, we bought fatty foods at the market and wolfed them down without restraint. We fattened up our old homesickness, it soaked up the hasty new meat. But even with the new meat, I fed myself the same old dream: Someday even I will stroll down elegant lanes. Even I.

Fundamental, like the silence

After the skinandbones time and the emergency exchange were all behind me—when I had balletki, cash, food, new flesh on my bones, and new clothes in my new trunk—we were released. It was hard to accept. For my five years in the camp I have five things to say:

1 shovel load = 1 gram bread.

Absolute zero is that which cannot be expressed.

The emergency exchange is a visitor from the other side.

Inside the camp, the we-form is singular.

Perimeters run deep.

But all five things have one truth in common: they are fundamental, like the silence that exists between them, and not the silence in front of witnesses.

The disabler

I came home from the camp at the beginning of January 1950. Once again I was in a living room, sitting in a deep square underneath a ceiling of white stucco, like snow. My father was painting the Carpathians, every few days a new watercolor, with gray-toothed mountains and fir trees smudged with snow, almost always in the same arrangement. Rows of firs at the foot of the mountain, groups of firs on the slope, pairs and single fir trees on the ridge, with birches sticking out here and there like white antlers. Evidently clouds were the most difficult to paint, they always wound up looking like gray sofa cushions. And the Carpathians always looked sleepy.

My grandfather had died, and my grandmother was sitting in his plush chair doing crossword puzzles. Now and then she asked for help: sofa in the orient, part of a shoe beginning with *t*, breed of horses, roof made of sailcloth.

My mother was knitting one pair of woolen socks after the other for her ersatz-child Robert. The first pair was green, the second white, and after that came brown, red flecked with white, blue, gray. My confusion started with the white pair—I saw my mother knitting clumps of lice, and with each new sock I saw our knitted garden between the barracks, the sweater tips at daybreak. I lay on the sofa, the ball of wool lay in the tin dish beside my mother's chair, it was livelier than I was. The yarn climbed and hovered and dropped. Two fist-sized balls of wool were needed for each sock, but it was impossible to tell how much that would be if laid out in a single strand, the total length for all the socks might cover the distance from the sofa to the train station, which was a neighborhood I avoided. At last my feet felt warm, they only itched on the instep, which was always where the footwraps first froze to the skin. The winter days turned gray as early as four o'clock. My grandmother switched on the light. The lampshade was a pale-blue funnel trimmed with dark-blue tassels. The lamp didn't cast much light on the ceiling, which stayed gray as the stucco-snow began to melt. The next morning it was once again white. I imagined that it froze during the night, while we were sleeping in the other rooms, like the icy lace in the empty field behind the zeppelin. The clock ticked away beside the wardrobe. The pendulum flew, shoveling our time in between the furniture: from the wardrobe to the window, from the table to the sofa, from the stove to the plush chair, from the day into the evening. On the wall, the ticking was my breath-swing, in my breast it was my heart-shovel, which I missed very much.

Early one morning at the end of January, Uncle Edwin came by to take me to the crate factory and introduce me to his boss. Out on the street, I saw a face in the window at Herr Carp's, who lived next door in the Schulgasse. The face was cut off at the neck by the frost pattern on the windowpane. Strands of icy hair twined around a forehead, a sliding greenish eye, and there was Bea Zakel in a white-flowered robe, her braid now heavy and gray. Herr Carp's cat was sitting in the window the way it always did, but I felt sorry for Bea, that she had aged so quickly. I knew the cat could only be a cat, that the telegraph pole wasn't a guard, that the blazing white of the snow wasn't the camp street but the Schulgasse. I knew that nothing here could be anything other than itself, because everything had stayed at home. Everything except me. Among all these home-sated people, I was dizzy with freedom. I was jumpy, my spirit conditioned for catastrophe, trained in doglike fear, my brain geared to submission. I saw Bea Zakel in the window waiting for me, and I'm sure she saw me walk by. I should have greeted her, at least nodded or waved. But that didn't occur to me until it was too late, we were already two houses farther down. When we reached the end of the street and turned the corner, my uncle hooked his arm into mine. I was walking close to him but he must have sensed how far away I was. He was probably just hooking his arm into his old coat, which I was wearing. His lungs were whistling. There was a long silence, and then he said something I felt he didn't really want to say. His lungs seemed to be forcing him to speak, which is why he had two voices when he said: I hope they take you on at the factory. It seems things are a bit grouchy at home. He was referring to the disabler.

Right where his fur cap touched his left ear, the crease of skin above his lobe flattened out just like mine. I wanted to see his right ear too. I unhooked my arm and crossed to his right side. His right ear was even more like mine than his left. There the crease smoothed out farther down, the lobe looked longer and wider, as if ironed flat.

They took me on at the crate factory. Every day I left the

disabler at home and returned to him after work. Each time I came home, my grandmother asked:

Are you back.

And I said: I'm back.

Each time I left the house she asked:

Are you leaving.

And I said: I'm leaving.

When she asked me these questions she took a step toward me and placed three fingers on her forehead as though she couldn't believe what I was saying. Her hands were transparent, nothing but skin with veins and bones, two silk fans. I wanted to fling my arms around her neck when she asked me that. The disabler stopped me.

Little Robert heard my grandmother's daily questions. When it occurred to him, he imitated her, he took a step toward me, placed his fingers to his forehead, and asked all at once:

Are you back, are you leaving.

Each time he touched his forehead I saw the folds of fat at his wrists. And each time he asked, I wanted to squeeze my ersatz-brother's neck. The disabler stopped me.

One day I came back from work and noticed a tip of white lace peeking out from the cover of the sewing machine. Another day an umbrella was hanging from the handle of the kitchen door, and a broken plate was lying on the table in two even pieces as though it had been cut down the middle, and my mother had a handkerchief tied around her thumb. One day Father's suspenders were lying on the radio and Grandmother's glasses in my shoe. Another day Robert's stuffed dog Mopi was tied to the teapot handle with my shoelaces, and a crust of bread was in my cap. Maybe they moved the disabler out when

I wasn't home. Maybe then everything came to life. The disabler at home was like the hunger angel in the camp. It was never clear whether there was one for all of us or if each of us had his own.

They probably laughed when I wasn't there. They probably felt sorry for me or cursed me. They probably kissed little Robert. They probably said they needed to be patient with me because they loved me, or else they just thought it to themselves and went about their business. Probably. Maybe I should have laughed when I came home. Maybe I should have felt sorry for them or cursed them. Maybe I should have kissed little Robert. Maybe I should have said I needed to be patient with them because I loved them. Except how could I say that if I couldn't even think it to myself.

During my first month back home I kept the light on all night, because I was afraid without the old barrack light. I believe we don't dream at night unless the day has made us tired. I didn't start dreaming again until I was working at the crate factory.

Grandmother and I are sitting together on the plush chair, Robert is on a chair next to us. I'm as little as Robert, and Robert is as big as I am. Robert climbs on his chair next to the clock and pulls some stucco off the ceiling. He gets down and drapes it around my grandmother and me like a white shawl. Father kneels on the carpet in front of us with his Leica, and my mother says: Why don't you smile at each other, let's get one last picture before she dies. My legs barely reach over the edge of the chair. From his position my father can only photograph my shoes from below, with the soles in the foreground, pointing toward the door. Because of my short legs, my father has no choice, even if he'd prefer another angle. I brush the stucco off my shoulder. My grandmother hugs me, puts the stucco back around my neck, and holds it in place with her transparent hand. My mother uses a knitting needle to conduct my father in a countdown: three, two, and then, at one, he clicks. My mother sticks the knitting needle in her hair and brushes the stucco off our shoulders. And Robert climbs on his chair and puts the stucco back on the ceiling.

Do you have a child
in Vienna

For months my feet had been at home, where no one knew what
I had seen. Nor did anybody ask. The only way you can talk
about something is by again becoming the person you're talking
about. I was glad that no one asked anything, although I was
also secretly offended. My grandfather would have asked, but
he'd been dead for two years. He died of kidney failure the summer after my third peace, but unlike me he stayed with the dead.

One evening our neighbor Herr Carp came over to return
the level he'd borrowed. He couldn't help stammering when
he saw me. I thanked him for his yellow leather gaiters and
lied that they'd kept me warm in the camp. Then I added that
they'd brought me good luck, that thanks to them I'd once
found 10 rubles at the market. He was so excited, his pupils slid
from side to side like cherry pits. He rocked back and forth on
his toes, crossed his arms and stroked them with his thumbs,
and said: Your grandfather never stopped waiting for you. On
the day he died the mountains disappeared into the clouds,
flocks of clouds drifted into town from faraway places like suitcases from all corners of the globe. They knew that your grand-

father had traveled the world. One of the clouds was definitely from you, even if you didn't know it. The funeral was over at five o'clock and right afterward it rained quietly for half an hour. I remember it was on a Wednesday, I still had to go into town to buy glue. On my way home I saw a rat without hair right in front of your house. It was cowering next to your wooden door, all wrinkled and shivering. I was surprised the rat didn't have a tail, or maybe the tail was under its belly. As I was standing there I noticed a toad covered with warts. The toad looked straight at me and started puffing out two white sacs attached to its throat, first one and then the other. The whole thing looked hideous. At first I wanted to shove the toad away with my umbrella, but I didn't dare. Better not, I thought, after all it's a toad, and he's sending some kind of signal, obviously something to do with Leo's death. People thought you were dead, you know. Your grandfather kept waiting for you. Especially at first. Less so toward the end. But everyone thought you were dead. You didn't write, that's why you're alive now.

One thing has nothing to do with the other, I said.

My breath was trembling because I could tell Herr Carp didn't believe me, he just chewed on his frayed mustache. My mother squinted out the veranda window at the courtyard, where there was nothing to see except a bit of sky and the tar-paper roof on the shed. Watch what you're saying, Herr Carp, my grandmother spoke up. You told me something different back then, you said that those white sacs had to do with my dead husband. You said the toad was sending a greeting from my dead husband. What I'm telling you now is the truth, Herr Carp mumbled, more to himself than anyone else. Back then I couldn't exactly bring up poor dead Leo, not right after your husband died.

Little Robert dragged the bubble level across the floor and went tch-tch-tch. He put Mopi on the roof of his train, tugged Mother by the dress, and said: All aboard, we're going to the Wench. The sliding green eye moved left and right inside the level. Mopi sat on the roof of the train, but inside the level Bea Zakel stared out the window at Herr Carp's toes. Herr Carp hadn't said anything new, he'd merely expressed what everyone else had been too polite to say out loud. I knew they'd been more frightened than surprised when I came back—there had been relief but no joy. By staying alive I had betrayed their mourning.

Ever since I came back, everything had eyes. And all the things saw that my ownerless homesickness was not going away. The old sewing machine with its wooden cover and its bobbin and that damned white thread still sat in front of the biggest window. The gramophone was back inside my worn-out suitcase and in its old spot on the corner table. The same green and blue curtains hung in the windows, the same flowery pattern snaked through the carpets, which were bordered by the same frayed fringe, the cupboards and doors squeaked as always when they were opened or closed, the floorboards creaked in the same places, the railing of the veranda stairs was cracked in the same spot, every stair still sagged from use, the same flowerpot dangled inside its wire basket on the landing. Nothing had anything to do with me. I was locked up inside myself and evicted from myself. I didn't belong to them and I was missing me.

My family and I had been together for seventeen years before I went to the camp. We'd shared the large objects like doors, cupboards, tables, carpets. And the small things like cups and plates, salt shakers, soap, keys. And the light from the windows and the lamps. Now I was someone else. We knew each other in a way we no longer were and never would be again. Being a stranger is hard, but being a stranger when you're so impossibly close is unbearable. My head was in my suitcase, I breathed in Russian. I didn't want to leave the house and I smelled of far away. I couldn't spend the whole day at home, I needed to find some work to escape the silence. I was twenty-two years old but had no training. Is nailing crates a profession—I was back to fetching and carrying.

One late afternoon in August I came home from the crate factory and found a letter for me lying opened on the veranda table. It was from the barber Oswald Enyeter. My father watched me read it the way you watch someone eat. I read:

Dear Leo! I hope you're back in Hermannstadt. There was no one left for me at home, so I kept on going, all the way to Austria. Now I'm here in Vienna in the Margareten district, lots of people from our part of the world. If you get a chance to come someday I can shave you again. I found a job as a barber, the shop is owned by someone from home. Tur Prikulitsch spread a rumor that he was the barber in the camp and I was the kapo. Bea Zakel keeps on repeating it even though she broke things off with him. She christened her child Lea. Does that have anything to do with Leopold? Two weeks ago some construction workers found Tur Prikulitsch under one of the bridges over the Danube. His mouth had been gagged with his tie and his forehead split down the middle with an axe. The axe was left on his stomach, no trace of the murderers. Too bad it wasn't me. He deserved it.

When I folded up the letter, my father asked:

Do you have a child in Vienna.

I said: You read the letter, it doesn't say that.

He said: Who knows what you all did in the camp.

Who knows, I said.

My mother was holding my ersatz-brother Robert by the hand. And Robert was carrying Mopi, the dog stuffed with sawdust, on his arm. My mother took Robert to the kitchen, and when she came back, she was holding Robert by one hand and a bowl of soup in the other. And Robert was pressing Mopi to his chest and holding up a spoon for the soup—obviously for me.

After I started my job at the crate factory, I'd roam through town when I got off work. The winter afternoons protected me since it got dark so early. The shop windows were bathed in yellow light like tram stops. Two or three plaster people, newly decked out, waited for me inside the displays. They stood close together, with price tags at their feet, as if they needed to watch where they were stepping. As if the price tags at their feet were police markers at a crime scene, as if a dead man had been taken away shortly before I showed up. Porcelain and tin dishes were crammed into smaller display windows at shoulder height, so that I carried them off as I walked past. The goods on sale waited in their sad light, all of them destined to last longer than the people who might buy them. Perhaps as long as the mountains. Crossing the main square I felt drawn to the residential streets. Lighted curtains hung in the windows—an enormous variety of lace rosettes and labyrinths of thread, all reflecting the same black tangle of branches from the bare trees. The people inside didn't realize how alive their curtains were, as the white threads mixed with the black wood in patterns that shifted every time the wind blew. The sky kept out of sight except at the street crossings, I saw the evening star melt and hung my face on it. By then enough time had passed and I could be sure that everyone would have finished eating by the time I came home.

I had forgotten how to eat with a knife and fork. My hands twitched, and so did my throat when I swallowed. I knew how to go hungry, how to make food last, and how to wolf it down when you finally have some. But I no longer knew how to eat politely, how long to chew, and when to swallow. My father sat across from me, and our tabletop seemed as big as half the world. He squinted as he watched me and hid his pity. The horror shone in his half-closed eyes just like the rose-quartz skin inside his lip. My grandmother understood better than anyone how to be kind to me without making a fuss. She made soup that was extra thick, probably so I wouldn't have to agonize over knives and forks.

On the day in August when the letter came we had a soup made with green beans and pork ribs. After the letter I lost my appetite. I cut a thick slice of bread and picked at the crumbs on the table. Then I dipped my spoon in my soup. My ersatz-brother was kneeling on the floor of the veranda, he stuck the tea sieve on the stuffed dog like a cap and set the dog astride the edge of the cabinet drawer. Everything Robert did made me uneasy.

He was a child assembled from different parts—his eyes came from Mother, old and round and evening blue. His eyes will stay that way, I thought. His upper lip came from Grandmother, like a pointed collar under his nose. His upper lip will stay that way. His fingernails were curved like Grandfather's and will stay that way. His ears were like mine and Uncle Edwin's, with the turned-in folds that smooth out at the lobes. Six identical ears made of three different skins, and the ears will stay that way. His nose won't stay the way it is, I thought.

Noses change as they grow. Later it may have a bony bridge, like Father's. If not, then Robert won't have anything from Father. And Father won't have contributed anything to his ersatz-child.

Robert walked over to me at the table, holding his Mopi with the tea sieve in his left hand, and grabbed my knee with his right, as if my knee were the corner of a chair. Since that first embrace when I came back home eight months ago, no one in our house had so much as touched me. For them I was unapproachable, for Robert I was a new object in the house. He grabbed hold of me like I was a piece of furniture, to steady himself or to put something in my lap. This time he stuffed his Mopi in my coat pocket, as if I were his drawer. And I kept still, as if that's exactly what I was. I would have pushed him away, but the disabler stopped me. Father took the stuffed dog and the tea sieve out of my pocket and said:

Take your treasures.

He led Robert downstairs to the courtyard. My mother took a seat across from me and stared at the fly on the bread knife. I stirred my soup and saw myself sitting in front of Oswald En-yeter's mirror. Tur Prikulitsch came in the door. I heard him say:

Little treasures have a sign that says, Here I am.

Bigger treasures have a sign that says, Do you remember.

But the most precious treasures of all will have a sign saying, I was there.

I was there—DA WAR ICH—the German words sounded in Tur's mouth like tovarishch. I hadn't been shaved for four days. In the mirror of the veranda window I saw Oswald Enyeter's black-haired hand pulling the razor through the white lather. And behind the razor a strip of skin stretched from my mouth to my ear like a rubber band. Or perhaps it was the long slit mouth from hunger already beginning to show. The reason that Father and Tur Prikulitsch could go on like that about treasures was that neither one of them had ever had a hunger mouth.

The fly on the bread knife knew the veranda as well as I knew the barber room. It flew from the bread knife to the cabinet, from the cabinet to my slice of bread, then to the edge of the plate, and from there back to the bread knife. With each flight it rose steeply into the air, sang as it circled around, and touched down in silence. It never landed on the brass top of the salt shaker with all the little holes. And all of a sudden I understood why I hadn't picked up the salt shaker since I came back: Tur Prikulitsch's eyes were twinkling in the brass. I slurped my soup, and my mother listened as though I were going to read the letter from Vienna one more time. The fly's stomach sparkled as it danced on the bread knife, now like a drop of dew, now like a drop of tar. Dew and tar and how the seconds drag, when a forehead has been split in two. Hase-veh, but how could a whole tie fit into Tur's short snout.

The cane

After work, instead of going home I went in the opposite direction, away from the residential streets and across the main square. I wanted to look inside the Holy Trinity Church to see if the white alcove and the saint with the sheep around his neck were still there.

A fat boy was standing on the square, wearing white kneesocks, short houndstooth-patterned pants, and a white frilled shirt, as if he'd run away from a party. He was shredding a white bouquet of dahlias and feeding the pigeons. Eight of them were convinced it was bread: they picked at the white dahlias on the cobblestones and then gave up. A few seconds later they'd forgotten everything, they jerked their heads and started picking at the flowers all over again. How long did their hunger believe that dahlias would turn into bread. And what was the boy after. Was he playing a trick on them or was he as dumb as the pigeons' hunger. I didn't want to think about the tricks that hunger plays. I wouldn't have stopped at all if the boy had been feeding bread to the pigeons instead of shredded dahlias. The church clock showed ten of six. I hurried across the square to make it to the church before it closed.

Then I saw Trudi Pelikan walking toward me. It was the first time I'd seen her since the camp. She was using a cane. We noticed each other too late for her to avoid me, she put her cane down on the pavement and bent down over her shoe. It wasn't even untied.

Both of us had been back in our hometown for more than half a year. For our own sakes we preferred to act as though we didn't know each other. There's nothing to understand about that. I quickly turned my head, but how gladly I would have put my arms around her and and let her know that I agreed with her. How gladly I would have said: I'm sorry you had to be the one to bend down, I don't need a cane, next time I can do it for both of us, if you'll let me. Her cane was polished and had a rusty claw on the bottom and a white knob on top.

Instead of going inside the church I made a sharp left onto the narrow street I'd come from. The sun stabbed at my back, the heat ran straight into my scalp as if my head were bare metal. The wind was dragging a carpet of dust, the treetops were singing. A little whirlwind formed on the sidewalk and swept through me, then touched down, leaving the pavement speckled with black. The wind droned and flung the first few drops. The storm was here, I heard the rustle of glass beads, and suddenly ropes of water went whipping past. I fled into a stationery shop.

As I stepped inside I wiped the water off my face with my sleeve. A salesgirl came out through a narrow curtained doorway. She was wearing worn-out felt shoes with tassels that looked like paintbrushes growing out of the insteps. She went behind the counter. I stayed next to the display window for a while, watching her with one eye and looking outside with the other. Suddenly her right cheek swelled up. Her hands were resting on the counter, her signet ring—it was a man's ring—was much too heavy for her bony fingers. Her right cheek went flat again, even hollow, and then her left cheek swelled up. I heard something clicking against her teeth and realized she was sucking on a candy. She closed one eye and then the other, her eyelids were made of paper. She said: My tea water's boiling. She disappeared through the little door and at that moment a cat slipped out from under the curtain, came up to me, and nuzzled my pants as if it knew me. I picked it up, it weighed practically nothing. This isn't a cat at all, I told myself, just gray-striped boredom that's grown fur, the patience of fear on a narrow street. The cat sniffed at my wet coat. Its nose was leathery and rounded like a heel. When it set its front paws on my shoulder and peered inside my ear, it wasn't even breathing. I pushed its head away, and the cat jumped to the ground. It jumped without making a sound and landed like a scrap of cloth. The cat was empty on the inside. The salesgirl's hands were also empty when she came back through the door. Where was the tea, she couldn't have drunk it that fast. And her right cheek was swollen again.

Her signet ring scratched against the counter.

I asked for a notebook.

Graphed or lined, she asked.

I said: Lined.

Do you have something small, I can't make change, she said. She puckered her lips and both cheeks went hollow. The candy slipped out onto the counter. It had some transparent pattern, she stuffed it quickly back in her mouth. It wasn't candy at all, she was sucking on a polished drop of glass from a chandelier.

Lined notebooks

The next day was Sunday. I began to write in the lined note-books. The first chapter was titled: FOREWORD. It began with the sentence: Will you understand me, question mark.

By you I meant the notebook. And seven pages had to do with a man named T.P. And another man named A.G. And one named K.H. and O.E. And a woman named B.Z. I gave Trudi Pelikan the alias SWAN. I wrote out the name of the factory Koksokhim Zavod and the coal station Yasinovataya. Also the names Kobelian and Kati Sentry. I even mentioned her little brother Latzi and her bright moment. The chapter ended with a long sentence:

In the morning after I washed up, a drop of water fell out of my hair and ran down my nose into my mouth like a drop of time—I really ought to grow a trapezoidal beard so no one in town will know who I am.

Over the next weeks I expanded the FOREWORD into three notebooks.

I didn't mention the fact that Trudi Pelikan and I had trav-eled back home in separate cattle cars. We did this deliberately but without any prior discussion. I also left out my old gramophone suitcase. I described my new wooden trunk and my new clothes precisely: the balletki, the paneled cap, the shirt, the tie, and the suit. But I said nothing about my sobbing fit on the way home, when we arrived at the receiving camp in Sighetul Marmaţiei, the first Romanian train station. Or about the weeklong quarantine in the freight depot at the end of the platform. I had broken down because I was afraid of being sent into freedom, afraid of the abyss that loomed so close by, and my fear made the way home shorter and shorter. I sat there nested between my gramophone suitcase and my new wooden trunk, in my new body and my new clothes, with my slightly swollen hands. The cattle car wasn't sealed, so we had the door wide open as we pulled into Sighetul Marmaţiei. The platform was covered with a film of thin snow, I stepped over sugar and salt. The puddles were frozen gray, the ice was scratched like the face of my sewn-on brother.

When the Romanian police handed out the tickets for the rest of the trip home, I held my farewell to the camp in my hand and sobbed. Home was at most ten hours away, with two changes, one in Baia Mare and one in Klausenburg. Our singer Loni Mich snuggled up to Paul Gast the lawyer, focused her eyes on me, and thought she was whispering. But I understood every word she said:

Look how he's bawling, he's falling apart.

I thought about that sentence a lot. Then I wrote it down on an empty page. And the next day I scratched it out. The day after that I wrote it down again underneath. Scratched it out again, wrote it down again. When the page was full I tore it out. That's memory.

Instead of mentioning my grandmother's sentence, I KNOW

YOU'LL COME BACK, or the white batiste handkerchief or the healthy milk, I went on for pages triumphantly describing my saved bread and the cheek-bread. And my persistence in the emergency exchange with the horizon and the dusty streets. When I got to the hunger angel I went into raptures, as if he'd only saved me and not tormented me. That's why I scratched out FOREWORD and wrote AFTERWORD above it. I was now free, but it was an immense personal disaster that I was irrevocably alone and bearing false witness against myself.

I hid my three lined notebooks under my bed, in my new wooden trunk, which had been serving as my dresser ever since I came home.

I'm still the piano

I nailed crates for a whole year. I could squeeze twelve little nails between my lips and flick twelve through my fingers at the same time. I could nail as quickly as I could breathe. The boss said: You have a gift for this, because your hands are so flat.

But they weren't my hands, just the flat breath of the Russian quota. 1 shovel load = 1 gram bread was transformed into to 1 nail head = 1 gram bread. I thought about deaf Mitzi, Peter Schiel, Irma Pfeifer, Heidrun Gast, and Corina Marcu, all lying naked in the earth. As far as my boss was concerned they were butter boxes and eggplant crates, but for me they were little fir-wood coffins. For me to meet my goal the nails had to fly through my fingers. I managed 800 nails an hour, no one else even came close. Every little nail had its hard head, and every nail was under the supervision of the hunger angel.

In the second year I enrolled in a night class on concrete manufacture. By day I was a concrete expert at a construction site on the Ucea River. That's where I made my first design for a round house, on blotting paper. Even the windows were round, everything with corners reminded me of a cattle car. With every line I drafted, I thought about Titi, the foreman's son.

Late that summer, Titi came with me to the Alder Park. An old peasant woman was standing at the entrance with a basket of wild strawberries, fiery red and tiny, like tongue tips. And each had a stem on its green collar like very thin wire. A few had three-fingered serrated leaves. She gave me one to taste. I bought two large bags for Titi and myself. We walked around the carved wood pavilion. Then I lured him farther and farther along the stream and through the bushes, behind the short-grass mounds. After we'd eaten the strawberries Titi crumpled his bag and wanted to throw it away. I said: Give it to me. He reached out his hand, I took it and wouldn't let go. He looked at me coldly and said: Hey. That couldn't be brushed off with laughing and talking.

The fall quickly colored its leaves and was soon over. I kept away from the Alder Park.

My second winter home the snow came early and stayed, by November the small town was packed in a padded suit. All the men had women. All the women had children. All the children had sleds. And they were all fat and home-sated. They ran through the white in tight-fitting dark coats. My coat was home-sated too since it was the same worn-out coat from Uncle Edwin. But it was light-colored and slightly dirty and much too big. All the people passing by were home-sated, but the scraps of breath flying out of their mouths showed the truth: here they were, going about their lives, but life was flying away. And they all watched it go, their eyes glistening like brooches of agate, emerald, or amber. One day, early or soon or late, onedroptoomuch-happiness awaits them too.

I was homesick for the lean winters. The hunger angel was

273

running around with me, and he doesn't think. He led me to the crooked street. A man was coming from the opposite end. He didn't have a coat but a fringed plaid blanket. He didn't have a wife but a hand cart. The cart didn't have a child but a black dog with a white head, which bobbed loosely in time with the turning wheels. As the plaid blanket came closer, I saw the outline of a heart-shovel on the man's right breast. As the cart went by, the heart-shovel turned into a singe mark from a flatiron and the dog into a metal canister with an enameled funnel in its neck. As I watched him walk away the canister with the funnel turned back into a dog. And I had arrived at the Neptune Baths.

The swan on the sign had three glass feet made of icicles. The wind rocked the swan, one of the glass feet broke off. On the ground, the shattered icicle was the coarse-grained salt from the camp that still needed breaking up. I stamped on it with my heel. When it was fine enough to sprinkle, I went through the open iron gate and stood in front of the entrance. Without thinking, I passed through the door into the hall. The dark stone floor reflected everything like still water. I saw my light-colored coat swimming below me to the cashier's booth.

The woman at the register asked: One or two.

I hoped it was only the optical illusion speaking out of her mouth and not suspicion. I hoped all she saw were the twin coats and not the fact that I was on my way to my old life. The woman was new. But the hall recognized me, the shiny floor, the middle column, the leaded-glass windows of the cashier's booth, the water-lily tiles. The cold decoration had its own memory, the ornaments hadn't forgotten who I was. I had my wallet inside my jacket, but I pretended to search for it in my coat pocket and said:

I left my wallet at home, I don't have any money.

The cashier said: That doesn't matter. I've already torn the ticket, go ahead and pay next time. I'll just take down your name.

I said: No, absolutely not.

She reached out of her booth and tugged at my coat. I shrank back, puffed out my cheeks, lowered my head, and shuffled backward in the direction of the door, narrowly avoiding the middle column.

She called after me: I trust you, I'll just take down your name.

Only then did I notice that she really did have a green pencil behind her ear. I backed into the door handle and yanked at the door. I had to pull hard, the metal spring wouldn't give. I slipped through the crack, the door squeaked shut behind me. I rushed through the iron gate and into the street.

It was already dark. The swan on the sign was sleeping white, and the air slept black. Under the lantern at the street corner it was snowing gray feathers. Although I wasn't moving, I heard my steps inside my head. Then I started to walk and stopped hearing them. My mouth smelled of chlorine and lavender oil. I thought about the etuba. And all the way home I talked to the snow that was dizzily flying from one lantern to the next. But the snow I was talking to wasn't the snow I was walking in, it was a famished snow from far away, a snow that recognized me from going door-to-door.

That evening, too, my grandmother took a step toward me and placed three fingers on her forehead, but asked:

You're back so late, do you have a girl.

The next day in the schoolyard I met Emma. She was taking a class in accounting. She had light eyes, not the same brass

yellow as Tur Prikulitsch, more like a quince. And like everyone else in town she had a dark home-sated coat. Four months
later I married Emma. Since Emma's father was deathly ill we
didn't have a celebration. We moved in with Emma's parents.
All that was mine I carried on me, my three lined notebooks
and clothes all fit inside the wooden trunk from the camp.
Emma's father died four days later. Her mother moved into
the living room and gave us the bedroom with the double bed.

We lived with Emma's mother for half a year. Then we left
Hermannstadt and moved to the capital, to Bucharest. The
number of our building was 68, like the number of bunks in
the barrack. Our apartment was on the fifth floor, it had just
one room and a small kitchenette, with a toilet out in the hall.
But nearby, twenty minutes by foot, was a park. When summer came to the city, I used a dusty path as a shortcut. Then
the park was only fifteen minutes away. While I waited in the
stairwell for the elevator, two light-colored woven cables moved
up and down inside the wire cage, as if Bea Zakel's braids were
rising and falling.

One evening I was sitting with Emma at the Golden Jug
restaurant, two tables away from the orchestra. As the waiter
poured the wine he covered his ear and said: You hear that, I
told the boss over and over that the piano's out of tune. So
what does he do, he throws out the piano player.

Emma gave me a sharp look. Yellow gears were turning
inside her eyes. They were rusted, her lids caught on them when
she blinked. Then her nose twitched, the gears freed up, and
Emma said, with clear eyes: See, it's always the player that gets
it and never the piano.

How come she waited until the waiter left before she said

that. I hoped she didn't know what she was saying. At that time my nickname in the park was THE PLAYER.

Fear is merciless. I stopped going to the nearby park. And I changed my nickname. For the new park, which was far from our apartment and close to the train station, I took the name THE PIANO.

One rainy day Emma came home with a straw hat. She'd gotten off the bus near the small hotel DIPLOMAT, where a man was standing under the awning. He was wearing a straw hat. As Emma walked by, he asked if he could share her umbrella, just to the bus stop on the corner. He was a head taller than Emma even without the hat, so Emma had to hold the umbrella very high. He didn't offer to take it, just stuck his hand in his pocket, practically shoving her into the rain. He said that whenever the drops make bubbles it rains for days. It had rained like that when his wife passed away. He'd put off the funeral for two days, but the rain didn't stop. He'd set the wreaths outside at night so they could drink the water, but that didn't help the flowers, which got soaked and rotted. After saying that, his voice grew slippery and he babbled something that ended with the sentence: My wife married a coffin.

When Emma said that marrying and dying were two different things, he said that they were both things to be afraid of. When Emma asked why, he demanded her wallet. Otherwise I'll have to steal one in the bus, he said, from some frail prewar lady, with nothing inside but a picture of her dead husband. As the man ran away his straw hat flew into a puddle. Emma had given him her wallet. Don't scream, he had told her, or I'll have to use this. He was holding a knife.

When Emma finished her story, she added: Fear is merciless. I nodded.

Emma and I often agreed on things like that. I won't say any more, because when I speak, I only pack myself in silence a little differently, in the secrets of all the parks and all the agreements with Emma. Our marriage lasted eleven years. And Emma would have stayed with me, I know. What I don't know is why.

Around that time CUCKOO and NIGHTSTAND were arrested in the park. I knew the police managed to get nearly everyone to talk and that nothing could help me if someone mentioned THE PIANO. So I applied for permission to travel to Austria. To speed things up I wrote the invitation from Aunt Fini myself. Next time you'll go, I told Emma—married couples were never allowed to travel to the West together. She agreed. While I was in the camp Aunt Fini had married and moved to Austria. She'd met a confectioner from Graz named Alois aboard the DINOSAUR, on her way to the salt baths. I had told Emma all about Aunt Fini's curling iron, the wave in her hair, and the locusts under her gauzy dress, now I led her to believe that I wanted to see my aunt again and meet her confectioner.

To this day nothing weighs more on my conscience. I dressed as though for a short trip, boarded the train with a light suitcase, and traveled to Graz. From there I sent a card the size of my hand:

Dear Emma,
Fear is merciless.
I'm not coming back.

Emma didn't know what my grandmother had told me. We'd never talked about the camp. I deliberately used her words, adding NOT on the card in the hope that even the opposite of my grandmother's sentence would be of some help.

That was more than thirty years ago.

Emma remarried.

I remained unattached. Wild animal crossings, nothing more.

The urgency of lust and the fickleness of luck are now long past, even if my brain still lets itself be seduced at every turn. Sometimes it's a certain way of walking on the street, or a pair of hands inside a shop. In the streetcar it's a certain way of looking for a place to sit. In the train compartment the prolonged hesitation when asking: Is this seat taken, and then a certain way of stowing the luggage that confirms my intuition. In the restaurant it's a certain way the waiter has of saying: Yes, sir, no matter what his voice is like. But to this day nothing seduces me so much as cafés. I sit at a table, sizing up the customers. With one or two men it's a certain way of slurping their coffee. And the way their lips glisten on the inside like rose quartz when they put down their cups. But only with one or two men.

One or two men can set off the patterns of arousal inside my head. The old habits act young even if I know they're frozen in place like figurines in a display window. Even if they know I no longer suit them because I've been ransacked by age. Once I was ransacked by hunger and didn't suit my silk scarf. Against expectation I was nourished with new flesh. But we have yet to come up with a new flesh that can counter the ransacking of age. I used to believe it wasn't entirely in vain that I let myself be deported into the sixth, seventh, or even eighth year of camp. That I might recover the five stolen years, that the process of aging might be postponed. It didn't happen that way, the flesh reckons differently when it surrenders.

It's barren inside and on the outside it glints in your face as eye hunger. And the eye hunger says:

You are still THE PIANO.

Yes, I say, the piano that no longer plays.

On treasures

Little treasures have a sign that says, Here I am.

Bigger treasures have a sign that says, Do you remember.

But the most precious treasures of all will have a sign saying, I was there.

I WAS THERE was what Tur Prikulitsch claimed should be written on treasures. My Adam's apple bobbed up and down under my chin as though I'd swallowed my elbow. The barber said: We're still here. That's five coming after nine for you.

Back then in the barber room I thought that if you didn't die in the camp then everything later would be After. That we'd be out of the camp, free, possibly even back home. Then we could say: I WAS THERE. But five comes after nine, we've been lucky, but our luck is a little balamuc, and we have to explain where and how. So why should someone like Tur Prikulitsch go back home and claim he never needed any luck.

Perhaps even back then someone from the camp had already decided to kill Tur Prikulitsch. Someone who was running around with the hunger angel while Tur Prikulitsch was strutting in his shiny patent-leather purselike shoes. Perhaps during the skinandbones time someone standing at roll call or locked up inside in the concrete box was rehearsing how he might split Tur Prikulitsch's forehead in two. Or was this someone up to his neck in snow beside a train embankment or up to his neck in coal at the yama or in sand at the kar'yer or inside the cement tower. Or did he swear revenge when he was lying on his bunk, unable to sleep in the yellow light of the barrack. Maybe he planned the murder on the day that Tur, with his oily gaze, was at the barber's, talking about treasures. Or at the moment when he asked me in the mirror, so how are things in the cellar. Or at the very instant I was saying: Cozy, every shift is a work of art. I guess a murder with a tie in the mouth and an axe on the stomach is also a work of art, a belated one.

By now I've realized that what's written on my treasures is THERE I STAY. That the camp let me go home only to create the space it needed to grow inside my head. Since I came back, my treasures no longer have a sign that says HERE I AM or one that says I WAS THERE. What's actually written on my treasures is: THERE I'M STUCK. The camp stretches on and on, bigger and bigger, from my left temple to my right. So when I talk about what's inside my skull I have to talk about an entire camp. I can't protect myself by keeping silent and I can't protect myself by talking. I exaggerate in one case just as I do in the other, but I WAS THERE doesn't fit in either. And there's no way of getting it right.

But there are treasures, Tur Prikulitsch was correct about that. The fact that I came back is a stroke of crippled luck that's permanently grateful, a survival top that starts spinning at the least damned thing. It has me in its grip just like all my treasures, which I cannot bear but also can't let go of. I've been using them now for over sixty years. They are weak and pushy, intimate and disgusting, forgetful and vindictive, worn out and new. They are Artur Prikulitsch's dowry and I can't tell one from the other. When I list them, I start to stumble.

My proud inferiority.

My grumbled fear-wishes.

My reluctant haste, I jump from zero all the way to a hundred.

My defiant compliance, I acknowledge that everyone is right so I can hold it against them.

My fumbled opportunism.

My polite miserliness.

My wearied envy of yearning, of others who know what they want from life. A feeling like stiff wool, cold and frizzy.

My steep-sided hollowness, I'm all spooned out, hard-pressed on the outside and empty on the inside ever since I no longer have to go hungry.

My lateral transparency, that I fall apart by going inward.

My burdened afternoons, time moving with me in between the furniture, slowly and heavily.

My fundamental leaving in a lurch. I need much closeness, but I don't give up control. I'm a master of the silken smile even as I shrink back. Since the hunger angel, I don't allow anyone to possess me.

The most burdensome of my treasures is my compulsion to work. It is the reverse of forced labor, an emergency exchange. In me sits the merciful compeller, a relative of the hunger angel. He knows how to keep all my other treasures in line. He climbs into my brain, pushing me into the enchantment of compulsion, because I am afraid of being free.

From my room I can see the clock tower of the Schlossberg here in Graz. At my window is a large drawing table. My latest blueprint is lying on my desk like a faded tablecloth. The paper's full of dust, like the summer on the streets outside. When I look at it, it doesn't remember me. Every day since spring a man has been passing in front of my apartment walking a short-haired white dog. He has a black walking stick, extremely thin, with just a slight curve for a handle, like a giant vanilla bean. If I wanted to, I could greet the man and tell him that his dog looks exactly like the white pig that my homesickness used to ride through the sky. The truth is I'd like to have a word with the dog. It would be good if the dog went on a walk by himself for once, or just with the vanilla bean and without the man. Maybe that will happen someday. In any case, I'll be staying where I am, and the street will stay where it is, and there's a lot of summer left. I have time, and I wait.

What I like best of all is sitting at my little white formica table, one meter long and one meter wide, a square. When the clock tower strikes half past two, the sun falls into the room. The shadow on the floor from my little table is a gramophone suitcase. It plays the daphne song or the pleated Paloma. I pick up the cushion off the sofa and dance into my awkward afternoon.

There are also other partners.

I've danced with the teapot.

With the sugar bowl.

With the biscuit tin.

With the telephone.

With the alarm clock.

With the ashtray.

With the house key.

My smallest partner is a torn-off coat button.

Not true.

Once a dusty raisin was lying underneath the little white formica table. And I danced with the raisin. Then I ate it. And then there was a distance deep within me.

Afterword

By the summer of 1944 the Red Army had advanced deep inside Romania; the Fascist dictatorship was overthrown, and its leader, Ion Antonescu, was arrested and later executed. Romania surrendered and in a surprise move declared war on its former ally, Nazi Germany. In January 1945 the Soviet general Vinogradov presented a demand in Stalin's name that all Germans living in Romania be mobilized for "rebuilding" the war-damaged Soviet Union. All men and women between seventeen and forty-five years of age were deported to forced-labor camps in the Soviet Union.

My mother, too, spent five years in a labor camp.

The deportations were a taboo subject because they recalled Romania's Fascist past. Those who had been in the camp never spoke of their experiences except at home or with close acquaintances who had also been deported, and then only indirectly. My childhood was accompanied by such stealthy conversations; at the time I didn't understand their content, but I did sense the fear.

In 2001, I began having conversations with former deportees from my village. I knew that the poet Oskar Pastior had been deported, and I told him I wanted to write a book on the subject. He offered to help me with his recollections. We began to meet regularly; he talked, and I wrote down what he said. We soon found ourselves wanting to write the book together.

When Oskar Pastior died so suddenly in 2006, I had four notebooks of handwritten notes, in addition to drafts of several chapters. After his death I felt paralyzed. His close presence in the notes made the loss even greater.

A year passed before I could bring myself to say farewell to the We and write a novel alone. But without Oskar Pastior's details about everyday life in the camp I could not have done it.

Herta Müller
March 2009

Translator's Note

Amid all the upheavals and mass movements of the 1940s, Leo Auberg is doubly displaced—as an ethnic German deported from his home in Romania and as a man with poetic and erotic sensibilities at constant odds with his surroundings. As he says: "I carry silent baggage. I have packed myself into silence so deeply and for so long that I can never unpack myself using words."

In one novel after the other, it has been Herta Müller's special calling to find words for the displacement of the soul among victims of totalitarianism. When the words cannot be found, she invents them. And when words do not suffice, she alloys the text with silence, creating striking prose of great tensile strength.

Translating this prose requires unpacking it in one language and repacking it in another. New coinages such as *Nichtrührer* or *Atemschaukel* defy literal rendering: "non-stirrer" and "breath-swing" fail to convey the layers of meaning lurking in these compound words that echo the wordplay in Oskar Pastior's poetry. Even uninvented words strain against a single

289

definition: *Geschirr* may be a bowl or a dish or a tin plate or a mess kit or simply a vessel waiting to be filled with something that will determine its meaning, like words themselves, especially in Leo Auberg's world, where innocent expressions are frequently filled with lethal content. Words, too, can be displaced. My task was to preserve this fundamental displacement without adding undue dislocation.

In matters of style and punctuation I have kept close to the original, where the abandonment of question marks and semicolons reflects the unpunctuated thoughts of the narrator, the simultaneity of insight and experience, the blurring of past and present. Similarly, I have followed the author's use of small capitals to mark certain words of iconic significance to the narrator.

All of these matters require careful consideration. Fortunately I have not been working alone, and I'm thankful to my family and friends for their kind assistance. Thanks to Herta Müller for indulging my many queries and to the staff at Metropolitan Books for their ongoing support. I am indebted to Ed Cohen for his usual creative scrutiny of the text and to Joana Ocros-Ritter for her invaluable ear in various languages. Finally, I am deeply grateful to Sara Bershtel for her consistently remarkable insights and generous engagement.

—Philip Boehm

ABOUT THE AUTHOR

Born in Romania in 1953, HERTA MÜLLER immigrated to Berlin in 1987 after suffering repeated threats for refusing to cooperate with Ceauşescu's secret police. The author of *The Land of Green Plums* and *The Appointment*, among other novels, she has received numerous honors, including the International IMPAC Dublin Literary Award and the 2009 Nobel Prize in Literature. *The Hunger Angel* has been translated into forty-seven languages.

ABOUT THE TRANSLATOR

PHILIP BOEHM has won numerous awards for his translations from German and Polish, including works by Franz Kafka, Christoph Hein, Gregor von Rezzori, and Stefan Chwin. He also works as a theater director and playwright: produced plays include *Mixtitlan*, *The Death of Atahualpa*, and *Return of the Bedbug*. He lives in St. Louis, where he is the artistic director of Upstream Theater.